THE
MOTHER
TREE

BY
HEATHER W. COBHAM

Managing Editor: Katie Elzer-Peters

Copy Editor: Susan Miller

Designer: Nathan Bauer

Front cover image: Alan Welch

Back cover image: Will Conkwright

ISBN 13: 978-0-9914085-1-1

Printed in the United States of America

For Maya "Doodle Bug" Brewer
in our lives July 14, 2007 - January 5, 2018
My muse, teacher, and best girl forever

ACKNOWLEDGEMENTS

Maya, Bay, Doodle Bug, and the members of the women's circle that meet around the Mother Tree entered my life 11 years ago when I began writing *Hungry Mother Creek*. Four years ago, Sloan and Nellie joined my fictional world when I started *The Mother Tree*. I'm grateful to my characters who've taught me new things about myself and increased my empathy as I sought to understand the perspective of women whose experiences were different from my own. This is one of the gifts of being a writer and all you need to receive it is your imagination, pen, paper, and time. And speaking of time, I need to acknowledge the impact that having more time to write has had on my life. In 2013 my husband and I became full-time residents of Oriental, N.C., and simplified our lives. With less "to do" to maintain my life there was more time "to be," reading, writing, staring at the water. This conscious shift in priorities and how I use my time increased my peace and focus, which in turn fueled my creativity.

I spent over 1,000 hours alone with pen and legal pad to write *The Mother Tree*, but you wouldn't be holding this book in your hands if it weren't for the love, support, and knowledge I received from others. With deep gratitude to Gaye and Ann, my writer's group, for your inspiration and feedback, but mostly for your love and friendship. We are writers! To Zelda Lockhart, whose workshop helped tighten the plot as I neared the end of my first draft. To Amy Rogers, from the

North Carolina Writer's Network, for her editing that strengthened *The Mother Tree*. To Katie Elzer-Peters and her amazing colleagues at The Garden of Words for final editing, formatting, and cover design. To Janice Allen, of the North Carolina Coastal Land Trust, for her feedback on my portrayal of the N.C. Coastal Land Trust and for showing me the first Venus flytrap I'd even seen in nature when we toured the Gales Creek Preserve. To Tracy Pollert Pardieu, for her lifelong friendship and for providing thoughtful feedback as a beta reader. To Tracey Lantz, for her belief in my writing and superb editing as a beta reader. To my first women's circle, whose love and wisdom over the past 22 years has made me a better person. To my new, Oriental women's circle, for reminding me that there are amazing women everywhere and for providing a safe and loving place to speak my truth and continue my spiritual journey. To Julia Brandon, my soulmate friend, for answering my calls in the middle of a bike ride and for having bigger dreams for me than I have for myself. To my mother and father, whose unconditional love over the past 50 years has given me the courage to follow my dreams. To my sister, Christie, who always understands me and whose love and support undergird my life. To my husband, Bobby, for too many things to name but mostly for loving me with "everything he's got." And to my beloved Labrador, Maya, who died just before I sent this manuscript to be published, for lying beside me while I wrote and edited every word of *The Mother Tree*, for taking me on walks when I had writer's block, for teaching me how to love unconditionally and live in the moment. You will always be my best girl.

And finally, I have to thank the wonderful village of Oriental for its support of *Hungry Mother Creek* and anticipation for *The Mother Tree*. Nautical Wheelers, Inland Waterway Provision Company, Paul's Produce Stand, The New Village Brewery, and the Front Porch Music Festival have all allowed me to sell *Hungry Mother Creek* and have been enthusiastic in their support. Thank you to local book clubs for selecting *Hungry Mother Creek* as one of your reads and for supporting a local writer. And I am immensely grateful for the friends, acquaintances, and strangers who stop me to say they enjoyed *Hungry Mother Creek* or to ask about the progress on *The Mother Tree*. Your interest, support, and positive feedback were appreciated more than you will ever know and provided a source of inspiration when my motivation lagged.

THE MOTHER TREE

A woman in harmony with her spirit is like a river flowing. She goes where she will without pretense and arrives at her destination prepared to be herself and only herself.

-Maya Angelou

THE MOTHER TREE

CHAPTER 1

At 3:20 Sloan woke by instinct. Except for the rise and fall of her chest and the rapid motion of her eyes as they scanned the dark room, she lay perfectly still. Had someone come in? She lifted her head a few inches off the pillow and listened. The familiar sounds of the window air conditioner and Peter's heavy breathing reoriented her. She'd had another nightmare. She put her head back on the pillow and took some deep breaths.

Would she ever stop waking before dawn? Sloan had hoped her move to the quiet sailing town of Oriental, North Carolina, and a new house on the Neuse River would change this pattern, but it hadn't. She closed her eyes but sleep wouldn't come. Worries clambered over each other to get her attention, and for the past 10 years, Deidre always landed at the top of the pile. If she'd been a better mother, would Deidre still be an addict? Like a gymnast performing a well-practiced routine, Sloan ran through all the reasons she'd contributed to Deidre's drug addiction. At least now she had something positive she could focus on: Deidre was alive, had finally agreed to get help, and Sloan was able to pay for it. This immediately spiked her next worry. Where would she get the money to renovate her new home into a retreat center? She'd set it aside but now it was paying for Deidre's rehab.

The whole purpose of moving to Oriental was to create a retreat center for businesses and other groups, and without it she'd have no income. Peter'd reduced his teaching load at North Carolina State in Raleigh to spend more time painting here, and was counting on her to pay half the mortgage. Had she made a mistake giving up her real estate business in Raleigh? Would she lose everything she'd worked so hard for? Could a biracial woman even create a successful business in rural North Carolina?

Sloan turned on her side, away from Peter, and tried to relax. She'd used numbers all her life to make decisions. This strategy provided her financial security in exchange for the time she could have spent with Deidre and her older brother, Anthony. But if you looked at the numbers, it hadn't made sense to buy Magnolia Bend and come to Oriental. Now in her 50th year and with encouragement from Peter, she'd made a decision based on feelings, not numbers; on the peace she felt being by the water here in Pamlico County and the connection she felt to this area, where she spent childhood summers with her mother's family.

How she loved those summer months. Time filtered out boredom, arguments, and sickness and all she remembered was the time outside, good food, storytelling, and most importantly, feeling safe and accepted. During the day she spent hours exploring the creek behind the small family home. Sometimes her great Uncle Jake, who lived next door, would join her and teach her the names of trees and birds and how to recognize the subtle tug of a flounder at the end of her fishing line. She always spent part of the day reading one of the books Grandma Rose selected for her. She and Pa-Pa stressed the importance of doing well in school and going to college, and they didn't want her academic skills to wane over the summer. Her grandparents had met while students at Central University and were the first in their families to attend college. Now as an adult, Sloan better understood the challenges her grandparents must have faced as a college-educated, black couple trying to build a middle-class life in the 1940s. Part of her desire to excel was fueled by their examples.

Most summer evenings were spent on the front porch. Her grandparents usually talked about politics, memories from their life in Durham, or the books they were reading, and the conversation was punctuated by silence to listen to the night sounds. Sloan would sit on the floor in front of her great-grandmother's rocking chair while GG braided her hair. Sometimes GG pulled too hard and hurt her, and Sloan would have to remind her that her hair was different, more fragile than her cousins' whose parents were both black. She didn't mind though. It made her feel good that GG thought of her as the same, even though she had a white father, and her skin was brown, not black like the rest of her mother's family. As a child, this was one of the only places she felt accepted. In school, white classmates treated her as black but her black classmates never fully welcomed her, either, leaving her alone in a liminal space.

Sloan lay on her back and stared at the ceiling. Her great-grandmother's home-place was less than half the size of Magnolia Bend with twice the people but she'd never felt crowded. In fact, as an only child whose parents were busy with their restaurant, she savored the proximity of her mother's family. She didn't even mind sleeping on a cot on the screened-in porch, but once she was 10 she couldn't sleep through the night there, either.

Sloan slid her long legs out from under the sheets and walked to the closet for her silk robe. She moved carefully across the bedroom and out to the hall. She and Peter had moved into Magnolia Bend at the beginning of May and in the three weeks since then, she'd stubbed her toes and bumped her head too many times to count. The house was built in the early 1800s, when people were smaller, and it would take a while for her almost 6-foot frame to adapt.

Sloan rested her right hand on the banister and fluidly moved down the staircase with her white bathrobe trailing behind her. The years of ballet lessons had infused her body with grace and balance. These qualities combined with her stature gave her a strong physical presence. Sloan was aware of this and used it to her advantage in her Wake County real estate practice.

Being a biracial woman automatically made Sloan a minority in a roomful of corporate realtors and businessmen, but her confidence and ability to look the white men in the eye helped equalize the power differential somewhat. Sloan didn't miss that part of her real estate job. The negotiations were exhausting, being twice as prepared as anyone else, monitoring eye contact and body language for prejudice and censoring her speech to avoid the slang she'd picked up as a teenager from her cousins.

In the kitchen, Sloan removed a bottle of water from the fridge to take outside. She paused with her hand on the French doors that led to the patio. She saw herself on the other side, peeking into the kitchen through this exact door 40 years ago. Magnolia Bend was just down the road from GG's home and several times each summer she would explore the abandoned property, looking into every window she could reach. The home was in disrepair then, with plaster coating the floors like snow, and vines growing in through the cracks. GG had told her there were chains and shackles in the basement, left from when this had been a plantation, so she'd crawled along the foundation until finally she found a small window. On her hands and knees she looked in and saw four sets of shackles bolted to the wall. She immediately wished she could un-see it. It was more than her 10-year-old mind could comprehend and she threw up in the boxwoods, overcome with anger at what half of her ancestors had endured and shame at what the other half had inflicted. That was the last time she'd been here until she came with the realtor back in March.

Sloan realized she was shaking and sat down at the kitchen table. She hadn't shared this memory with Peter or her realtor, but knew it had influenced her decision to buy Magnolia Bend. She couldn't erase the past, but now had the opportunity to write a new chapter in the history of Magnolia Bend. It would become a sanctuary, a place to restore and create rather than to suffer.

Sloan stood and went out to the patio. Her plan had been to sit in one of the Adirondack chairs, but now she needed the river to soothe her emotions. The crescent moon was rising in the east and lit her way as she walked across the backyard to the pier. She'd forgotten to put on shoes and stepped gingerly. The dew was heavy, and she left a trail of wet footprints as she walked to the end of the pier. She heard an owl hoot and the gentle lap of the water on the shore, but otherwise it was quiet. The moon continued its ascent and threw moonbeams into the water to dance. She watched the moonlight waltz on the water, and the distress created by her dream and memory of the chains eased. Sloan closed her eyes and breathed in the moment.

Suddenly she felt another presence. Her heartrate doubled and she turned away from the water. She looked back to the house and saw a woman walking down the pier toward her. Sloan's pulse returned to normal as the woman approached. She was petite, close to 5 feet, with a pleasant expression on her face. She wore a loose-fitting gingham house dress, similar to what Sloan's grandmother used to wear.

"Good morning," Sloan called out, more in the form of a question than salutation as she wondered who this woman was and why she was walking down her pier in the predawn hours. Sloan tucked in a few strands of hair that had loosened from her French twist during the night, and cinched her robe tighter, suddenly aware of what she must look like.

"Hello," the woman said. Her voice was soft, but clear and friendly with no discernible accent. "I hope I didn't startle you. I couldn't sleep and came out to walk. When I saw you out here I thought I'd say hello and welcome you to the neighborhood."

Sloan looked around, trying to figure out where this woman had been walking and how she'd seen her. The only way she could have gotten to the pier was by walking from Magnolia Bend Road through Sloan's yard or by coming from the backyard of one of her neighbors. The woman was barefoot like her, so she couldn't have walked too far.

"Do you live in one of these houses?" Sloan asked, sweeping her hand to include the homes on either side of Magnolia Bend.

The small woman was now at the end of the pier and leaned back into the railing directly across from Sloan. "Yes. You could say we're neighbors. I'm Nellie."

Sloan instinctively put her hand out and then adjusted her robe instead when Nellie didn't respond. "I'm Sloan, Sloan Bostwick. It's nice to meet you. I've been out of town and busy unpacking so you're the first neighbor I've met."

"You're unpacking? Wonderful. That means you're going to live here. Magnolia Bend's had several owners in the past 20 years but no one lived here full time. It'll be nice to have someone in the house."

Now that only the width of the pier separated them, Sloan looked more closely at Nellie. It was hard to discern her age, but Sloan guessed her to be younger than she. Nellie's skin reminded Sloan of a pearl, pale and smooth, like someone who spent more time inside than out. Her eyes were striking in their almond shape but the color nondescript. In contrast, her hair was distinctly black, so black it was hard to determine where her hair ended and the night sky began. It was long and wound up in a loose bun at the back of her head.

A heron honked and took off from the shore, causing Nellie to look back toward the house. The left side of her neck was now exposed, and Sloan saw a dark purple and blue bruise encircling the entire left side. Even in the moonlight, the contrast between the bruise and her otherwise pale skin was striking. When Nellie looked back and saw Sloan's line of vision, she immediately turned to hide the bruise. Sloan read her body language and didn't ask questions.

"Sloan, now tell me, what inspired you to buy Magnolia Bend? It's not the kind of house you buy on a whim." Nellie leaned toward Sloan to devote her full attention.

Sloan was surprised by her question. Usually when people first met her, they wanted to know where she was from. The combination of her father's aquiline nose, her brown, coppery skin and light brown eyes made it difficult for people to categorize her. Before they could get to know her as a person, it seemed they wanted to put her in a box: white, black, Hispanic, Indian.

Sloan smiled at Nellie and then began her story, only planning to share the basics. Nellie's attentive gaze and the moonlight softened Sloan's usual defenses and details about Peter, summers with her mother's family, her career in real estate and plan of a retreat center spilled out.

"What will your retreats focus on? Will you be leading them?" Nellie asked.

"No. Not at first. I'll be marketing Magnolia Bend to businesses or other groups who already have their agenda. I'll coordinate the food, kayaking, massage, and yoga to complement their time spent in meetings or classes. Maybe once I get the hang of it I'll create my own retreats, but Peter will definitely be having some week-long painting classes here."

Nellie smiled at her and said, "I bet you couldn't sleep this morning because you're excited about your new life."

Sloan, still under the spell of Nellie's attention, answered honestly, but without details of Deidre's overdose and subsequent treatment.

"I was thinking about my new life, but am more anxious than excited," she confided. "I can't get enthusiastic about the future until I have the money to finance it. I've got to come up with money for renovations, furniture, and marketing." Sloan sighed and in that pause realized she'd been monopolizing the conversation.

"I'm sorry, I got carried away and have talked way too much," she added. Nellie smiled forgivingly. "Now how about you? What brought you to Oriental? You don't sound like you're from here."

Nellie continued to angle herself to hide the bruise on her neck. "Oh, I've been here a while," she said. "Came here with my husband and son years ago."

Sloan waited for Nellie to add more but she didn't.

Nellie pointed toward the eastern horizon where the pink terra cotta of dawn layered the black water. "With this view, your property is the perfect place for people to get away on a retreat," she said, diverting the subject away from herself. "Magnolia Bend has seen its share of pain so it's nice to know it will be used for something positive."

Sloan wondered if Nellie knew some of the history of Magnolia Bend, but before she could ask, Nellie stepped toward her and said, "From what you've told me about your real estate career, it sounds like you're a determined and resourceful woman. I'm sure you'll get the money you need, and this time next year Magnolia Bend will be full with a group on retreat."

Nellie didn't break eye contact with Sloan and in those moments Sloan saw the east ballroom full of people listening to a motivational speaker. Nellie's declaration was reassuring and amplified Sloan's intuition that she could make this work.

Nellie took a few steps backward in the direction of shore. Sloan stepped forward to close the distance. "Thank you."

Before Sloan could say anything else, Nellie lifted her hand in a wave goodbye and said, "I need to get home. It was great to meet you." She turned and walked down the pier toward the house.

Sloan called out, "Do you want to exchange phone numbers?" but Nellie didn't seem to hear her and continued down the pier. A pelican dove for its breakfast and took Sloan's attention to the water. When she looked back toward land, Nellie was already halfway across her yard, heading to Magnolia Bend Road. Sloan paused at the end of her pier to watch Nellie. She was happy they'd met but concerned about the bruise on her neck. This was only their first meeting so she shouldn't jump to conclusions, but she resolved to keep her eye out for other bruises the next time they were together.

Sloan walked toward the house and admired the pink glow of dawn reflecting in her windows. Bolstered by her talk with Nellie, she was determined that today she'd find a way to make the money she needed.

***

Peter folded *The Pamlico News* and laid it on the kitchen table. He stretched his legs out in front of him.

"Are you going to walk the land before it's logged for timber?" he asked. "Seems like it would be good to look it over before the logging road is put in."

"I guess I could, but I don't see the point," Sloan said, stirring the onions and peppers she was sautéing for their spaghetti sauce. "You know I need money to start renovations and have in reserve if Deidre needs more rehab. Logging that piece of property is the only way to get it." Sloan stabbed at the vegetables and several onions flew out of the pan onto the stove top. "Damn," she said and threw them back. "Peter, that land is 5 miles away and whether those trees are there or not won't make a difference to us."

Peter stood and his height filled the space between floor and ceiling. "I know," he said. "It's just a thought, but don't worry about it. The retreat center is your baby and I support whatever you have to do to get it going."

Peter took a few steps toward her and Sloan smiled. Even after 15 years she was still surprised at his unconditional support, something she didn't have when she was married to Deidre and Anthony's father. She turned back to the stove and Peter stepped behind her. He slid one hand around her waist and kissed the back of her neck. Sloan leaned into him and their fingers interlaced, creating a weave of brown and black. She let her body relax. Part of the reason she loved him was his ability to calm her. She hated that she'd been tense the past few weeks. One of the main objectives for moving here was to slow down and reduce her stress.

Without being asked, Peter stepped to the counter and poured diced tomatoes into the pan and placed the basil and oregano by the stove for Sloan. Cooking was something they loved doing together and over the years they'd learned to follow each other's lead in the kitchen, like partners on a dance floor. Sloan finished the seasoning and put a lid on the pot.

They walked out to the patio. It'd been a hot and steamy day, typical for mid-June, but now with the breeze and setting sun it was tolerable. Sloan settled back in the Adirondack chair and angled herself west.

"Peter, do you think I'm making a mistake by logging that piece of property?" she asked, not taking her eyes away from the horizon. "I don't want to take on more debt with a loan, and with the current real-estate market it would take several years before I could sell it. This is really the only option." Sloan's shoulders tensed and she questioned herself again. She wasn't usually ambiguous. She'd make a decision and follow through, but ever since she'd signed the papers to purchase Magnolia Bend, she felt more hesitant. She was in uncharted territory. After 20 years in real estate, she was confident about her skills to handle whatever challenge presented itself. Now, she was outside her comfort zone.

"No, I don't think you're making a mistake, but I find it interesting that that 50 acres is still on the Magnolia Bend deed," Peter replied. "I know it was a part of the plantation years ago, but I wonder why it's never been sold. But, like you said, it's 5 miles away and doesn't adjoin this property so the logging won't have any impact on us."

Sloan gripped the end of her Adirondack chair. She knew Peter wasn't trying to dispute her decision but he did have a point.

"Maybe there is something about that land, but right now my priority is getting the retreat center up and running to have income," she said. "That will help Pamlico County more than a bunch of trees, and anyway, the logging company will plant new ones that'll grow back."

"Well, you have a point there, babe," Peter said gently. "Now that you know where the money's coming from, how quickly can the renovations get started?"

Sloan silently thanked Peter for ending talk of the logging. The decision was made and she was ready to move on.

"I'm meeting with a contractor on Friday to discuss the changes I want and to make sure the building meets code," she said. "I have some money to get started and the logging company said they'd probably get to my property in September, and after that I'll have the money to complete everything. Hopefully, I'll have my first retreat next March when the weather begins to warm up."

As Sloan talked, she felt her enthusiasm rise. She could see it now:

people listening to a motivational speaker. Sun streaming through the windows. Folks scattered in Adirondack chairs meditating by the water.

Peter's voice brought her back to the moment. "Sloan. You've been staring out at the water for the past couple of minutes."

"Oh, sorry. I was thinking that this would be a great spot for people to meditate."

"That's quite all right. I'm happy to see you dreaming, but you may want to get more comfortable chairs to meditate in," Peter said and shifted in his seat. "These aren't made for anyone over 6 feet." The humidity made Peter's ebony skin glisten and he took a handkerchief from the pocket of his jeans and wiped his face and head.

Sloan laughed, "Maybe I should buy you a sweatband to help with that." Before Peter could answer she got a whiff of garlic and remembered the sauce. "Oh! We better get inside. I'm sure the sauce is ready and the water's boiling for spaghetti."

They stood to go inside, and Peter put his hands around Sloan's waist. He pulled her to him and she slid her arms behind his neck. He looked down at her and said, "I know the finances are causing you stress but remember how lucky we are to be here. Once things are settled, we'll have a slower pace of life, more time together, and a gorgeous place for me to paint, and you to have your retreats." He leaned down and kissed her firmly on the lips. She returned the kiss as the sun sank into the Neuse River.

CHAPTER 2

Maya woke a millisecond before her alarm went off. She propped on an elbow and looked out the French doors leading to the second-story porch. Dawn was only a glow in the east. The robins and blackbirds began their morning chorus and Doodle Bug's doggie snores provided backup accompaniment from the floor beside her bed. Maya slid the pillow behind her and leaned back against the wrought iron headboard, letting the impact of the day settle in. Today was the solstice and the longest day of the year. Well, officially it was yesterday, but today was Saturday and the day her women's circle would meet at the Mother Tree to celebrate the solstice. Today would also have been Hazel's 80th birthday. Maya's throat tightened and tears pricked at the back of her eyes. It had been three and a half months since Hazel's death of lung cancer and Maya was still adjusting to the loss of her friend and mentor and to the fact Hazel had left her as executor of her family's $4 million philanthropic fund. Maya hadn't even begun to figure out the ins and outs of managing that.

Maya missed Hazel's physical presence, morning coffee on the porch, tea in the late afternoons, playing with Doodle Bug under the oaks in the back yard—but she felt her spiritual presence everywhere. How could she not? Thanks to her generosity, and the fact Hazel's son had no desire to move to Oriental, Maya was now living in Hazel's 19th-century farmhouse on Beards Creek in Oriental. It was mostly furnished with Hazel's family heirlooms, which was a blessing because Maya'd lost all her possessions in Hurricane Katrina. When Maya lived in Hazel's boathouse, she'd gotten by with some of her sister's old furniture and inexpensive pieces from Craigslist, so now she appreciated the quality of what Hazel had left her. Every time she made a cup of tea in the rosebud china or dusted the face of the antique grandfather clock, Maya could feel Hazel's presence.

The most challenging part of settling in Hazel's home had been clearing out the remnants of her years of hoarding. Hazel had tried to fill the hole left from her mid-life abortion with stuffed animals, magazines, kitchen appliances, and children's clothes. Each bag that left for the dump, church yard sale, or Goodwill released a piece of Hazel's pain and regret and the house felt more peaceful as a result. Maya held her own yard sale in May and used the profits to replace some floors and carpet that had rotted and molded from the years of being covered.

Maya glanced at the clock. Seeing the time, she swung her legs over the edge of the bed to get up. She had 45 minutes to get dressed and paddle to Hungry Mother Creek to meet the women's circle. She pulled on shorts and a T-shirt and threaded her shoulder-length brown hair through a baseball cap. Her hair was highlighted with blond, and her arms and legs were tanned and firm from the hours she spent running and kayaking out in the sun.

She ran down the steps and into the kitchen and quickly let Doodle Bug out. She picked up the bag she'd prepared for the circle gathering and headed down the path to the water. There was a light on in the small boathouse next to the pier and Maya wondered why Bay was up so early on a Saturday. The boathouse had been the first place Maya'd lived when she moved to Oriental. Now Bay Witherspoon lived there.

Maya smiled at how life works itself out. Eight months ago, Bay was living in a 3,600-square-foot custom home, in the exclusive River Dunes neighborhood, and Maya was in the 950-square-foot boat house. At first Maya could barely tolerate Bay, but after an accidental meeting on a run led to regular running dates, she realized Bay's haughty attitude was a cover for her insecurities and that they had more in common than she'd guessed. After Bay's husband, Holden, 22 years her senior, had a severe stroke, they became even closer. Maya stood by Bay as she struggled with whether to fight Holden's daughter for custody after he was deemed incompetent, or leave him, and end a marriage that'd been suffocating her even before her husband's need for 24-hour care. Bay chose to divorce Holden and this coincided with Maya's move into Hazel's spacious farmhouse. It only made sense to offer Bay the boathouse to start her new life.

Maya reached her kayak at the water's edge. She stowed her bag behind the seat and then held either side of the blue kayak, her biceps tensing with the effort. Her core strength and balance made her entry into the boat look effortless. Maya adjusted herself in the seat and then saw Bay walk out of the boathouse in her running clothes.

"Hey, Maya? Is that you?" Bay asked and walked to the edge of the water. As usual, she was well put together with black Nike running shorts and a black-and-white tank top with her blond hair pulled back in a high ponytail. She was 42 but could easily pass for 30.

"Of course. Who else would be out here in my backyard getting in my kayak?" she said playfully. "I'm paddling to my women's circle. What are you doing up so early on a Saturday?"

"I'm going for a short run and then I'm working all day at Marsha's Cottage. Remember? I started there Monday. It's the little clothing boutique in town."

"Oh, that's right. How do you like it so far?"

"Oh, I love it. I can't believe I get paid to play with clothes and dress people up and it will look good on my application to the school of design at N.C. State. You'll have to stop by sometime."

Maya laughed. "I'm your biggest fashion project, aren't I?" Maya looked at her watch and pushed her kayak away from land. "I have to go. Sunrise isn't far away. Have a good run. Maybe I'll stop by this afternoon."

Bay waved and began a slow trot down the driveway.

Maya turned her kayak toward Hungry Mother Creek, falling into an easy rhythm of paddling. She'd been paddling regularly for almost a year now and her body was as comfortable with the pull of the water against the paddle blade as it was with the strike of her foot on the earth when she ran.

She paddled steadily so she would reach the Mother Tree before sunrise. The hum of a boat motor gained volume behind her. It must be Violet's husband bringing her to the circle, she thought. At the mouth of Hungry Mother Creek, Maya steered her kayak to the right side to get out of their way. She turned around to wave good morning and was surprised to see only Violet in the boat. Violet slowed the skiff so her wake wouldn't swamp Maya's kayak.

"Violet!" Maya called, "Where's Ben? When did you learn how to drive the skiff?"

"Morning. Ben's been teaching me. I'm getting more comfortable driving it, but will need your help getting the anchor up before I leave today."

"No problem. See you at the beach in a second."

"OK."

Violet throttled up the engine and drove the quarter mile to the beach.

The pink and yellow of dawn gained altitude and prompted Maya to increase her cadence. She slowed her pace when she got to the beach and saw Lilith and Ella were already there, helping Violet secure her boat.

"Morning, everyone," Maya called. Her kayak slid onto the sand between Ella's and Lilith's. Before Maya got out of her kayak, she sat for a moment looking at the scene in front of her. The three women on the beach were framed by live oaks draped in Spanish moss. The saw palmettos behind them provided a low wall between the beach area and a clearing at the edge of the woods, worn down by years of use. Presiding over this scene with outstretched limbs was the Mother Tree, a huge live oak that got its name from the feminine eyes and gentle mouth created by the natural contours of her bark. The Mother Tree had stood on this spot for over 200 years, the wind and weather no match for her strength and flexibility. Their circle met around her trunk on the solstices and equinoxes.

Violet sat in her camp chair and was drying her feet before she slipped on the Keds she always wore with her wraparound skirt. Her short gray hair, full bosom, and easy smile exuded grandmotherly charm. Lilith, her curly brown hair made unruly by the humidity, was stowing her tent and sleeping bag in the storage compartment of her kayak. Weather permitting, she always camped here on the beach before their gatherings. And finally, Maya's gaze fell on Ella, who was sitting on the bow of her kayak watching the others. As usual, Ella looked beautiful in an effortless way. The breeze and humidity seemed to have little impact on her long, smooth blond hair pulled back into a low ponytail. She wore a black skort and purple technical T-shirt and looked like she was on a photo shoot for Athleta catalog. Maya wished she'd worn something else now. Her shorts were wrinkled from lying on the floor and there was oily stain on the front of her shirt, thanks to a splatter of Italian salad dressing. She rethreaded her hair through her baseball cap and then twirled the copper band in her spinner ring.

Lilith's voice brought Maya out of her self-appraisal.

"You guys ready to get started?"

"Yes," Maya said. She stepped out of her kayak and then took her bag of supplies and ran up the beach to join the others. She hugged the women in greeting. This was only the second time since Hazel's death that they'd met at the Mother Tree and Maya still expected to hear Hazel's skiff coming down the creek. It didn't feel like the circle was complete with only four women.

"Before we go back to our circle," Maya said, "I'd like us to do something here on the beach in remembrance of Hazel." The women paused and turned to Maya. She dug her toes into the sand, uncomfortable being the center of attention. Maya continued, "You probably know this, but if Hazel were alive, today would be her 80th birthday. While I was caring for Hazel before her death, she shared a beautiful birthday tradition. She and her grandmother had the same birthday and her grandmother taught her this sunrise ritual."

Maya could tell she had the women's attention. She didn't see any flashes of recognition and realized Hazel must not have shared this with the others. She reached into her bag, opened a Tupperware container and pulled out a chocolate cupcake with a pink rosebud on the top. She continued, "Hazel would take a cupcake with a candle down by the water." Maya reached in her bag again and drew out a candle to stick in the middle of the rosebud. "She would light the candle and hold it up as the sun broke the horizon. The flame from the candle would blend with the glow of the rising sun. She would make a wish, blow out the candle and then eat the cupcake." Maya paused and looked east. The timing was perfect.

"I thought it would be nice to repeat this ritual today in honor of Hazel and then each of us send our own birthday wish to her."

Maya handed out cupcakes and candles to the women. As she handed Lilith hers, Lilith took her free hand and gently squeezed Maya's arm. "What a wonderful idea. Thanks for initiating this."

Maya blushed at the compliment, still unaccustomed to them after growing up with parents who rarely seemed to notice her and her sister, Kate. Her mother was distanced by depression and her father by his business during the day and bottles of wine at night. She'd been in the circle for only nine months and felt more love and acceptance here than she ever had with her parents.

The horizon had gone from pink to orange and the four women walked down to the water's edge and lit the candles in their cupcakes. They faced east to more clearly see the sun. Maya saw the top edge rise gracefully above the tree line as if a magician were overhead, orchestrating this feat with her wand. Maya, Violet, Lilith, and Ella all held their cupcakes up and aligned the flame on the candle with the sun that now lit the creek with a buttery glow.

Maya said, "To you, Hazel." And in unison each woman blew out her candle. A weight pressed against Maya's chest and she swallowed hard to avoid crying. Her wish for Hazel was that she could see all the good she'd done in her life and forgive herself for having the abortion.

The women stood in silence by the creek's edge. As the sun rose, the bird song increased in intensity and volume and several mullet threw themselves out of the water in their version of a sun salutation. Lilith was the first to take a bite of her cupcake. Maya giggled at the line of chocolate frosting on her upper lip. The others finished their cupcakes and then followed Violet back to the worn circle around the Mother Tree.

The diameter of their circle had decreased with Hazel's absence. Maya took her place on the ground between Ella and Lilith, while Violet placed a fat pillar candle in the center and lit the four wicks. She sat down in her camping chair across from Maya, creating more of a square than a circle. Maya wondered when there would be five women again.

Violet began, "I'm honored to be the elder of our circle and continue the tradition of women meeting around the Mother Tree. For over 100 years, women have come here to glean wisdom from Mother Nature, God, and one another and to live more mindfully and intentionally." Violet paused and the women instinctively took several deep breaths to honor this sacred space.

Maya looked at the Mother Tree and remembered the fall morning when she first saw it, and how the feminine features outlined in the bark and the melted candles at her base had disconcerted her. After she'd sat in silence in front of it, her discomfort had transformed into peace. Today she was grateful for the Mother Tree and the women around her for creating a safe place to heal from the trauma of Hurricane Katrina and to resolve her conflicted feelings about her husband's death from a diabetic coma immediately after the hurricane.

Violet continued, "For the spring equinox, we shared what seed of intention we wanted to plant in our lives. Today we'll share how our intention has grown and if it has born fruit or if it's more like asparagus and will take several seasons to mature." Violet smiled at each of them and blushed.

She smoothed her skirt over her knees. "Being a leader doesn't come naturally to me and I'm still nervous serving as the elder of this group. I'll do my best to not let the circle down." Violet reached into the center of the circle and picked up the talking stick she'd placed there a few minutes ago. "Because of my new role as elder and because I want to expand my comfort zone, the intention I planted was to become more independent. I spend a good amount of time with Ben, or my daughters and grandchildren, and often put their needs before mine. It makes me happy to care for them but I want time that's totally mine. Since we last met, I've been taking Wednesday mornings and sometimes that entire day for myself."

Violet held the talking stick up in a gesture of victory and the others laughed. "I may take a day trip or sit around and read all day. Whatever I want. Of course, I've had plenty of days to myself before this, but it was only by default. It feels good to create space for myself. Ben has taught me how to navigate our boat, too, and now I can motor out to see the sunrise or follow a pod of dolphins on my Wednesdays."

Violet glowed as she talked, and Maya could tell she was thrilled with her newfound time and independence. Violet's perspective was different from her own. Maya was almost always alone and all the decisions were hers to make, from how she spent her time to how she would allocate Hazel's money to charity. Sometimes this was overwhelming, and she wished for a partner to share her life with, but someone different from Steven. She remembered the hopes she'd had at the beginning of their marriage eight years ago, how they'd dimmed with his drinking and emotional abuse, and then extinguished with his death after Hurricane Katrina. Six months ago, this line of thought would have sent Maya into a panic attack but now she took a couple deep breaths, twirled her spinner ring, and allowed the regret and hurt to pass. Since the winter solstice ritual when she'd spread Steven's ashes in the creek, she was better able to manage the anxiety that accompanied the memories of her marriage.

Maya brought her attention back to the circle and watched the four flames on the pillar candle flicker in the light morning breeze. Ella and Lilith were both still, so Maya reached for the talking stick Violet had laid beside the candle. Violet, Ella, and Lilith looked toward Maya and waited for her to speak. She took a moment, wanting to speak her truth and not what she thought sounded right or what others wanted to hear. She was becoming more comfortable speaking in the circle and the butterflies in her stomach had decreased with each circle gathering.

"The intention I planted this spring was to get back in touch with who I am and what my dreams are. I think I've lost that over the past few years." Maya's voice cracked. "I spent much of my marriage adjusting who I was to try and keep Steven happy. After his death, as you all know, I focused on healing from my marriage, the trauma of Hurricane Katrina, and then three months caring for Hazel. The last six weeks, I've been cleaning, purging and organizing Hazel's house," Maya corrected herself, "my house. I'm trying to make the house my own, so I guess that's a start. Violet, I must be the asparagus. I'm sending down roots—planted exactly where I'm meant to be, but no spears yet. Not sure what the magic formula is to figure yourself out, but not always basing my decisions on someone else is a start."

Maya wanted to add that deciding what causes she would support with Hazel's philanthropic fund would also be a part of this process but honored Hazel's request to keep this confidential and didn't mention it.

Maya replaced the talking stick in the center of the circle, happy to have something positive to share. The fall equinox and winter solstice circles had been difficult as she revealed the pain of her unhappy marriage and the guilt of finally being free from it when Steven died. In the silence after her sharing, Maya's eyes filled with tears. It felt good to focus on herself. The past five years she'd been in survival mode and not able to look inside and connect with her own desires. Now, Maya's mind raced with possibilities for her life and a tingle ran up her spine in anticipation of what may lie ahead. The call of a heron brought her attention back to the circle, where Ella reached for the talking stick.

Ella held it silently and stared at the Mother Tree. It was only 6:30 but the forest was already well lit by the summer sun. The air hummed with insects, bird calls, and the rustle of leaves from the scurrying squirrels. Maya, Lilith, and Violet waited for Ella to begin, honoring the time and space that was hers.

Ella's gaze left the Mother Tree and returned to the women in the circle. She caught Maya's eye and Maya smiled. No matter how many times she looked Ella in the eyes, their sapphire blue color always struck her.

"Well, a lot has happened since March, as Maya already knows," Ella said, and Maya nodded, remembering their dinner in New Bern and kayak trip to Goose Creek where Ella shared some of the recent developments in her life. Although she enjoyed her work as a regional sales manager for a pharmaceutical company, she was desperate to slow the pace of her life.

"The intention I set in March was to redesign my current job or find another one so I wouldn't have to travel as much. I want to grow my social circle in New Bern," Ella paused, "and even start dating. Traveling most of the month leaves me little time for building relationships."

Maya found it difficult to understand why someone as beautiful as Ella had to even think about finding a date.

Ella continued, "I'm happy to report that I have a job offer as an event coordinator at the New Bern Convention Center and have also negotiated with my boss to cut my travel in half. The convention center job would be fun, and I could walk to my office from my condo downtown, but it would be a huge pay cut. Staying in my current job would keep my income stable, but as time passes, I'm worried I'll be pressured to pick up my travel again and be right back where I started. I have to give the convention center an answer by Monday. I hope to gain some clarity here this morning."

Ella's eyes filled with tears and Maya knew she was struggling with her decision, feeling the opposing pull of financial security and simplicity. Why is there always a choice between the two? Of course, Maya had chosen simplicity by moving to Oriental. She'd taken a pay cut but then decreased her expenses equally and was financially stable. Things had become more complicated since she inherited

Hazel's home. Taxes, flood insurance, upkeep of the house and dock all required more money than the $350 rent she'd paid at the boathouse. Thankfully, Hazel had thought of this and included a housing fund of $10,000 to help Maya initially, but she knew she'd need to keep adding to that fund to be prepared.

Maya thought about her new financial responsibilities. She uncrossed her legs and folded them under her. What if a hurricane hit Oriental? Would she have the money to repair the dock, the boathouse? What about saving for retirement? Her chest tightened and Maya realized she was focused on her own internal drama rather than Ella. She was ashamed and looked at Violet and Lilith, wondering what they were thinking. Were they focused on Ella's decision or did they use her dilemma as a catalyst to obsess over issues they were facing?

Ella stared at the water and gripped the talking stick as if she could squeeze an answer out of it. After a few minutes she brought her attention back to the circle. Her tears had dried and she looked more peaceful. Ella gently placed the talking stick back in the circle.

Lilith reached for the stick, immediately passing it back and forth between her hands. Her back was toward the creek and the sun backlit her curls, creating a brown halo around her head. As usual, Lilith's eyes sparkled with mischief and Maya wondered if she was always happy and playful. At recent circles, Lilith had focused on having more sex and expanding her bread baking business. Both laudable goals but hardly the intensity of some of the others' issues. Maya knew from her talks with Lilith that she'd suffered and lost her way, but she seemed to have culled wisdom from her past and made peace with it. Now she could focus on the simpler pleasures in life. Or so it seemed to Maya.

Lilith began, "This spring, we met a couple weeks after Hazel's death and our circle felt small without her. I thought of the other women in our circle who've died and how little we know about them. The seed

I planted was to create a way to honor the women who've sat in our circle. We have a strong oral history, but nothing written that can be passed to the future generations who will sit around the Mother Tree. I've decided to write a book that includes stories and wisdom from the women who've been in our circle. Obviously, many stories are lost, but I'll do my best to find family members and friends who knew past members. I'll record how the circle started and the lives of its members over the last 50 years or so. Violet, I'll definitely be picking your brain." Violet smiled and nodded in agreement.

Lilith continued, "I'll do as much as I can and from here on out, the circle will add accounts after the death of a member."

Lilith paused and Maya felt awkward, trying not to look in Violet's direction, knowing that chronologically, the older woman was the next to die. Of course, as Maya was avoiding Violet, Lilith addressed her directly.

"Now Violet. Don't get all melancholy about being the next entry in the book. None of us are getting out of here alive and there's no need for us to focus on the inevitable."

Lilith chuckled to herself and Violet smiled. Leave it to Lilith to convey a harsh truth using wit and honesty.

"Anyway," Lilith continued, "I plan to get started right away while I'm energized and focused. I'll keep y'all up to date on how things are going and Violet, let's plan on a lunch date at my house this week if you can."

Maya could see Lilith's enthusiasm oozing from her pores. She admired Lilith's zest for life and hoped she would learn to put less energy into worrying and more into creating.

Lilith smiled at each of the women and put the talking stick back into the center. They sat quietly for a moment to honor Lilith's words. Maya felt a bead of sweat forming on the back of her neck. The air was already heavy with humidity. To signal the circle was over, Violet blew out the four flames on the large pillar candle.

The women stood. Violet folded her small camping chair and the others brushed dirt and stray leaves off their shorts. Before Maya headed down to the beach, something bright pink from behind the Mother Tree caught her eye. She wondered if it was some sort of wildflower, like the wild roses she'd seen growing in the ditches. She walked about 10 feet into the thicker forest behind the Mother Tree to investigate, hopeful Lilith would know what kind of flower it was. Maya stepped carefully with her bare feet through the tangle of vines and roots on the forest floor and then bent back several small saplings growing in front of the pink that had caught her eye.

Disappointed not to find a new kind of wildflower, Maya realized she'd only seen the end of a pink ribbon fluttering in the breeze. She wondered why someone would tie this around a large pine tree. Maybe to mark a property line. That was an interesting thought. She'd never considered who owned the property that contained the Mother Tree. It felt like it belonged to everyone. There was something written on the ribbon, so she stepped closer. Across the trunk of the tree she read, "Stream side measurement zone." Wonder what that means, she thought to herself.

Maya felt a presence behind her and Lilith pressed into her back. Maya opened her mouth but before she had a chance to ask Lilith what the pink ribbon meant, Lilith looked at her and nearly spit out the words, "Logging. This pink ribbon marks the creek-side boundary of a logging tract. Whoever owns this property must be getting ready to log it for timber."

Simultaneously Maya and Lilith turned back toward the Mother Tree and saw it was aligned with this tree. Did that mean the Mother Tree would be cut down? Would there be nothing by their circle but stumps and gouges in the earth left by the heavy equipment? A lump formed in

Maya's throat as she thought of losing the Mother Tree and this sacred space. She looked over to Lilith and saw her neck was flushed red and her hands were balled into fists.

Lilith said, "Maya, this can't happen. We have to do something. I'm going to tell Ella and Violet." Lilith strode purposefully past the Mother Tree and down to the beach where Ella was helping Violet load her boat. Lilith motioned with her arms as she told Ella and Violet. Immediately they all looked up toward the Mother Tree and then Violet covered her face with her hands.

On her way to join them, Maya paused at the Mother Tree. She placed her palms against the bark and closed her eyes. She thought of the hundreds of years it had taken the Mother Tree to reach her current size, a tiny acorn to almost 70 feet tall. It could be gone in a day. She thought of the stories and tears that women had shared here. The lump in her throat grew and she leaned further into the tree for reassurance. The bark was warm from the morning sun and the edges pricked her palms. Maya's hands pulsed with energy from the tree and her emotions calmed. They must find a way to save the Mother Tree and this sacred space. She hoped that the wisdom of their circle would show them how. Maya stepped back from the tree and jogged to the beach to join the others.

THE MOTHER TREE

CHAPTER 3

Maya let Doodle Bug off her leash to run around back and jump in the creek. The morning air was muggy and Maya'd felt the weight of it pressing against her during her morning run. Sweat dripped from the end of her ponytail. Her jog bra, tank top, shorts waist band, and even her socks were saturated with sweat. She'd managed to run eight miles but had only taken Doodle Bug on the last two because of the heat.

Maya left her shoes and socks on the front porch and when she got inside went straight to the refrigerator. Not wanting to drip sweat on the new hardwoods, she hurried down the hall and out the back door. She took two bottles of water because she knew he'd be there and she was right. Maya waved to Buster as she walked toward the creek in her bare feet. His skiff was at the end of the pier and Buster was casting out into the deeper waters of the creek. Doodle Bug was lying in the shallows, but when she saw Maya she bounded up to meet her, running several circles around her and then back into the water to cool off.

"Hey, Buster," Maya called.

"Hey there, Maya Lou. Lord, girl, did you go for a swim with Doodle Bug? You look like a wet dog yourself."

Buster smiled at her and caught the bottle of water she threw to him from the dock.

"I'll take that as a compliment, Buster, since I think Doodle Bug is the cutest thing in the world, wet or dry."

Maya had known Buster almost a year and knew his teasing was a sign of affection. She'd become more comfortable dishing it back to him. Buster's fishing pole bent and he instinctively jerked it to set the hook, then reeled in the line. Maya watched as he concentrated on getting the fish to the boat, something that must be innate after 40 years as a commercial fisherman. He worked to reel in the fish. The sweat trickled down his face, channeled through the crevices in his weathered skin, and landed in his gray beard.

Doodle Bug joined Maya at the end of the pier and watched with rapt attention as the fish jumped and splashed on its way to the boat.

"Stay, girl," Maya said, not wanting her to jump in after the fish and end up with a hook in her mouth. Doodle Bug sat obediently next to Maya as Buster netted the fish onto his skiff. He held it up proudly.

"Looks like flounder for dinner. Might be a bit smaller than regulation but the perfect size for my frying pan so it's all good, as far as I'm concerned." Buster took the hook out and threw the flounder in his cooler full of ice. He sat down on the bench seat and took a swig of the water Maya'd brought him. "Whew. Now I know why you're dripping wet. How far did you run in this?"

"Eight miles, but it felt like 20," Maya replied. "My head's clear though, so it was worth it. No matter the weather, I'm always happier if I run instead of staying in bed an extra hour."

Maya sat on the edge of the dock and finished her water as Buster continued to cast. She swung her feet back and forth over the top of the water and felt the pleasant fatigue from her run. This was becoming a Sunday tradition, meeting here after her run while Buster fished. She and Buster had grown close during the three months she'd cared for Hazel. Buster would come over every morning so she could run and have a few hours to herself. She missed seeing him every day and looked forward to their Sunday mornings. They'd talk about their week, missing Hazel, their families, and sometimes just sit quietly together. Buster was in his mid-60s and Maya appreciated his fatherly advice and support—and the fact she could depend on him.

Buster kept his eyes on his fishing line. Maya swirled her feet in the brown water. Doodle Bug lay beside her, wet head on her paws. A couple of birds called back and forth from the shade of the live oaks. The insects hummed. No fish jumped this morning, held in place underwater by the weight of the humidity.

Buster broke the silence. "Maya, how was your women's circle yesterday? I imagine it feels incomplete without Hazel."

"Yeah. It does. But at the same time her presence is strong when we're gathered around the Mother Tree so she's not totally absent."

"What exactly do you ladies do when you meet at the solstices and equinoxes? Do you dance naked around the Mother Tree?" Buster started to laugh.

"Sorry to disappoint you, but no naked dancing." Maya joined in as she conjured the visual to accompany Buster's comment. "Now, if I tell you what we do, I'd have to kill you, and I definitely want to keep you around, so you'll have to use your imagination. That's probably more interesting than what we really do, anyway."

"OK," Buster said, "but I really think you should ask them about adding naked dancing." Buster grinned and cast his line out again.

"Buster, I have a question," Maya said, swatting a mosquito on her arm. "You know the land the Mother Tree is on, behind that beach area on Hungry Mother Creek?"

"Sure. I fish down there in the fall and hunted deer and turkey there with my grandpa when I was young," Buster replied. He was quiet for a moment while he thought about the past. "I remember the Mother Tree and the circle of stones. Grandpa told me it was there even when he was young."

"Do you know who owns it now?"

Buster looked her way inquisitively.

"After our circle I saw something pink behind the Mother Tree," Maya explained. "I thought it was a wildflower but when I went to investigate I saw it was surveyor's tape. We saw more tape making a boundary a couple hundred feet from the creek. Lilith said a logging company put it there and that land will probably be logged for timber."

Buster reeled in his line, put his fishing rod in the rod holder and leaned in toward her.

"What did you say? Logging the property on Hungry Mother Creek? Well, that can't happen. People from Oriental have been using that land for years. Not only for the women's circle, but for hunting, fishing, camping. It'd be ruined if it were logged."

Maya had seen this same intensity in Lilith. She'd only been in Oriental a year and already the land on Hungry Mother Creek was special to her.

"I know," she agreed. "The circle is devastated that we could lose the land. We want to figure out a plan to save it and that's why I asked if you knew the owners. Seems like that would be the first place to start. Maybe we could talk with them and change their mind."

As Maya was talking, Buster leaned back, arms folded across his chest. Maya could tell he was listening to her with one part of his brain but the other was busy working on a solution.

"I remember my grandfather telling me there that the Hungry Mother Creek property belonged to the people who owned the Magnolia Bend house," he said.

"But Magnolia Bend is miles from Hungry Mother Creek," Maya said, scratching the quickly emerging red welt on her arm. "Why would they own it?"

"Magnolia Bend was a huge plantation back in the early 1800s and they owned acres and acres of land on the Neuse River and the creeks near Oriental, including Hungry Mother Creek," Buster explained. "Over the years, the property's been sold off to small farmers and folks who built homes next to Magnolia Bend on the river."

"Do you know who owns Magnolia Bend now?"

"Hold on a minute, Maya. We don't even know if that property is still connected to Magnolia Bend, so we need to find that out first. The last time I drove by there, there was a For Sale sign out. Hmm." He paused, wiping sweat from his forehead with the back of his hand. "Maybe the house has sold and the new owners have no idea about the value of the land on Hungry Mother Creek."

Maya could hear the wheels turning and knew Buster had an idea.

"OK Maya, tomorrow on your lunch break, go to the courthouse in Bayboro and they can help you find the deed for Magnolia Bend. This should tell us who the owners are and what land is connected with that property. I'll call a realtor I'm friends with and I can guarantee you that she'll have some background information on the new owners that would be helpful."

Maya stood. Her legs were stiff after her run. She tapped her empty water bottle against her thigh. "Thanks, Buster. Sounds like we have the first couple of steps in our plan. I'll call Lilith this afternoon and let her know. Once we know who the owners are, we can discuss our next step."

"Sounds good, Maya Lou," he said, using the affectionate nickname he'd given her. "Let me know what you find out."

"Will do. Have a great week."

Buster started his engine and slowly pulled away from the pier and pointed toward home, probably stopping somewhere for a country breakfast. Maya turned and walked down the pier with Doodle Bug right on her heels. Her stomach growled and she anticipated the whole wheat blueberry pancakes she'd make after her shower. Instinctively Maya turned left down the path to the boathouse and then caught herself. That was Bay's home now, not hers. She redirected to the main house, stopping to pick some hydrangeas for her desk at work.

**

Maya took her coffee bean freeze and went to the high-top table at the back. Because of the heat this morning, she hadn't been able to think about hot coffee. The dull headache began around noon, letting her know she needed a caffeine infusion, so she retreated to The Bean, the quaint coffee shop right across from Oriental's public dock. Bay was working again today and Maya thought she'd take her up on her invitation to stop by and visit her at Marsha's Cottage. She even brought some money in case Bay helped her pick something out.

Maya hadn't brought anything to read and leaned back against the wall to people watch. The coffee slushy slid down easily, cooling her off and satisfying her addiction. The door opened and in walked a woman with a miniature version of herself that must have been her daughter. The woman looked a few years older than Maya and the little girl about 7 or 8. They stood in front of the cooler, deciding what flavor of ice cream to have. The mother stood behind the little girl, her hands on her shoulders. She leaned in and whispered something to the little girl, who giggled. The sound of the child's laugh was contagious, and Maya smiled. She continued to watch as they took their ice cream cones to a table close to the door. The mother was affectionate with her daughter, holding her hand, tousling her hair, putting an arm around her shoulder. Their heads leaned toward one another and they took bites of each other's ice cream. They laughed at their sticky hands and noses. It seemed like there was no place they'd rather be than there together.

Maya's eyes filled with tears and she looked away. She'd never felt that type of intimacy with her mother. She couldn't even recall a time she and her mother went somewhere together unless it was to the doctor, dentist, or some other necessary appointment. She definitely didn't have a memory of going to an ice cream parlor together. If they had, her mother wouldn't have gotten ice cream because it was fattening, and she would have wiped Maya's hands every few minutes to keep them from getting sticky.

Maya twirled a piece of hair that escaped her ponytail and looked out the window at the boats tied up at the town dock. She felt empty in the pit of her stomach, a homesick feeling, a longing for something she'd never had. And then she thought of Lilith's hugs and playfulness, Hazel's understanding, Violet's nurturing, the feeling of connection and acceptance sitting in front of the Mother Tree alone and with the circle. At 39, she was being mothered by other women and by nature. Maybe it didn't always have to come from your biological mother, she thought. She looked back at the woman and her daughter, now standing to leave, and wondered how different her life would have been if her mother hadn't been depressed. Would her mother have provided the love and acceptance Maya craved? If she'd gotten these things from her mother when she was young, would she have ever married someone like Steven?

"God damnit Maya. Why are you so needy? You can't expect me to stay home with you and that dog every night." Steven rinsed his razor in the sink full of water and continued to shave.

Maya leaned against the doorway of the bathroom and a vise tightened around her chest. She struggled for enough oxygen to speak.

"I'm not asking you to stay home every night," she said, trying to make eye contact in the mirror. "It's just that you've worked late all week and

it's Friday, when we usually go out for pizza." Maya tentatively placed a hand on Steven's bare back. "Can't you go out with your friends another time?"

Steven stepped away from her and took a long drink from the beer sitting on the vanity. He continued shaving.

"What the fuck difference does it make when we have pizza?" he said. "I've already made plans to meet the guys. We can go out tomorrow." Steven finished his beer, crumpled the can and threw it in the trash. He pushed past Maya into the bedroom. She put her forehead on the bathroom door frame and watched the water, thick with shaving cream, circle down the drain.

A loud gurgle and slurp from the bottom of her cup startled Maya. She blinked to reorient herself to The Bean but her mind kept racing. Why had she stayed with Steven? By the end of their marriage, his highest priority was drinking with his friends, but she'd kept hoping things would change. Even when Katrina was bearing down on Bay St. Louis, he chose to go to New Orleans for his guys' weekend and left her and Doodle Bug to fend for themselves. If she'd left him sooner, she wouldn't have had to experience the trauma of Katrina.

Maya's breath quickened and sweat formed at her hairline. She sat up straighter in her chair and uncrossed her legs. She watched the person at the table in front of her filling in the Sunday crossword puzzle. Instinctively her right thumb twirled her spinner ring and she slowed her breath. She looked out the window and watched a fishing trawler maneuver away from the dock beside the fish house and out into the small harbor.

Maya took the lid off her cup and drank the last of her bean freeze. It'd been a while since she felt like this, but thankfully she'd avoided a full-blown panic attack. *I can't change anything about my childhood or my marriage,* she thought to herself, *but I can buy a new outfit.* She slid off her stool and headed out the door to see Bay, happy for a distraction.

Maya walked into Marsha's Cottage and the mannequin wearing gold palazzo pants and a black lace top made her feel out of place in shorts and flip-flops. It seemed quiet in here compared to The Bean, any sound muffled by the thick carpet on the floor and the designer clothes lining the walls. Maya scanned the small shop for Bay and saw her off to the left with her back to her. Bay must have felt Maya's presence and turned around. She broke into a smile and walked over to Maya to give her a hug.

"You came!" Bay said with genuine surprise.

"Well, you invited me. How'd you get so tall all of a sudden?"

"It's my heels," she said, lifting her foot to show a gold sandal with 2-inch heels. Bay wore a blue and green block-print dress that complemented her gorgeous figure and she definitely looked the role of a fashion consultant.

"What are you working on?" Maya asked, curious as to exactly what Bay did here all day.

Bay pulled Maya over toward the jewelry case under the window. There was a blue silk blouse with white polka dots lying across it. "I'm looking for a necklace to pair with this blouse for a new window display. I was thinking of this one," Bay said, pointing to a statement necklace with large red stones. "What do you think?"

Bay unlocked the case and took the necklace out. Maya draped it across the blouse and thought Bay was asking the wrong person about statement necklaces. The door chimed and both she and Bay looked up. Bay immediately turned her back to the door and twisted her gold hoop earring. She motioned for Maya to move closer and whispered softly, "The two women who just came in are the wives of Holden's golfing buddies. I haven't seen them since Holden's stroke and our divorce. Pretend you're a customer so I don't have to help them."

Maya feigned interest in the jewelry case while keeping the women in her peripheral vision. She and Bay held their breath when they heard the women speak.

"You'd think she'd at least have the decency to leave town. It's as if she doesn't think she's done anything wrong."

"I know," the second woman said, her voice hushed. "It's obvious now that she married Holden for his money. As soon as he has a stroke and needs her, she divorces him and leaves him in a nursing home. I sure hope he had a prenup."

Bay whispered to Maya through clenched teeth. "Do they think I'm deaf? I knew they always hated me. I can't tell you how many times I had to ignore sexual comments his friends would make about me, including the husbands of those two. I should walk over there and give them a piece of my mind."

Maya put her arm around Bay's waist. "Take a deep breath," she said, inhaling and exhaling deeply as if to serve as a model. "Nothing you say will change their minds."

"I know, but they need to know that I did love Holden. I probably wasn't in love with him for the last few years, but I tried to do what was best for him."

"You did the right thing," Maya said, loosening her hold around Bay's waist. "It's better that his daughter has guardianship of him. Now he's close to her and his grandchildren and getting excellent care in Raleigh. Being defensive will only confirm their thoughts about you. And besides, you don't want to get in an argument with a customer and get fired."

Bay's breath slowed and she stopped fidgeting with her earring. "You're right," she said. "This time next year I'll be at N.C. State working on my degree in fashion design. I'll probably never see them again, anyway."

Maya and Bay turned slightly to watch the women. They continued to peruse the sales rack and whisper to one another. A woman came out from the back of the store.

"Uh oh," Bay said. "That's Marsha, my boss. I hope she's not angry I didn't wait on them."

Marsha asked the women if she could help them and then looked questioningly at Bay.

Maya saw this and said, "I came prepared to buy something. Help me pick out a cute top to wear with my white jeans. Hopefully you won't get in trouble if you're helping a paying customer."

Bay took Maya by the arm and led her over to a rack of summer blouses. "Thank you," she said, and began flipping through the clothes. "Guess I should tell Marsha my story in case this happens again."

"They must've been only looking," Maya said. "There're already leaving."

"Good," Bay said, and continued to look through the blouses. "Here," she said, pulling a plum-colored shirt from the rack. "This would look great on you. Go try it on."

Maya walked out of Marsha's Cottage with the plum shirt, a floral skirt that matched it, and a new pair of earrings. She spent more than she'd planned but hoped her purchases would keep Bay from getting in trouble. Maya peeked into the bag, happy with her new outfit, and smiled at Bay's enthusiasm when she picked it out. Maybe she'd wear it to work tomorrow and brighten up her Monday.

***

Maya crossed her slim ankles over one another and adjusted the waistband of her new skirt. She slid her heels in and out of her white flats and wished she was in shorts and flip-flops. The door chimed and

41

the first patient of the week walked into the chiropractor's office where Maya worked. Maya refocused on the computer screen in front of her and checked in the patient.

"What a beautiful arrangement of hydrangeas, Maya. Those must be from the bushes around Hazel's—I mean your house," the patient commented.

Maya was still amazed by how much people know about you in a small town. She had no idea how her patient, Anna, knew Hazel had hydrangea bushes at the back of her house.

"Thanks," Maya said, pulling her chart. "I thought it would be nice to have a bit of summer inside. How've you been? Back pain any better?"

While Anna went into a detailed description of her pain over the past two weeks, Maya nodded and smiled in the right places all the while making a mental list of what she needed to do today. Remind Dr. Allan she was leaving early, stop by the courthouse to find out who owned Magnolia Bend and the Hungry Mother Creek property, and be in Oriental by 3:00 for her first meeting with Trident Investments. She'd been so preoccupied with cleaning and organizing the house after Hazel died, she'd barely thought about the philanthropic fund. Today she'd learn the process for getting the money to the charities she decided to support.

Maya handed Anna the receipt for her co-pay and ended her soliloquy on pain. "Dr. Allan will be right with you," she said in her polite work tone. "I'll let him know you're here."

Maya pressed the button for the buzzer in Dr. Allan's office and looked at her watch. 9:15. Had she only been here 45 minutes? Thank goodness she was leaving at 1:00 today. It'd been almost a year since Maya started work at the chiropractic office. She'd enjoyed the challenge of organizing the office, but now that things were running smoothly, she was bored. Checking patients in, filing, billing insurance, paying the office bills. There were plenty of tasks to complete, but with little challenge or meaning. She'd never felt restless in her job before. Why now, she wondered? In fact, when she was married to Steven, her job was a refuge, safe and predictable, but now she wanted more. The door chimed again and instinctively Maya reached for the next patient's chart. She glanced at her watch again. 9:30.

The morning dragged by and finally Maya left for the courthouse. She presented the address for Magnolia Bend to the register of deeds and in a few minutes had the name she needed: Sloan Bostwick.

Maya drove out of Bayboro toward Oriental and tried to imagine the woman who owned Magnolia Bend and the Hungry Mother Creek property. Why did she come to Oriental? Why within months of closing on Magnolia Bend did she want to harvest her land for timber?

Maya slowed when she reached Oriental city limits and turned right into the small retail center containing a gift shop and health foods store. Trident Investments was located above them. Maya pulled into a parking space with time to spare since it hadn't taken long at the courthouse. The register of deeds quickly found the information on Magnolia Bend. Maya saw that Sloan Bostwick had purchased Magnolia Bend on April 30 for $750,000 from a man who had an address in London, England. Maya asked if Ms. Bostwick's phone number would be listed anywhere on the deed. No, the register of deeds told her, but she knew the realtor who'd sold the property and a phone call procured the cell phone number in a matter of minutes. Having dealt with patient privacy issues for most of her professional life, Maya was amazed at how easily she got this information. She felt sure some privacy agreement must have been breached.

Maya rolled down the car windows and, since she had time, called Lilith to share Sloan's name and phone number.

"Well, look at you. Becoming a detective," Lilith said.

"It wasn't that hard. Buster sent me to the register of deeds and in a matter of minutes she found the information I needed. What should we do now?" Maya asked.

"We need to schedule a meeting with Ms. Bostwick," Lilith said. "Hopefully she's a reasonable woman and we can figure out a compromise that will spare the property around the Mother Tree. I'll call Violet if you can call Ella. Let's get dates that work for us and then I'll schedule a meeting with Ms. Bostwick."

"How can you be sure she'll even meet with us? I doubt she'll have any interest in hearing our opinion on what she should do with her property," Maya said.

"All I know is we have to talk to her to save the Mother Tree," Lilith said. "Let me worry about how to make this happen. I can be creative when I need to." Maya felt Lilith's smile through the phone before she hung up.

Trident Investments was an auspicious name, but when Maya walked into the office she immediately felt comfortable. It was one large room with a desk and filing cabinets in the back half and the front was set up with a conference table and sitting area. As soon as she walked in, a man in his late 50s hurried from his desk to greet her, holding out his hand.

"Maya Sommers," he said, shaking her hand enthusiastically. "I'm Jeff O'Neal. I've been looking forward to meeting you ever since Hazel told me you'd be taking over her fund." He immediately blushed, his alabaster skin now redder then his hair. "Sorry. I didn't mean to sound excited about meeting you. It makes it seem like I'm happy Hazel died, which of course I'm not." His blush deepened and he pulled up his pants that were already sitting way above his waistline.

Maya smiled. "I didn't take it that way. It's nice to meet you, too."

She followed him to the conference table that had two water bottles and a large manila folder on it. Mr. O'Neal fumbled to open a water bottle and Maya thought he must be more comfortable with numbers and profit and loss statements than he was with people. He handed her the water and sat down. Immediately he stood back up and rushed toward her to pull out her chair like she was being seated at a five-star restaurant. Before she was fully seated, he pushed the chair in toward the table and she almost slipped out. He didn't seem to notice and Maya suppressed a giggle and situated her small frame in the large office chair.

Mr. O'Neal sat back down and looked at her, waiting for her to speak. Maya's mind was blank. She'd been focused on the Mother Tree and Sloan Bostwick and hadn't given this meeting much thought. Hazel had entrusted her with the family's philanthropic fund. Hazel's grandmother created it and passed responsibility for it to Goldie, Hazel's mother, and then to Hazel. The intent was for the fund to always be managed by a female descendent, but Hazel didn't have a daughter and selected Maya as the beneficiary. It was an honor, but she hadn't found the time to even prepare questions for today, much less think about where she'd donate the money. Maya tried to ignore the feeling she was letting Hazel down. She blurted out, "So, how do I get money from you to give to charity?"

Mr. O'Neal's face lit up and he opened the manila folder. "I figured you'd ask that question, so I printed out a summary for you to take home. Now let me explain the steps."

Maya relaxed in her chair and listened to Mr. O'Neal outline the process, his demeanor confident, now that he was in his area of expertise. Before she knew it, an hour had passed. Once they'd gotten started she had plenty of questions for him and realized she actually had given the fund some thought.

"So, if I understand correctly, there's no limitations on how I donate the money other than it has to go to a nonprofit organization?" Maya asked.

"That's correct," Mr. O'Neal said. "Remember, you can't donate more than 5% of the principal though, but that was never an issue for Hazel. She was pretty tight with this money, if you ask me. She'd request pages of documentation from agencies, have them travel halfway across the state to meet with her, and then only donate $1,000. She was old and probably thought $1,000 went farther than it did." Mr. O'Neal's face glowed again. "Of course, I respected Hazel, it's just that sometimes, well it doesn't matter what Hazel did. I know she wanted you to donate the money however you see fit."

"Thanks for taking time with me today," Maya said, gathering her papers to take home. "I'll give you a call once I'm ready to make my first donation."

Mr. O'Neal reached across the table to help, knocking over her water. Luckily Maya swiped the papers out of harm's way. She watched with amusement as Mr. O'Neal did a combination of a hop, walk, and shuffle to get paper towels from the bathroom, stopping several times to hike his pants. Well, at least she'd be entertained when she had her quarterly meetings.

Maya opened her front door and Doodle Bug bounded out to greet her, so filled with delight that her entire body wiggled, not just her tail.

"Hey, girl. How are you? Did you have a good day?" Maya said, rubbing her ears, head, and back. She hated to leave Doodle Bug home all day but wouldn't have wanted her to sit in the hot car this afternoon when she was at her appointments. She missed having Hazel here to let Doodle Bug out during the day.

Maya walked into the kitchen with Doodle Bug right on her heels. She threw her purse and papers on the kitchen table.

"Let me change and then we'll go for a walk and swim," she said.

Doodle Bug danced in anticipation and Maya smiled, grateful for her love and companionship.

Maya threw the stick into the middle of the creek and Doodle Bug swam wildly for it again and again. The repetition gave Maya time to gather her thoughts from the day. The philanthropic fund was a big responsibility. Maya knew she'd like her donations to go to organizations serving Pamlico County but didn't know where to start. She threw the stick again and then it dawned on her she'd have to be discreet if she donated locally to keep knowledge of Hazel's fund from becoming widespread. Hazel had requested anonymity and had maintained that by donating only to state or national agencies with no local ties. Hmm. Maya hadn't thought about that. How could she research agencies without people knowing it was her making the donation?

Doodle Bug let the last stick Maya'd thrown float away and she lay in the shallow water panting. Her tail wagged, creating a tiny wake in the water and she looked adoringly up at Maya on the bank. Maya sat down, trying not to get overwhelmed with the responsibility of the fund. The ground was warm and she lay back, noticing where each part of her body came in contact with the earth. She watched a sliver of a cloud move across the sky, the blue now softened by the setting sun. She heard the lap of water from Doodle Bug's tail, the croak of several nearby frogs and the evening bugs warming up for their concert. She twirled her spinner ring each time she took a breath. She would figure it out, and a call to her sister would be a good place to start since Kate was the only person she'd told about the fund.

Maya stood and Doodle Bug followed suit, stopping to shake and getting Maya's legs wet in the process.

"Come on, girl. Let's go make some dinner and then call Kate."

Like "swim" and "walk," dinner was a word Doodle Bug knew, and she ran ahead of Maya and up onto the back porch. Maya smiled, always amazed at the joy Doodle Bug found in the simple routines of life, a trait she'd like to replicate in her own life.

CHAPTER 4

Sloan heard the click as the latch disengaged from the doorframe and watched the hall light on the bedroom wall grow from a sliver to a rectangle and then shrink until her room returned to darkness. She kept her back to the door and curled her prepubescent body tighter into itself, like a young fern frond. The doorknob clicked back into place and then came the sound of the lock. The faint tick of the lock engaging would have been easy to miss in most circumstances but was deafening to her.

The next sound was the rush of heavy breath behind her as he knelt by the bed. He pulled back the covers and fumbled with her nightgown. She'd begun wearing long flannel nightgowns, wanting a thicker layer of protection around her. She'd hoped her mother would inquire about her sudden preference for flannel when she'd always preferred short, cotton ones, but her mother never asked. She wondered if she'd even have the courage to tell her mother what was happening if she had. Her 11-year-old mind knew it was wrong. If she told, would she get in trouble? Had she done something bad to make this happen? How come her mother never checked on her at night?

She felt his sweaty hands on her back and then around her waist. Their width easily spanned her stomach. Tears slid from her eyes. She mentally transported herself through the wall and into her front yard to lie on the grass and watch the stars, trying to ignore what was happening to her body in her locked bedroom.

Sloan woke suddenly and was disoriented. Her hairline was damp with sweat and her heart was pounding with such force that she felt its reverberations in her fingertips. She looked toward the door. It was closed. Sloan took a deep breath and rolled onto her back, reaching for Peter, but then remembered he was in Raleigh to teach his summer school class at N.C. State. She didn't have to look at the clock to know it was after midnight and already Tuesday. It would be close to 3:30. It always was. Since living at Magnolia Bend she'd continued with her early-morning awakenings. In Raleigh she'd wake with her mind racing about her latest real estate deal or worrying about Deidre, but since living here she'd been having more flashbacks from her 10th and 11th years when her Uncle Tommy, her father's younger brother, had lived with them while attending law school in Chapel Hill.

Sloan turned on her left side, away from the door, and pulled Peter's pillow into her chest. She inhaled his scent from the pillow and this grounded her in the present. After several minutes she unfurled herself and stretched out her legs, aware of her 6-foot, middle-aged body that only a few minutes ago had felt small and vulnerable. Experience had taught her that lying in bed would intensify the thoughts, so she got up and grabbed her bathrobe at the foot of the bed. When Sloan came to the window she paused and looked out to the river. It must be overcast, she thought, because she didn't see the moon or stars but something was at the end of her pier. She watched for a minute and thought she could make out the shape of a person. Nellie! Maybe she couldn't sleep either. Sloan hadn't seen her since their early-morning meeting almost a month ago. It would be nice to talk with her again.

Sloan took a few steps to the bedroom door and then froze with her hand on the doorknob. The door was locked. She never locked the bedroom door. Being in locked rooms gave her panic attacks. It didn't make her feel safe. She felt trapped and vulnerable. Sloan twisted the knob several more times to be sure she wasn't imagining it. No, it was definitely locked. Sloan found the light switch on the wall and flipped it, surveying the room for an intruder but nobody was there. She took a few breaths to calm herself and unlocked the door. Maybe she'd done it by accident. No one else was in the house and that was the only explanation she could find.

Sloan took two bottles of water from the fridge and went outside. Her eyes adjusted to the light and she saw a few stars peeking through the clouds as she walked to the pier. It was humid. No breeze stirred and the Neuse was black glass. Nellie was at the end of the pier, leaning against the railing. Sloan raised a hand in greeting before she got to her.

"Hey Nellie. You couldn't sleep either?"

"No, and I took a chance and came out here in case you were awake, too."

Sloan approached Nellie. "Here. I saw you from inside and brought you a bottle of water." Sloan waited for Nellie to take the water but she stood there, ignoring Sloan's gesture, much like she'd ignored Sloan's attempt to shake her hand last time. Finally, Sloan put the bottle on the railing and opened her own to take a sip.

"How've you been? I was happy to see you from my bedroom window. I hate it's been so long since we last talked," Sloan asked after swallowing.

"Me, too," Nellie smiled. "Well, guess that's obvious since I came out on your pier uninvited. Hope you don't mind. Tell me, have you figured out a plan to get money for the renovations?"

"Yes. Things are coming together," Sloan said. "There's a piece of property that's deeded to Magnolia Bend, about 5 miles from here. I'm going to log it for timber in September. I've got enough money to get things started and then once I get the money for the timber, I'll have more than enough. It's taken a load off my mind." Sloan continued to leave out the financial impact of Deidre's rehab.

"Then what woke you up this morning?" Nellie asked. "Last time, you couldn't sleep worrying about the finances, and it sounds like that's resolved."

Sloan stared at Nellie, not sure how to answer. She didn't want to lie but she didn't want to share the truth, something only her great grandmother and Peter knew. As Sloan looked at Nellie, contemplating her response, she couldn't help but notice that Nellie still had a bruise on the left side of her neck. The exact spot she'd had one when they last met. But that was almost a month ago. Surely it would have healed by now, or at least faded to a pale yellowish blue. Sloan drew the only conclusion she could and wondered if Nellie needed help to leave her husband.

Sloan realized she'd been staring when Nellie turned to lean on the railing and look directly out to the water, her left side now out of Sloan's line of vision. The long silence reminded Sloan she hadn't yet answered Nellie's question.

"I had a bad dream that woke me up and I knew I wouldn't be able to go back to sleep," Sloan said. "How about you? Why are you up so early?"

Sloan moved to lean on her elbows beside Nellie and gaze out at the water. Even in the dark, when you could barely see it, the water was a comfort. There were a few moments of silence and finally Nellie spoke.

"I miss my son," she said. "He died in February, and ever since, I haven't been able to sleep through the night." Nellie paused and said softly, "He was only 10."

Instinctively, Sloan tried to put her arm around Nellie to comfort her. There was no waist to encircle or shoulder to squeeze and Sloan's arm moved awkwardly, grasping at air. Nellie had slipped away and was sitting on the railing now, her feet resting on a lower rung. The way Nellie avoided touch reminded Sloan of a dog who'd been abused, cowering at even a friendly attempt to pet it.

"Nellie," Sloan said, her voice thick with emotion. "I'm so sorry. I ..." Sloan paused, fumbling for the right words, but anything she thought of felt inadequate and trite.

Before Sloan could say anything more, Nellie said, "Thanks, Sloan. Don't worry. Nobody knows what to say. Just being with you helps."

Sloan released the breath she'd been holding. She'd come close to losing Deidre to her drug addiction and could only imagine the excruciating guilt and sadness she'd have if Deidre had died. Sloan thought of her now, safe and getting help at the rehab center, and was immensely grateful. Immediately she felt guilty for having this thought as Nellie grieved her son a few feet away.

"Do you have any other children?" Sloan asked gently.

"No," Nellie replied. "Issac was my only one, and I won't be having any more."

From the tone in Nellie's voice, Sloan could tell this topic of conversation was over. Sloan knew she'd suffered, but compared to what Nellie was going through, she figured she'd had it easier.

"Do you and Peter have any children?" Nellie asked, her tone of voice back to normal.

"No. Peter and I aren't married, but we've been together for 15 years," Sloan said. "I've got two children from my first marriage. Deidre's 28 and Anthony is 30." Sloan hesitated, considering whether she should share the truth about Deidre since Nellie had easily opened up about her life. "Anthony lives in Chapel Hill and works for the newspaper there. He's a writer and also does some freelance work. Deidre's in the mountains right now getting treatment for her addiction to pain medication and alcohol." Sloan paused, took a sip of water, and continued. "She accidentally overdosed a couple nights after I closed on Magnolia Bend. I got a call from Wake Med in Raleigh and rushed up there to be with her. I'm actually thankful it happened. Those few days with her in the hospital were precious. We haven't had regular contact for a couple of years and I can't remember the last conversation I'd had with her when she wasn't high on something."

Nellie'd been listening closely. "I've never heard of someone abusing pain medicine, but the alcohol addiction I'm all too familiar with," she said. "I couldn't image it being your child, though, and not having the power to help her."

"It's been hard not seeing her the past few years, but it was worse seeing her high and not acting like herself," Sloan agreed. "I told her I'd be there for her 100% when she was ready to get sober but couldn't be a part of her life when she was using. Thank God the overdose scared her, and she finally agreed to treatment. Since Deidre doesn't have health insurance, I'm paying out of pocket for her rehab. That's the reason I was short on money to start my business."

"Oh. I'd been wondering about that," Nellie admitted. "I'm not a business woman, but it didn't make sense that you'd buy Magnolia Bend before you had money to start the retreat center. Two of your worries are gone: Deidre's in rehab and you have the money for your dream. You'll be sleeping through the night now," Nellie said, smiling.

Sloan knew that wasn't the case and wished she could figure out how to quell the nightmares and sleep past 3:30.

"I don't know about that, Nellie," she said. "I've always woken early. I'm sorry. I've been going on about myself again."

"Oh, don't apologize," Nellie reassured her. "Hearing about your life takes my mind off Issac." She sighed. "It's only been a few months since I lost him, but grief must age you. I feel 20 years older."

"How old are you?"

"33."

Sloan had known Nellie was younger than she, but now that she knew the age difference, Sloan's maternal instinct kicked in and she wanted to protect Nellie from whomever caused her bruised neck. Before Sloan could respond, Nellie turned and walked down the pier. Sloan glanced at her watch and saw it was 5:30. The sky was pink and cantaloupe as dawn broke.

Nellie raised her hand to wave goodbye and called back to Sloan.

"Have to get home to cook breakfast. See you soon!"

"Wait!" Sloan yelled, walking quickly to try to catch her. She didn't want to leave again without getting Nellie's phone number. Nellie kept walking as if she didn't hear her. Sloan jogged to catch up and walked beside her.

"Nellie, can we exchange phone numbers? I'd like to see you more than our chance encounters on my pier."

Nellie never stopped walking. "I don't have anything to write with," she said. "Can I give it to you next time? I really have to get home. Joe's expecting breakfast." Nellie picked up her pace.

Sloan sensed Nellie's fear and felt more confident that her husband was the cause of her bruises. "OK," she conceded. "We'll be sure to do that next time." Sloan felt like she needed to do something more, but wasn't sure what.

Nellie kept walking without saying anything or making eye contact. When they got to the edge of Sloan's property, Sloan slowed her pace. Nellie turned right down Magnolia Bend Road.

"Nellie, if you ever need anything, just show up at my front door," Sloan called after her.

Nellie didn't acknowledge Sloan and kept walking. Sloan's instinct was to follow Nellie so she could help her, but she didn't. Nellie was a grown woman, not a child like she'd been when she herself was abused, and she couldn't force Nellie to do anything she wasn't ready to. Sloan sighed and watched Nellie walk away before turning back to the house.

***

Maya hurried from the kitchen, down the hall, past the living room to the back porch. She pushed the screen door open with her hip. Her hands were full of napkins, silverware, and a candle for the table. Last month Maya'd bought a wicker table and two matching chairs for the back porch so she could eat outside. It was a good investment as she'd eaten most breakfasts and dinners outside since she'd bought it. She set the table for two and heard Doodle Bug whining from behind the screen door. In her haste she'd forgotten Doodle Bug was right on her heels and let the screen door slam in her face.

"Sorry, girl! I'm coming right back. Hold on."

She placed the napkins and utensils on the table and lit the fat, pink pillar candle. When Maya cleaned out the kitchen after Hazel died, she found a whole cabinet full of candles, some still in their UPS boxes. She wouldn't have bought a pink candle, but it was still usable and she hated to see it go to waste.

Maya headed back to the kitchen with Doodle Bug right behind her. She peeked out the window over the kitchen sink but didn't see Lilith's car. It was Monday night and Lilith's husband had Rotary club. She was going to drop him off and then join Maya for dinner. A few days ago, Lilith had called and told Maya that in her quest to chronicle the lives of past members of their women's circle, she'd found some interesting information she was dying to share. Maya'd jumped at the chance to have Lilith for dinner, but now was nervous. Lilith was a wonderful cook and hostess, and Maya hoped her meal would garner Lilith's approval. She'd made tabbouleh over the weekend with fresh tomatoes and parsley from the farmers market and then threw together a fruit salad when she got home from work this afternoon. Of course, Lilith was bringing the bread, her specialty.

Maya heard the car door slam. Doodle Bug barked and ran back to what had been Hazel's office. Maya followed and pushed the door open onto the driveway. Lilith's mound of curls bounced as she strode toward Maya, her arms full with a notebook, bread, and a bouquet of colorful zinnias.

"Hello, my love," Lilith said, leaning in so Maya could give her a kiss on the cheek.

"Come on," Maya said, leading Lilith back to the kitchen. "Let's get this bread in the oven to heat up."

Lilith looked around the kitchen, her eyes wide. "Wow! It looks totally different now that you can see the counters and the floor. It must have taken forever to organize this place."

Maya handed Lilith a glass of chardonnay and said, "It's been my focus since the funeral, but it was worth it. I'll give you the grand tour while we wait for the bread to warm." She was excited to show Lilith around her home. Besides Buster, nobody had been here since Hazel's death. Now that she'd cleaned every square inch, she felt more at home and less like a guest.

Lilith walked slowly around the living room and then into the dining room beside the kitchen. "This place looks amazing," she said. "I can't believe these hardwood floors and gorgeous antiques have been hiding here all these years."

Maya stood at the head of the dining room table, her hand resting on the back of one of the chairs. Lilith came up beside her and put her arm around Maya's waist.

"Hazel would be happy to see her home in this condition," Lilith said. "I imagine this is how it looked when she was growing up here."

She paused. "Has it sunk in that all this is yours?" she asked, sweeping her arm around the room.

"I'm working on it," Maya said. "It never even crossed my mind that Hazel would leave me her home and land. I assumed her son would inherit the property."

Lilith pulled out a dining room chair and sat down. Maya followed suit.

"I knew you two were close," Lilith said, "but it did surprise me that she left you the house."

Maya's eyes filled with tears and she went back to that moment in the attorney's office when she found out the house and property were hers. Even now she could feel the curve of the arm rests that she'd gripped in disbelief.

"Now that time has passed, it makes more sense," Maya said. "Even though she'd lived in Raleigh for close to 30 years, this house, the creek, Oriental, they were home for Hazel. The place she was safe, and loved, and close to nature. I guess she knew it meant the same to me." Maya paused and wiped a tear from the corner of her eye. "Her son never lived here and only came for his obligatory visits. At least that's what it felt like to Hazel. I think she knew I would appreciate and care for her property in the same way she, her mother, and her grandmother had."

"She must have thought of you like a daughter," Lilith said.

Maya thought a moment. "Maybe so. She certainly liked to take care of me. At least once a week she brought a casserole by for dinner. She watched Doodle Bug while I was at work and was always a good listener when I needed to talk about Hurricane Katrina or Steven."

Maya looked across at Lilith, whose eyes were wet with tears.

"I don't know if Hazel thought of me as a daughter, but she was a mother figure to me," Lilith said. "My mother died when I was 12."

Maya's hand went to her mouth in response to this new information.

"Oh, Lilith. I didn't know. I'm so sorry."

Lilith smiled, acknowledging Maya's awkward sympathy, and continued. "Hazel provided me with a role model for aging but most importantly she taught me how to nurture my spirituality."

Maya leaned down and rubbed Doodle Bug's head. "Yes, me too," she said. "Even amidst her own struggles and shame, Hazel never lost faith that there was a force greater than herself to sustain her."

"And only our Hazel could feed her faith in the family pew at the Baptist Church and in a camp chair around the Mother Tree," Lilith laughed.

Doodle Bug growled softly at Maya, indicating her dinner time was approaching.

Lilith stood and said, "I'm starving too, Doodle Bug. The bread's probably ready and I better put those flowers in some water so they don't wilt."

Maya lingered at the dining room table a minute more and allowed the hollow ache in her chest to pass, the physical manifestation of her grief and gratitude. Maya took a deep breath and sent up what was probably her thousandth thank you to Hazel and then followed Lilith into the kitchen.

They filled their plates with tabbouleh, fruit, and huge slabs of Lilith's rustic bread and walked out to the wicker table on the back porch. They sat down and Lilith reached across the table for Maya's hand.

"This is lovely, and such a treat to have someone cook for me," she said. "Let's take a minute of silence to appreciate our food before we eat."

Maya sat back in her chair and was aware of the warmth in her hand from Lilith's touch. She was beginning to get used to Lilith's spontaneous affection, something she rarely had growing up. Maya focused on her breath and gazed out to the water. It was after 7, and the sky in the east was grayish blue but darkness was still over an hour away. There was no breeze and despite the fact the sun was behind the house, Maya felt sticky from the humidity. A fish jumped down by the dock and the river grass rustled in the slight breeze. She was aware of Lilith across from her, Doodle Bug at her feet and fresh food on the table. She had much to be grateful for.

Lilith must have sensed Maya's thoughts and said, "Here's to the moment!" She raised her wine and clinked glasses with Maya.

After she put her glass down, Maya immediately reached for her piece of bread and took a huge bite, appreciating the flavor and texture. How she loved Lilith's bread.

Lilith laughed. "The way you're savoring that, it looks like you haven't eaten for weeks."

"Well, I haven't had your bread for weeks," Maya laughed.

A few minutes of silence passed as Maya and Lilith enjoyed their meal. Maya quickly finished off her first piece of bread and ran back to the kitchen to get herself and Lilith more. When she returned she said, "OK, Lilith. Spill it. What have you found out about our circle that's gotten you so excited?"

Lilith's eyes twinkled, and she gave Maya a sly smile. "I think I may have found the key to saving the Mother Tree," she said.

Maya leaned forward, interested in what Lilith was about to say. Besides knowing who owned the Hungry Mother Creek property and having a meeting with her next week, they had no real plan.

"Two weeks ago, I had lunch with Violet to discuss past members of our circle," Lilith continued. "We started with Florence Gupton, who was the elder prior to Hazel, and the last black woman to sit in our circle. She died a few years before I joined the circle."

Maya interrupted. "That's interesting that the circle was founded by Native Americans and then evolved to include white and black women.

Wonder why there haven't been any black women since Florence died?"

"I asked Violet the same question and she didn't know for sure," Lilith replied. "She said they never pressed the issue because the circle doesn't recruit new members but lets synchronistic events lead the right women to them, like how you became a member."

"Yes. There was some divine intervention that day I found the Mother Tree and then met you 30 minutes later. Anyway, back to Florence. How will her story help us save the Mother Tree?"

Lilith sat back in her chair. "Well, it isn't Florence's story that will help us, but what I learned from her daughter, Jana," she said. "I called Jana and told her about my research on the women's circle. She was very receptive and invited me over for coffee the following morning. After I gathered information on Florence, I showed Jana the names of the prior members Violet had given me, to see if she was familiar with anybody on it."

"But what about Florence?" Maya asked. "I want to hear what you learned about her."

Lilith smiled. "If you don't stop asking questions, I'll never get to how we can save the Mother Tree. At our fall equinox gathering we can set aside time to honor the women I've learned about and I'll share Florence's story then."

"I love that idea. OK. I'll be quiet now." And to emphasize her point, Maya took a big bite of fruit salad to keep her mouth occupied.

"So, as I was saying," Lilith said in a teasing tone, "I showed her the list of names and she knew the relatives of several and said that the great-granddaughter of one, Sadie Prince, had moved down to Oriental a few months ago. That great-granddaughter is Sloan Bostwick." Lilith paused and ate a forkful of tabbouleh to let Maya process this.

It took Maya about five seconds to make the connection. She grabbed both sides of the wicker table and leaned toward Lilith. Doodle Bug sat up and perked her ears, sensing Maya's excitement.

"Are you sure? Sloan Bostwick? Who owns Magnolia Bend and the Hungry Mother Creek property?"

Lilith shook her head yes.

Maya continued, "So, now we've found a connection between Sloan's family and the property around the Mother Tree. This could definitely help when we meet with her next week. Thank goodness you found this out."

Lilith said, "Let's call Violet and Ella and see if we can get together and work on a strategy for our meeting next Wednesday."

"Good idea." Maya stood to gather the dishes. "Now sit tight and let me clear the table and bring out dessert."

"My dear, that sounds lovely," Lilith said, inching her chair around to look out at the water. "Doodle Bug and I will sit here and enjoy the view."

Maya stepped away from the table with an armful of dishes.

"Oh, Maya . . ."

Maya paused, propping the door open with her hip.

"I also found out from Violet that Travis' grandmother was a member of the Mother Tree circle. Thought it would make sense for you to interview him and gather her history since you guys already know each other." Lilith smiled at Maya and then turned all her attention to the water, ignoring the look on Maya's face.

Maya'd met Travis on her first visit to Oriental when he'd been her kayak guide. After she moved here permanently they dated for several months, sharing a mutual love for paddling the creeks around Oriental. She ended their relationship last November because she needed more time to heal from her abusive marriage. She'd also been hurt that Travis hid the fact he was a minister. They occasionally got together as friends, but it'd been over a month since they'd seen one another. Their visits had dwindled once spring arrived and Maya'd thrown herself into cleaning and organizing her new home.

Maya stepped into the house and the screen door slammed behind her. She couldn't deny she felt a twinge of excitement to have a reason to see Travis. Damn that Lilith! Maya'd been consciously avoiding thoughts of Travis but as she served up the angel food cake and strawberries, that was all she could think about.

THE MOTHER TREE

CHAPTER 5

Maya called Ella to let her know they'd be late, and then knocked on the boathouse door. Bay was supposed to have met her in the driveway 10 minutes ago to leave for Croakerfest. The door swung open and Bay hurried back inside.

"I'm coming," Bay said, running back to the bedroom. "I need to grab some earrings and put on my lip gloss."

Maya walked into the living room to wait and felt a pang of nostalgia. It looked the same, since she'd left all her furniture here. Everything in Bay's home with Holden would have been too large for the boathouse and Bay hadn't kept anything except her clothes. All the money made from the sale of their house went toward Holden's nursing home expenses.

Maya looked at her watch. "Are you almost ready? We're meeting Ella in front of The Bean. She's probably already there."

"OK. I'm ready." Bay walked out in a pair of white Bermuda shorts and a blue and white boat neck short-sleeve sweater.

"You look cute. Where's your red to complete the patriotic theme?" Maya asked.

"Oh, you must not have seen my earrings, red stars," Bay said, laughing, and moved her blond hair away from her neck so Maya could see them.

They left the boathouse and walked together on the path to the driveway.

"Maya . . ." Bay began.

Maya interrupted, "I know. My shirt's untucked and I'm wearing flip-flops and a baseball cap but we're going to a Fourth of July arts festival on the water. I don't need to make a fashion statement."

Bay laughed. "Why did you think I was going to comment on your outfit? I've given up on you unless you ask me for help. What I was going to say, if you'd let me, was that I'm looking forward to meeting Ella."

"Oh. Sorry." Maya said, embarrassed that she'd jumped to that conclusion but happy they could joke about their differences. "Well, you won't have to worry about Ella's clothes. She's a lot like you in that way."

"Well, then I'm sure I'll like her."

Maya, Ella, and Bay wandered around Croakerfest trying to stay in either the shade or breeze to keep cool. Thankfully it was after 5 and there was a good amount of shade to be had. Booths lined both sides of the waterfront streets and clustered on the grass of Lou Mac Park. You could buy everything from paintings to T-shirts, with lots of nautical supplies mixed in. There was a stage in the middle of the street and a band was setting up. There'd be music until 9, and then the fireworks would start.

"I'm dying of thirst," Ella said. "You guys want to get a slushy and sit down for a minute?"

"Sounds perfect," Maya said.

They settled themselves into Adirondack chairs facing the water, each with a different flavored slushy. Maya was seated between Bay and Ella and, seeing them together, thought they could pass for sisters, even with the 15-year age difference.

"Bay, did you and Maya meet when you moved into her boathouse?"

Ella asked.

Maya looked over at Bay and saw her discomfort with the question. She probably didn't want to tell Ella about her divorce yet. For a moment, only the background noise of seagulls cawing and Fourth of July revelers shuffling about filled the space between them. The air smelled faintly of kettle corn.

"We've been running partners since the fall," Maya said. "When I was moving out of the boathouse into Hazel's, Bay needed a place to live, so it worked out perfectly."

"I bet you love the boathouse," Ella said. "My condo is on the water in New Bern but it's not as quaint as living here in Oriental. Where do you work?"

"I'm working part time at Marsha's Cottage. It's the boutique we passed on our way here. I also take classes at the community college and plan to transfer to N.C. State to get my degree in fashion design."

Maya watched Ella processing this with a puzzled expression and imagined she was questioning why a woman in her early 40s was going back to school. She wished she'd given Ella the story on Bay before they all got together. She knew how it felt to be asked questions you weren't ready to answer.

"What do you do in New Bern?" Bay asked Ella, tucking a stray strand of hair behind her ear to keep it from blowing into her slushy.

"I'm the East Coast sales director for Simmons Pharmaceuticals," Ella replied. "I was traveling a lot but thankfully that's about to change. I'll use video conferencing with my sales reps, which will cut my travel in half."

Maya interjected, "You made a decision! Congratulations. I've been wondering if you'd stay in that job or take the one in New Bern."

"The job at the convention center seemed like it would be fun, but I've worked hard to get where I am in my company. I'm not ready to give that up yet."

"How old are you?" Bay asked.

"27."

Maya saw Bay's posture stiffen. "Good for you. You've achieved a lot at a young age." The tone of Bay's voice did not imply this was a compliment.

Oh no, Maya thought, spinning the copper band on her ring. Maybe she'd made a mistake introducing these two. Ella was well established in her career and Bay, at 42, was starting over with hers. Ella didn't seem to notice Bay's tone and continued to sip her slushy and watch the people walking past. While Maya was trying to think of something to ease the tension, Ella asked, "What made you want to go back to school?"

Bay stood. "I really don't feel like talking about this. Maya, can Ella take you home? I'm gonna leave. I've got lots of studying to do. Y'all have fun." Before Maya could say anything, Bay had turned and was walking away.

Ella had tears in her eyes. "What did I do wrong? Why did I make her angry?"

Maya reached over and squeezed Ella's hand. "You didn't do anything," she reassured. "Bay's going through a hard time. She left her husband a few months ago and is adjusting to being on her own and back in school."

Maya empathized with Bay. She remembered doing the same thing to Bay when she stormed out of a restaurant after Bay'd asked her an innocent question about being married. She hadn't been ready to talk about Steven, like Bay wasn't ready to talk about Holden.

"Try not to worry about it," Maya said. "Bay'll be fine. I'll talk with her when I get home. Let's finish our slushies and go find Lilith. She's selling her pies at the Rotary Club's booth."

It was close to 10 when Ella dropped her off at home, but Maya saw a light on in the boathouse. She ran to her front door and Doodle Bug was there to greet her. Maya let her out to run, then walked down to the boathouse for the second time that day. Bay answered the door looking unusually casual in running shorts, a T-shirt, and bare feet. She wore her glasses and Maya could tell she'd been crying. Bay wouldn't look Maya in the eye and kept her gaze above Maya's head, probably watching Doodle Bug chasing her shadow in the flood light.

"Here," Maya said, handing a small box to Bay. "I saw this at one of the artist booths and thought you'd like it."

Bay reluctantly took the box and finally looked Maya in the eye. "I was rude to your friend and you buy me a present?"

"Can I come in for a minute?" Maya asked.

Bay didn't say anything but stepped away from the door to let Maya pass. Maya moved some books over to the coffee table and sat at one end of the couch but then hopped up to open the door. "You don't mind if Doodle Bug comes in, do you?"

"Of course not. She lived here before me, anyway," Bay said. She smiled and bent down to pet the dog.

Maya sat at one end of the couch, curling her legs under her, and Bay sat at the other end. Doodle Bug positioned herself on the floor next to Bay, intuiting who needed the most comfort. Bay still held the unopened box in one hand while she petted Doodle Bug with the other.

"I'm sorry I was such a jerk to Ella," Bay said. "She asked an innocent question, trying to get to know me, and I bit her head off. I don't know what's wrong with me. One minute I'm happy I'm following the path I'm meant to and the next I'm guilty and ashamed, thinking of Holden lying in the nursing home." Her eyes filled with tears.

Maya's heart ached. This time last year she'd been in a similar place, feeling guilty that her husband's death had released her from an abusive marriage.

"There's no need to apologize to me," Maya said. "I totally understand. Do you remember? I did the same thing to you last year."

Maya paused to give Bay time to think.

"Oh!" A look of recognition came over Bay's face. "We were in the middle of lunch and you suddenly left. I don't even remember what we were talking about."

"You casually asked me if I was married," Maya said. "At that point I wasn't comfortable talking about Steven's death and definitely wasn't ready to share it with someone I only knew casually, so I avoided answering altogether, like you did today."

Bay exhaled. "You do understand."

"Yes. And now you and I are friends and you'd almost forgotten that whole incident. I bet the same thing will happen with you and Ella. Don't you want to see what I got you?"

"Of course. I'd almost forgotten about this," Bay said, retrieving the box from the coffee table. She lifted the lid to reveal a delicate, handmade silver bracelet. A row of iridescent stones gleamed in the low nighttime light. "Maya! It's gorgeous!" she said, linking the bracelet around her wrist. "It will go with tons of my outfits."

"I know. That's why I bought it," Maya said, smiling. She looked at her watch and stood. "Come on, Doodle Bug. It's late. Time for bed." Doodle Bug slowly rose to her feet and followed Maya to the door.

Bay embraced Maya. "I can't thank you enough for coming over," she said, pulling back from the hug and grasping Maya's shoulders. "I feel much better."

"You're welcome. And Bay, this will pass, and you'll be OK."

Bay's eyes filled with tears again. "Thanks. Guess you're living proof of that."

Maya walked the path from the boathouse to her back porch. Before going in she sat on the top step and looked out toward the water. The moon's reflection undulated in the gentle ripples. The peepers and frogs filled the air with their call and response. I'm living proof of it, she thought. Was she worthy of being a role model for Bay? Yes, she wasn't having flashbacks from Katrina or Steven's rages anymore, and was grateful for all that was happening in her life. To Bay, she probably did look like she had resolved everything. She had a gorgeous home on the water, was financially secure, healthy, and had friends she could count on. Where did this sense of yearning come from? She was happy, but something was missing, and she had no idea what it was.

She saw Bay's light go out and knew it was late. She went inside and as she climbed the steps to bed, she wondered if the women in her circle had ever had a desire for something that couldn't be named. She'd bring it up when they were together again. Maybe they'd have wisdom to share from their experiences.

***

Maya watched the muscles in Travis' arms and back strain against his shirt as he paddled into the wind. A couple of brown curls escaped his baseball cap. They were paddling to Hungry Mother Creek so she could show him the Mother Tree. With a little pressure from Lilith, Maya had talked with Travis about the circle, his grandmother's involvement, and their quest to document the lives of the women who'd been members. Upon hearing all this, Travis immediately asked Maya if she'd show him the Mother Tree. That was Friday at Croaker Fest and today was Wednesday, Maya's day off. They'd left her property at about 8 this morning with plans to eat lunch after their paddle, where Travis would share details of his grandmother's life. It felt comfortable and familiar to be on the water with Travis, like their weekly outings last fall.

Travis slowed his kayak until it was even with hers. "Hey, Maya, how come you never told me you were in this circle?"

"I don't know," Maya paused to think. "Probably because last fall I focused on my marriage in the circle, and since I steered clear of talking about Steven with you, it never came up in our conversations. Plus, there's the expectation of confidentiality in the circle, so it was easier not to discuss it."

"Oh, that's right. Our fall of avoidance," Travis said. "You avoiding the topic of Steven and me avoiding that minor detail of being a minister." He laughed hesitantly and looked to Maya for her response.

Maya swallowed hard. She remembered the Sunday she'd accompanied Hazel to church. She was shocked to see Travis in the pulpit and devastated that he'd never told her about this, one of the most important aspects of his life. Travis was right though—they'd both hidden parts of themselves. Maya smiled and used the edge of her paddle to splash him. "Yeah, that minor detail. But you're forgiven."

Travis, serious now, said, "Thanks Maya." He held her gaze for a moment and then said, "Race you to Hungry Mother Creek!"

Maya looked ahead and saw the turn off for Hungry Mother Creek about a quarter mile away. Travis took off and his kayak created a small wake from the effort. Maya dug her paddle blades deep and increased her cadence to catch him. They reached Hungry Mother Creek together, short of breath and laughing. Spontaneously, they tapped their blades together in a kayak version of a fist bump.

Travis slowed to let Maya pass. "Lead the way, m'lady."

Maya took several strokes to glide in front of Travis. She tried to ignore the butterflies in her stomach. She was probably hungry. They paddled in silence until Maya pulled up to the beach in front of the Mother Tree. "Here we are."

Travis' kayak slid up on the sand beside her and they steadied their crafts as they stepped out. "I know this beach. I've paddled by it before and even stopped to rest here but never noticed a circle."

Maya walked away from the water. "Come on," she said, motioning with her hand. "It's back here, behind the Palmettos, where the trees start."

Maya stepped into the circle. Travis joined her and they faced the Mother Tree.

"It's beautiful but isn't much different from other trees around here," he said.

Without thinking, Maya grabbed Travis' hand and lowered herself to the ground, pulling him down with her. "Sit down. The face is more visible at eye level."

Travis sat beside her and took a deep breath, "Oh. Now I see." He seemed as mesmerized by the tree as Maya had the first time she discerned the face in the folds and curves of the bark. Maya watched Travis out of the corner of her eye. His eyes were closed and he was breathing deeply. She remained quiet and studied his profile: thick eye lashes, tanned cheeks, and the straight nose, an arrow to his full lips.

Maya looked away and tried to quiet her mind, but had trouble centering herself. A mosquito buzzed around her head and distracted her. It felt different being in the circle with Travis and not the other women. She almost felt like she was breaking a rule, bringing a man to the circle that's been sacred to women for many years. She looked at Travis again. He seemed to honor this space and had a connection to it through his grandmother so perhaps she wasn't committing a huge offense.

Travis opened his eyes and caught Maya looking at him. "Sorry," he said. "I needed to take a moment of silence. Not sure if it's because I know my grandmother used to sit here or something else, but this place is definitely special." Travis reached over and squeezed Maya's hand gently. His palm was warm and slightly callused. Maya didn't pull hers away. "Thanks for bringing me here."

"It's nice to share a new place with you after all the places in Pamlico County you've introduced me to," Maya said.

"Exactly what do you all do here in the circle? Gram never talked to me about it, and when I asked my mother last night she wasn't sure, although she did remember Gram coming to her circle meetings at the tree."

"You'll have to use your imagination," Maya said, smiling secretively. "We don't discuss the details of our meetings." She stopped, gazing at the Mother Tree, but Travis listened closely, expecting more. "It has to do with connection, connecting with our own truth, with each other and with nature."

"Sounds kind of like church if you substitute God for nature."

Maya thought about that for a minute. "Hmm. I guess you could be right. I wouldn't know, though, because I don't have much experience in church."

"Now that you know who the minister is, you should come one Sunday," Travis said with a smile.

Maya looked away and wiped the sweat from her forehead with the back of her hand, "Whew. It's getting hot. You ready to head back for lunch?"

"Sounds good to me," Travis said. Maya silently thanked him for not asking her about church again. She'd spent most of her life deflecting questions about church, always feeling judged when she said she didn't go.

He stood and extended a hand down to help Maya up. "Some air conditioning and sweet tea will hit the spot."

Before they left the circle, the pink surveyor's tape caught Maya's eye. She'd been focused on Travis and had forgotten about the logging. After the interview with him about his grandmother, she'd tell him. Maybe he could help.

Maya and Travis bypassed the screened porch at M&M's Cafe and chose to sit inside to soak up some AC. They paused to peruse the specials on the whiteboard and then Maya led the way to a table in what probably had been the family room when the building was a house. They sat in the corner at the last open table.

Maya leaned back in her chair, inhaling the aroma of fried flounder. "It sure feels good in here," she said. "I need to cool down a few degrees before I can even think about eating."

"Me, too. Bring on the iced tea."

"Happy to," the waitress said, appearing behind Travis to take their orders. "And what would you like, ma'am?" she asked, looking at Maya.

"I'll have water with lots of lemon."

"I'll be right back with those drinks."

"Travis, why don't we do the interview about your grandmother before we eat?"

"Great idea," Travis said, resting his elbows on the table. "Where do you want to begin?"

Maya picked up the legal pad and the list of questions she'd printed out from Lilith's email. "Why don't we start with the more structured questions and then while we eat you can share whatever you'd like about your grandmother."

Before Travis could answer, the waitress returned with their drinks. Immediately Travis and Maya grabbed their glasses and drained half their contents.

"OK, then," the waitress said. "Guess you'll be needing some refills. Y'all ready to order?"

After they ordered, Maya looked down at the list of questions Lilith and Violet had developed for the interviews. She looked up, ready to begin, and saw Travis watching her with a look of amusement. "What are you smiling at?"

"Just you. You look like a serious reporter with your interview questions and legal pad."

"Yeah. A serious reporter in a sun visor and flip-flops," Maya said with a laugh.

"And a good-looking one, too," Travis said, and the air between them immediately charged with electricity.

Maya blushed and shifted, so more of her bare legs were under the table. "OK. Let's get started." She dropped her pen and then bumped her head on the table when she bent to retrieve it. When she sat up, Travis smiled, never taking his gaze from her face. She took a breath to regain her composure. "I think I'm ready now. How did your grandmother end up in Oriental?"

Travis took a sip of his iced tea and leaned back in his chair, now focused on the task at hand. "She didn't end up here. She started here. Her father ran the general store that used to be in that old building on the corner of Broad and Hodges streets. To the best of my knowledge, she never lived anywhere else, so that would make 78 years that she lived here."

"Wow," Maya said, scribbling this info down. "I love Oriental but couldn't imagine living here all my life. Even Hazel left for college and her career. What did your grandmother do?"

"I don't have a memory of her working in a typical job, just being Gram and cooking our favorite things when my brother, sister, and I came to visit. I remember Mom saying that when she and her brother started school, Gram worked part time at her father's store until it closed."

Maya took notes and went through the other questions: favorite memory of his Gram, her hobbies, the biggest challenge she'd faced in her life. "OK. Last question. What life lesson did your grandmother teach you?"

"Hmm. Good question. I'll have to think about that one for a minute."

During this pause, the waitress appeared with their lunch. Travis continued to gaze out the window and Maya began eating, giving Travis all the time he needed.

"I have an answer, but I'm not sure how to put it in words. Surely Gram's life influenced me because I've been drawn back to live in her hometown and prefer to live in her house rather than the rectory. What comes to mind first is how special Gram made me feel. I guess my brother and sister felt the same way. On summer visits she would cook our favorite foods, let us choose what we wanted to do each day and then do it with us no matter if it was fishing, sailing, or reading on the porch. She would ask us questions about our dreams, and our opinions on various topics and listen without correcting or interjecting."

Maya understood exactly what Travis was talking about. She and her sister often felt like an afterthought to their parents, but when they were with their grandparents at Kerr Lake, they felt like the center of the universe. Before she could share this with Travis, he continued.

"You must have felt the same way. I remember you talking about how much you and your sister enjoyed summers with your grandmother."

"I can't believe you remember me telling you that."

"I guess that proves I learned the power of attention from Gram. When you give someone your full attention it's easier to remember what they say." Travis winked at her and took a bite of his shrimp wrap. They sat in silence for a few minutes while they ate.

Maya tried to focus on her lunch but was distracted by her thoughts. How did Travis remember that small detail about her grandmother she'd shared over their first dinner? That was months ago. And his comment about her being good looking. And her reaction.

A potato chip hit Maya in the nose. Travis was laughing. "Earth to Maya. Looked like you were somewhere else. Maybe you need to pay more attention to people you're with, like my Gram did."

Maya blushed. "You're right. I was lost in my thoughts. Sorry."

"That's all right." Travis took the last bite of his wrap. "I'm glad your circle's doing this project. It's been nice to talk about Gram and I don't think I would have distilled the lesson she'd taught me without you asking. When I think about it, I apply it daily, especially when I meet with members of my congregation. The simple act of holding someone in your attention is healing in itself."

"I know," Maya agreed. "That's what's powerful about our circle. When I told them about Steven's death and our marriage, I had the full attention of four compassionate women. I think that helped me heal more than anything."

"So, have you made peace with your marriage?"

A drawstring tightened at the top of Maya's throat. Her instinct to not talk about Steven tried to engage. Before she could answer, a woman, probably in her early 60s, approached them, stopping at the table on her way out of the restaurant.

"Travis. How are you? It's nice to see you out and about in town." She smiled at Travis and looked pointedly at Maya.

Maya guessed she must be a member of his church.

"Susan, this is Maya Sommers," Travis said, gesturing toward Maya.

"Oh, Maya. You're the one who inherited Hazel's house. Hazel must have thought a lot of you." She reached out to shake Maya's hand. "I'm happy to meet you. I'll let you two get back to lunch and I'll see you Sunday, Pastor."

There was a reminder. Travis was a minister. People looked to him for spiritual inspiration and direction. He must think she was a heathen sitting around a tree and not having church experience. She was thankful he'd never pressed her about her beliefs. She wasn't sure she could even put them into words yet.

Travis appeared unfazed by the interaction with his congregant. "Sorry for the interruption," he said, turning his attention back to Maya. A waitress scurried behind him. "You were about to tell me if you'd made peace with your marriage and Steven's death."

It was strange to hear Steven's name come out of Travis' mouth. She knew the healthy thing to do was to be honest with Travis.

"Yes," she said, perhaps speaking the truth and perhaps willing it to be so. "I think I have, for the most part. I spread his ashes with the circle, and that physical act helped me mentally let go. I've also accepted that I can't change my past and have forgiven myself for staying in an unhealthy marriage for so long." Maya blushed after she said this. She'd ended her relationship with Travis because she needed to heal from her marriage, but now this was mostly resolved. What if they started dating again? Would it work this time?

"Good for you," Travis said and brought Maya out of her daydream. "Sounds like the circle is meaningful. I wonder what my grandmother got out of her experience?"

"I'd say the lesson she taught you was one thing," Maya said. A toddler in hot pink shorts wobbled by their table with her young mother race walking to catch her. The pink reminded Maya that she wanted to talk with Travis about the logging of the Hungry Mother Creek property. "Oh, before we go, there's something else I want to talk about. Maybe you could help."

Travis put his arms on the table and leaned forward. "Sure. What's up?"

Maya gave Travis the rundown on what she knew about the potential logging of the property on Hungry Mother Creek. She finished by telling him about the circle's meeting with Sloan Bostwick next Wednesday and the connection Lilith had discovered between the circle and Sloan's great grandmother.

After Maya finished, Travis was quiet. She sat back in her chair and took a sip of water to wait for his response.

"Thanks for telling me about this," Travis said. "After seeing the Mother Tree today and knowing more about the history of the circle, I definitely want to help, but I'm not sure what I can do."

"I don't know, either," Maya said. "I'm hopeful our talk with Sloan will go smoothly and that maybe we'll convince her to look at other property to log. If not, at least we'll know where we stand and can work on a plan from there."

"OK. Let me know what happens next week when you meet with her."

"Sounds good." Maya looked at her watch. "It's already 2. I better get home and let Doodle Bug out."

"Thanks again for taking me to the Mother Tree. I had fun. I better get going, too. I need to prepare for church tonight."

Maya and Travis left money on the table and walked outside. They walked slowly through the heat to their cars.

"Bye, Travis. Have a good afternoon," Maya said and opened the door to her Saturn.

"Will do. Give me a call next week after your meeting with Sloan."

Maya suppressed her urge to touch Travis, who was only a few feet away. He continued walking to his car and waved before getting in his Jeep. Maya watched him drive off before starting her car.

***

His arm encircled her waist and pulled her toward him. The

pressure of his hand against her stomach flooded her bloodstream with adrenaline. She tried to pry his white fingers off her skin. This didn't work, so Sloan slid her left knee toward the edge the bed to gain momentum and then kicked behind her, her foot landing squarely on his knee. He released her and she scrambled away from him and out of the bed. Her feet got tangled in the sheets and she fell on the floor. She pulled the sheets and bedspread with her and covered her body protectively.

"Get away from me," she screamed, scooting herself away from the bed.

"Sloan. Sloan. Listen to me. You're OK. You're safe. It's me, Peter."

Sloan clutched the bedspread around her and tried to slow her breathing. Peter moved to sit at the edge of the bed, "Sloan, you've had another nightmare. It's not real. Everything is OK."

Peter. Magnolia Bend. Oriental. 50 years old. Safe. Sloan's brain recognized these facts and her fear subsided.

"Oh, Peter. Oh my God. I'm so sorry," she said, remembering she'd kicked him. Sloan gathered the sheets and bedspread and got back in bed with Peter. He held her from behind in the same position that had started all this, but this time Sloan saw Peter's black hand around her waist instead of her uncle's white one. Now she felt comfort instead of terror. Peter kissed her shoulder.

They didn't say anything for a few minutes. Sloan kept repeating to herself, "I'm OK. I'm with Peter." The adrenaline wore off and her body became heavy and relaxed. "Peter."

He cut her off. "You don't need to apologize. I hate to see you going through this. You've always woken up early, but you've had more nightmares since we moved here."

"I know," Sloan agreed "I've been trying to figure out why. The only two reasons I can come up with are that I'm not as busy as I was in my real estate job and that Oriental was the first place I talked about what my uncle did. Hopefully once I get the retreat center opened I'll have more to occupy my mind and the nightmares will stop."

"Or," Peter said softly, "you could look this thing in the eye and deal with it once and for all."

Sloan pushed him away and sat up on the edge of the bed, "Deal with it? Are you serious? I've dealt with it. I told my great-grandmother. I told you. I've had a successful career and raised my children mostly alone. I wouldn't have been able to do all that if I hadn't dealt with it. I just need to stop thinking about it and I'll be fine."

Sloan stood and grabbed her robe from the bottom of the bed. In four strides she was at the bedroom door and then almost broke the doorknob off because the door was locked. She turned back to Peter. "And why the hell do you keep locking this fucking door? You know how I feel about being in a locked room. Are you trying to torment me?"

She didn't wait for an answer, unlocked the door and stormed out. She went down the stairs two at a time and a small voice at the back of her head said a locked door wouldn't bother her if she'd truly coped with her abuse.

The sound of Peter making coffee woke Sloan from where she slept on the couch in her office. She sat up and rubbed the back of her stiff neck. From the amount of daylight outside, she guessed it was about 7:30. At least she'd been able to go back to sleep and hoped Peter had too. She heard him frying an egg and smelled toast. She wrapped her arms around her waist and stared out the windows at the front lawn. She needed more time to think before she talked to him.

She knew he was right. She'd never coped with her uncle's abuse. She'd locked it away, hoping time would dilute the intensity of her memories and emotions. It'd been 38 years and last night it felt like it was still happening. Obviously, her way of coping was not working.

But what should she do? See a therapist? Was there even one in Oriental? How would sitting across from someone and sharing the details of what she'd experienced help, anyway? Sloan felt her anger rising. It wasn't fair that she had to deal with this. She often wondered if her uncle would have abused her if she'd been white. Did her brown skin give him a sense of privilege?

Her cell phone rang, interrupting her thoughts. It was her mother. She let it ring a few more times to mentally prepare for their conversation.

"Good morning, Mom."

"Sloan, honey, is everything OK? You don't sound good. Is everything alright with Deidre?"

"Why do you always think something is wrong? I'm fine. Deidre's fine. I didn't get much sleep last night." If her mother intuited over the phone this morning that something was wrong, how did she miss the signs that she was being molested by her uncle all those years ago?

"I hope you can take a nap later today," her mom continued. "You've had trouble sleeping through the night since you were a teenager. Maybe you should see a doctor about that."

For what felt like the thousandth time in her life, Sloan thought about telling her mother the truth, that she regularly woke at 3:30 because that was when Uncle Tommy always came to her room, locked the door and, and what? How could she give voice to what really had happened to her? It felt too powerful for either her or her mother to handle. Somehow, she'd been able to share the truth with GG, maybe because her great-grandmother wouldn't blame herself like Sloan knew her mother would.

"Sloan. Are you there? Are we disconnected?"

"Sorry, Mom. I'm here."

Her mother's voice softened. "Sloan, are you sure everything is OK? I know this must be a difficult time with Deidre in rehab and you trying to start your own business."

"Everything's good, Mom. Deidre will be home in a month and in a couple weeks the renovations on the house will begin."

"OK. If you say so. I was calling to see if you could stop by your great-grandmother's house. I want to know if it needs any repairs or maintenance."

"Sure, I can do that. I'll try to go in the next week."

"Have you at least driven by lately? Does it look like anyone's been trespassing? I don't want people thinking they can take up residence there. I wish you'd go by today and check things out."

"I will try, Mom."

"Well now you sound angry. If it's too much trouble just forget about it. I can hire someone to go check on the place."

Sloan's chest tightened and she stood up to walk around her office. Why couldn't they have a normal conversation without one of them getting angry or defensive? Sloan tried not to sound irritated. "Mom, I'm not angry. I'll go by this afternoon and give you a call. I haven't noticed anything out of sorts when I drive by."

"Thank you, sweetie. Next time I'm there, I'll walk through the inside. I should probably get it ready to sell. No point to keep it now that we can stay with you if we come to Oriental."

Sloan's stomach dropped. "You can't sell the place. It's been in our family for four generations."

"I know that, but what's the point in holding on to it?" her mother asked. "I never lived there, and only visited my grandmother when I was young, and then mother and father when they moved back there. It doesn't mean that much to me."

"But it does to me," Sloan blurted out and then regretted it. She hoped her mother didn't ask her why. How could she put into words the refuge it provided her when she was younger?

"Well, we can discuss this another time," her mother said dismissively. "I need to get ready for my lecture at the culinary school." Sloan heard her father in the background. "Your father says hi and he loves you."

"Tell him I love him, too."

"I will. Thanks for helping with GG's house and I hope you can get a good nights sleep tonight."

"Thanks Mom. Have a good class."

"OK. Talk to you later."

When Sloan hung up she heard Peter washing his breakfast dishes. She should apologize before he started painting. What was wrong with her? She was always the one having to say I'm sorry. Her anger would go from zero to 100, like it did this morning, but Peter rarely lost his temper. She wondered if he'd get tired of dealing with her moods. Sloan sat down and rubbed her temples, trying not to think about losing him. She had to control her emotions.

Peter was still at the sink when she got to the kitchen. Sloan walked behind him and slid her arms around his waist, resting her head on his back. He put down the sponge and rubbed her arms, then turned and hugged her. Over the top of her head he said, "Sloan, neither one of us can live like this forever. You have to do something."

Tears slid down her cheeks. "I know." They'd had this conversation before, and Sloan knew it had to be the last one, but wasn't sure how to help herself.

THE MOTHER TREE

CHAPTER 6

Ella slid in the back seat beside Lilith and slammed the door of Maya's Saturn. "Sorry I'm late," she said hurriedly. "One of my sales people had a crisis and I had to help them problem solve."

"That's fine," Maya said. She turned right, toward town, and glanced at the car's clock. "It'll only take 10 minutes to get to Magnolia Bend so we'll still be on time." Maya pulled the visor down to block the sun.

Violet, who was sitting up front next to Maya, angled herself to see Ella and Lilith in the back. "Lilith, you never told me what you said to Ms. Bostwick when you set this meeting up," she said. "I'm surprised she agreed and even invited us to her home."

In the rearview mirror, Maya saw Lilith break eye contact with Violet and look out the window.

"Please don't be angry," Lilith began hesitantly, "but I may have sugar-coated the truth just a little to make our meeting more enticing to her."

"You usually speak the truth without much of a filter. What made you change your tactic now?" Maya asked.

"The truth without a filter would have sounded something like this: Ms. Bostwick, there's a group of women who meet regularly on your property on Hungry Mother Creek," Lilith spoke in a mockingly high-pitched voice. "While meeting here, without your permission, we noticed surveyor's tape. We were devastated to learn you're planning to log land that's sacred to us. We'd like to set up a meeting to change your mind. If I'd said it like that she'd probably have hung up or had us arrested for trespassing."

"Now Lilith, you wouldn't have had to say it that harshly, to be honest," Violet said. "What did you tell her? Probably good we know so we're all on the same page."

"Paul found out from someone in the Rotary Club that Ms. Bostwick plans to remodel Magnolia Bend and create a retreat center, so I decided to frame our visit in a way that would sound helpful to her. I told her I represented a women's group that's been in existence for over 100 years and that we'd love to learn more about her plans for her property."

"I don't know. That sounds a little sneaky to me," Maya said.

"You have to agree though, those are all true statements," Lilith said.

"I think Lilith is right," Ella said. "From my experience in sales, I've found that being creative with the truth can get you in the door. Once you're there, you should be respectful and understand how you can help the customer achieve her goals. In this case, it'll be important for us to understand why Ms. Bostwick wants to log the land and then maybe we can provide options to achieve her goal without disturbing the Hungry Mother Creek property."

Maya smiled. That was probably the most she'd heard Ella talk at once outside the circle. "Was that what you were discussing with your sales person earlier?" Maya asked.

Ella blushed and twirled a piece of her hair. "Something like that. Seemed like it would apply here, too."

"It most definitely will," Violet said. "Thanks for sharing that."

Maya turned left on Magnolia Bend Road and then right into the driveway of the plantation home. The house was three stories, with two dormers on the third floor and a chimney at each end. It was butter yellow with black shutters and had a small covered front porch. When she rounded the bend in the driveway, Maya noticed the two-tiered porch on the back, facing the water, like Hazel's house.

Maya parked in a spot about 50 feet from the front door and turned the car off. Immediately sweat prickled her scalp and the back of her neck. The four women angled themselves toward one another. Lilith leaned forward and squeezed Violet's shoulder.

"I know I'm the one who got us here," Lilith said, "but you're our elder and more tactful than I am. I think you should be our spokesperson."

Maya and Ella nodded in agreement.

"I'll be happy to start things off, but want you all to contribute," Violet replied. "And Lilith, you definitely need to be the one to talk about Ms. Bostwick's great-grandmother's involvement in the circle."

"OK," Lilith said. "Maya, were you able to get the map of the land to show her exactly where the circle and Mother Tree are?"

Maya held up a manila folder. "Yep. Got it right here."

By instinct, the four women sat silently and took several deep breaths in unison. Maya couldn't help but think of Hazel and wished she was here to guide them.

Violet broke the silence. "Everyone ready?" Without waiting for an answer, she continued, "Let's treat this meeting like our circle, be respectful and honor Ms. Bostwick's point of view. When it's our time to talk, we'll speak from our hearts about the significance of the Mother Tree and the land around her, and remember, she's a woman like us, so no need to be nervous."

No one had said anything about being nervous, Maya thought, and then realized that Violet must be. Being the elder didn't come naturally to Violet, even after several months in this role.

The four women walked toward the front door. Before they were on the porch, the door opened, and Maya saw Sloan Bostwick for the first time. She was first struck by Sloan's height, which took up most of the doorframe. Then her attention was drawn to Sloan's skin. It was light brown with copper undertones, lighter than Maya expected since Sloan's great-grandmother was African American. Sloan wore white linen pants and a rose-colored silk blouse, and her hair was swept up in a twist. She presented a sharp contrast to their group—Lilith, with her unmanageable curls was in flip-flops and khakis; Violet in her usual wrap-around skirt today paired with sandals instead of Keds; and Maya, who thought she'd dressed up, wearing a casual skirt and T-shirt. Ella was the most dressed of them all in a turquoise shift dress and gold open-toed shoes.

Before Ms. Bostwick could say anything, Lilith stepped forward. "Ms. Bostwick, I'm Lilith. We spoke on the phone. Thank you for meeting with us today."

Sloan shook Lilith's hand and then stepped back from the door to let them come in. "I'm glad you're here, and please, call me Sloan."

Once they were in the foyer, Lilith introduced Maya, Violet, and Ella. It was silent after the introductions as the women took in their surroundings. A staircase rose directly in front of them with 10 steps that went to a landing and then a shorter flight of stairs to the second floor. The side of each step had a wave-like pattern carved in it. The plaster walls were painted willow green and there was a white chair rail.

Maya guessed the others were also struck by the beauty of the home. Sloan noticed, and said. "I take it you've never been inside Magnolia Bend? I'd be happy to take you on a tour after our meeting."

"That'd be lovely," Violet said. "I've lived in Pamlico County all my life and have passed by here in car and boat but have never gotten the chance to come inside. In fact, until now, I wasn't sure anyone lived here."

"From my research," Sloan said, "it looks like the last few owners lived out of state and never made it their home. I think it's been 15 years since someone actually lived here full time."

"Rumor has it that it's haunted and that's why no one wanted to live here," Lilith said with a smile.

Sloan laughed. "Well, I don't believe in ghosts, so I don't need to worry about them bothering me. Come. I have a table set up in the east ballroom where we can meet. That's the room I'll be updating to serve as the main meeting room for my retreat center."

Hearing Sloan laugh helped Maya relax. They walked past the staircase on the right and a closed door on the left that Maya guessed was either a lavatory or a coat closet. She could see a swinging door straight ahead and imagined the kitchen was behind it. She followed Sloan left into the spacious ballroom. Wide pine boards made up the floors and the walls were covered in a faded blue-gray paint with a white chair rail.

"Sloan, this room is perfect for a retreat. Look at the view," Maya said, pointing to the wall of windows looking across the 4-mile expanse of the Neuse River. "I appreciate my creek view, but this is amazing. I bet you love watching the sunrise."

"I do and imagine my retreat groups doing sunrise yoga here or even outside on the patio in good weather. But that's a ways off," Sloan said, her eyes traveling around the room, appraising its current state. "There's quite a bit I need to do to get the room ready, primarily updating the electrical system, installing wi-fi, and getting partitions to create smaller rooms for break-out sessions."

"Oriental needs something like this. I bet it will draw more people down here and help local business. When will it open?" Violet asked.

"I hope to have it ready for my first retreat next March, when the weather begins warming up. I should have financing for the renovations by the fall, and then it will depend on how quickly the work can get done."

Maya caught Lilith's eye and knew she'd heard it, too. Sloan needed the money from logging to renovate her retreat center. Maya immediately starting thinking of other ways Sloan could raise money besides destroying the tree they cherished.

Sloan motioned them to a rectangular folding table set up in the middle of the ballroom. A pitcher filled with water sat in the middle. Its condensation created a wet circle on the white tablecloth. Goblets were placed in front of each chair. Sloan sat down and poured herself a glass of water. "Please, help yourself."

Maya poured herself a glass of water and waited. She looked to Lilith beside her and then across the table to Ella and Violet, but no one made eye contact. She twirled her spinner ring and wondered if she should speak up. She began formulating an opening sentence in her mind when Sloan said, "Thanks for asking to meet with me. I'm glad you have an interest in my retreat center. Lilith said you wanted to hear more about my plans for Magnolia Bend, which I'm happy to share, but first tell me more about your group. Lilith told me it's been in existence for over 100 years."

Maya shifted in her chair, uncomfortable with the false pretense Sloan had about the meeting. She thought they were here to support her efforts when, in fact, they were defending their own interests. Maya's body tensed as she anticipated conflict. She tried to come up with ways to help Sloan understand their point of view. Suddenly Maya realized Violet was speaking. She placed her arms on the table and leaned in, bringing her attention back to the meeting.

Violet was saying, "It's hard to put into words the exact nature of our women's group. Actually, we refer to it as a circle, a women's circle." Violet paused. "There's nothing in writing that defines our circle, only the tradition that's been passed down orally and in our practices. Through ritual and speaking truthfully about our lives, we help each other heal our wounds and grow stronger. Our circle connects us to one another, nature, and our spirituality."

Maya thought Violet was doing a good job succinctly sharing what was meaningful about the circle. Sloan, who appeared to be paying close attention, said, "That's an interesting concept. How did the circle get started? It's hard to imagine something that loosely structured would exist for 100 years."

Maya saw Violet take a deep breath and look across the table at Lilith. In the next few sentences, she'd have to mention the Mother Tree and then Sloan would know the real reason for their visit.

"We don't know the specifics of how the circle started, but the story that's been passed is that Native American women began meeting around a sacred tree for ritual," Violet explained, caution in her voice. "Over time, white women and African-American women were included. The rituals have evolved over the years to meet the needs of whomever is in the circle at the time."

"So, your group, I mean circle, meets outside around a tree?" Sloan asked incredulously.

"Yes. We call it the Mother Tree. She's a huge, ancient live oak that sits just off the bank of Hungry Mother Creek. Our circle meets there at sunrise on the solstices and equinoxes."

Maya, Ella, Lilith, and Violet were all watching Sloan closely to see if she had a reaction to the mention of Hungry Mother Creek. She didn't, and appeared to be processing the information she'd just received.

"How can my retreat center help you, then?" Sloan asked. "I assumed when you asked to meet, you were interested in using my retreat center for your meetings. I even thought you may be a part of a state or national organization who'd want to use Magnolia Bend. Your circle is unique and sounds important to you, but I'm not sure how I can be of help."

Maya sensed Lilith fidgeting beside her and knew she was trying to contain the passion bubbling beneath her surface. Violet didn't answer Sloan's question and poured herself a glass of water. Maya took Violet's hesitation as a sign she wanted someone else to speak. Maya took a breath and thought of the Mother Tree, the accepting eyes in the contours of the bark and her limbs spread protectively over the circle. Maya knew she had to speak the truth like she did in the circle, even if it resulted in conflict.

"Sloan, you're right," Maya said calmly. "Our circle doesn't need to use your retreat center. We're here to talk with you about the parcel of land that's deeded with the Magnolia Bend property. Your property on Hungry Mother Creek."

Sloan sat back in her chair and crossed her arms over her chest. Maya guessed she made the connection. In a taut voice Sloan asked, "And why should you have an opinion about what I do with my property?"

Maya felt the tension thicken. Ella and Violet were quiet, their eyes on the table. Lilith was at the edge of her seat, ready to pounce. Quickly, before Lilith could jump in, Maya said, "As you've probably figured out, the Mother Tree is located on the property you're planning to log on Hungry Mother Creek. That land has been sacred to women in Pamlico County for generations."

Maya paused for a sip of water and Lilith used this opportunity to jump in. "Sloan, I've been researching the life stories of some of our past members, and you actually have a connection to our circle and the Mother Tree."

Sloan pushed her chair away from the table and crossed her legs. "I know I have a connection. I own the Mother Tree."

Maya put her left hand on Lilith's thigh as a reminder to stay calm, although she was having difficulty herself. She blinked back the tears that formed when Sloan said she owned the Mother Tree. Maya'd never considered who owned the Mother Tree. It was a part of nature and not something that could have imaginary lines drawn around it and given to one person.

Lilith squeezed Maya's hand and said, "The connection I found was that you have a family member who was part of our circle. Your great-grandmother Sadie was in our circle for over 20 years. From what I've been told, she stopped coming a few years before her death because she was too weak to get there."

The women watched Sloan, waiting for her reaction, hoping the mention of her great-grandmother would soften her resolve. Sloan's face didn't offer any clues. She pulled her arms in tighter across her chest and stared out the windows at the water. Maya watched a bead of sweat slip down the right side of her face, but she made no attempt to wipe it away.

Finally, after what felt like an eternity, Lilith asked, "Sloan, did your great-grandmother ever talk to you about the Mother Tree or her experience in the circle?"

Sloan's body was frozen and only her eyes moved to lock in on Lilith. "What my great-grandmother and I talked about is none of your business," Sloan said firmly, her voice unwavering. "Unless you all have the money to fund my renovations, I think this meeting is over. I've been in real estate most of my life and have cut down hundreds of trees to make space for a building that will serve more people than the trees did. I see this in the same light. I understand the Mother Tree and the land around it serves a purpose for you four, but ultimately logging that land will help me create a retreat center that will serve hundreds every year." Sloan stood. "Looks like our time has been wasted this morning. Let me show you out."

They all stood, and Maya realized she was still holding the plot map. She placed it in the middle of the table and said, "I'll leave this map of the Hungry Mother Creek property. We marked the Mother Tree and circle area with a red X in case you want to see it for yourself."

Sloan glanced down at the map and then walked toward the front door. Lilith, Ella, Violet, and Maya followed silently. Sloan opened the door and the heat and humidity rushed in. "I hope we can meet again on better terms," she said, not unkindly. "Soon my retreat center will be open; you'll have found another place for the circle to meet and this will have all blown over."

Violet reached out and shook Sloan's hand. "Thank you for your time this morning. If we come up with another way to finance your renovations, we'll let you know."

"The logging company is getting started in the next four to six weeks. I think it will be simpler on your part to start looking for a new place for your circle to meet," Sloan replied.

Lilith stepped off the porch and then turned and stood in front of Sloan, her hands clenched in fists by her side. "As a responsible property owner, you should at least walk the land on Hungry Mother Creek before you destroy it. Find the Mother Tree. Sit in the circle. Your great-grandmother felt the energy of that place, and you may feel it, too. I'm begging you, please go there before you begin the logging!" Lilith's voice cracked and she turned abruptly. She walked past Maya's car and strode forcefully toward the end of the driveway, her emotion needing an outlet.

Maya wasn't sure what to do next. Should she say something to support Lilith or try to smooth things over? Ella and Violet were taking the path of least resistance and walking to the car. Before Maya could make a decision, Sloan stepped backward into the house, totally ignoring Maya, and shut the door. Maya didn't move and listened to the click of Sloan's heels receding deeper into the house until there was silence. She turned back to the car where Violet and Ella were already seated, both looking straight ahead. Lilith was at the end of the driveway and turning onto Magnolia Bend Road. Their first attempt to save the Mother Tree had failed.

***

Maya took the lasagna out of the oven to let it cool and then sat down at the small kitchen table to wait for Travis. She was exhausted and now wondered if she should've waited to talk to Travis when she had more energy, but it was too late now. He'd be here any minute. Maya'd been upset after the meeting with Sloan and called Travis as soon as she got home. After hearing her version of the meeting, he suggested they have dinner to talk about the next step. Without thinking, she invited him over for dinner and then threw herself into making spinach lasagna to keep her mind off the Mother Tree.

Doodle Bug, lying spread eagle on the linoleum floor to absorb as much of the coolness as possible, lifted her head, ears perked. Maya guessed Travis was close and then had her answer when Doodle Bug jumped up and ran to the door, her tail wagging furiously. Maya walked through Hazel's office and opened the back door. Doodle Bug bounded out and ran to Travis, who was halfway to the front door.

"Hey there, Doodle Bug. How are ya doing, girl?" Travis said, bending down to pet Doodle Bug, who was doing her happy dance all around him.

Maya stood at the bottom of the back steps, watching Travis walk toward her. God, he was good looking. He wore flip-flops, jeans, and a royal blue T-shirt with the Pamlico Paddle logo on the chest. His hair was still damp from the shower. He held her gaze as he approached, and Maya's heart rate accelerated.

Without hesitation, he pulled her into a hug and said, "I'm sorry things didn't go like you wanted this morning. We'll figure something out."

Maya lingered in the hug a moment longer than she probably should have, but it was good to be held. She felt Travis' heart beating against her cheek and his body heat penetrating her thin cotton T-shirt. She quickly stepped back and smoothed her skirt. The space between their bodies held the same electrical charge she'd felt at lunch a few days ago, making it difficult for Maya to move. Suddenly, Doodle Bug ran between them and dropped a stick at Travis' feet. The moment was broken and Maya was thankful for Doodle Bug's interruption so she could regain her composure. Travis threw the stick down the driveway and Doodle Bug sped after it.

"She'll have you throwing that stick all night if you let her," Maya remarked.

"Oh, I know. Elvis is the same way," Travis replied. "Maybe next time I'll bring him, too, and they can play."

"Sounds like a plan. Now come on in. Dinner's ready. Doodle Bug! Come! Time for dinner."

Maya sat at the head of the dining room table with Travis to her right. She tried telling herself she'd just invited a friend over, but the linen tablecloth, arrangement of zinnias and petunias, and Bay's input on her outfit contradicted this.

"The lasagna smells amazing," Travis said, and grabbed his fork to begin. "It's a treat being here. When I knew Hazel, I worked outside and on the boathouse but never came in. It's gorgeous."

"I know. I still have to pinch myself to prove it's mine. It'll take a while before I stop referring to it as Hazel's."

As usual, Maya started her meal with Lilith's bread. She sliced a wheat loaf and spread garlic herb butter on it. The bread was soft and warm and the butter enhanced its flavor with garlic and parsley. Maya closed her eyes to savor the bread and when she opened them Travis was smiling at her.

"I take it the bread is good," Travis said, reaching for his own piece.

Maya blushed. "Yes. My friend Lilith makes it for me and it's usually my favorite part of the meal."

"I can see," Travis said. "Now Lilith. She's in your circle, right?"

"Yes," Maya said. "She's the one researching the lives of our past members and the one who found out your Gram was in our circle. I hope she's doing OK. She was more upset about the meeting than I was."

"So, speaking of this morning, it doesn't sound like Sloan was open to compromising, short of you all paying for her renovations."

Maya chewed and swallowed for a moment before she replied. "No. At first, things were going well, and she seemed genuinely interested in our circle, but as soon as Hungry Mother Creek was mentioned, and then especially after Lilith brought up her great-grandmother's involvement, she shut down. I've never seen anyone disconnect like that. It was almost like she wasn't in the same room with us. Obviously, that wasn't conducive to an open discussion."

Travis, listening attentively said, "So, after being engaged with you all, she suddenly withdrew, and you couldn't have a two-way conversation?"

"Yes," Maya said, nodding. "She never even said anything about us meeting on her land, but she was definitely defensive about her great-grandmother. After that, she basically said she owned the Mother Tree and we needed to find some other place to meet."

"Maya, I think there's more going on with her than needing the logging money for renovations."

"Why do you say that?"

Travis wiped his mouth with his napkin then placed it in his lap. "When someone's reaction is stronger than necessary, it's often because the situation triggered something negative from their past. Their intensity is more related to the past than what's going on in the moment."

Maya considered this for a minute and reflected on her own behaviors after Hurricane Katrina and Steven's death. "You could be right, but I don't see how that will help us save the Hungry Mother Creek property."

"It may not, but the better you understand Sloan, the greater the chance you'll find a compromise. She's not the bad guy trying to kill the Mother Tree, but probably someone with her own struggles."

Maya now felt guilty about being angry with Sloan. She pushed her chair away from the table and crossed her arms in front to her. Doodle Bug whined quietly at her side and looked up at her with wide, begging eyes. "Well, no matter what's going on with her, the end result was that she had no interest in compromising."

Travis smiled. "Sorry, I wasn't being judgmental of how y'all handled it. Does your circle have any ideas about the next step?"

"No," Maya said. "We hoped that after the meeting there'd be alternatives to explore, but like I said, we never got that far. We were all disappointed and frustrated after the meeting and didn't even discuss what we'll do next."

"Didn't you say that Sloan implied the Mother Tree had less value because it was special to only you four?"

"Yes. She said more people would be positively impacted by cutting down the trees and creating the retreat center."

Travis rested his chin in his hand and stared out the window toward the creek. Maya remained silent, sensing he was working on an idea. He sat up and leaned back in the chair. "So, what if we showed Sloan that the property was valuable to the community, and that more than your circle would feel a loss? I wonder if that would motivate her to look at other options?"

"I don't know," Maya shrugged, feeling pessimistic. "It might, but who else cares about that land? I know Buster does because he used to hunt there with his grandfather."

"After you showed me the Mother Tree and circle area I mentioned it to our youth director, who immediately knew where I was talking about," Travis said. "He's taken our high school youth there to camp. He's from Oriental, and said he and his friends hiked all around there growing up. He told me that boys still go out there to run, hunt with BB guns, fish, and be out in nature."

"So, it's not just women who are drawn to that area," Maya said.

"Doesn't seem to be. Anyway, after talking with him, I asked others in my church and neighborhood if they knew about the land on Hungry Mother Creek and almost everyone did and wanted to share a memory. My next-door neighbor who's in her 80s said her husband proposed to her on the sandy beach in front of the circle."

Maya was surprised at the number of people who knew about the property on Hungry Mother Creek. She was happy they might help save it, but had trouble knowing others spent time near the Mother Tree and their circle. When she and the women gathered, it felt like that spot was put there solely for them.

"How could we let Sloan know logging will affect more than the circle?" Maya asked.

"I was already thinking about that," Travis said, his enthusiasm growing. "Maybe we could organize a gathering, a rally, to honor the Hungry Mother Creek property and invite Sloan to come. We could have folks share their memories and how its destruction would impact them. It would take some organizing."

"But Travis, wouldn't that put Sloan on the defensive?" Maya said, the concern and doubt in her voice evident. "If she shut down with only four women, I don't know if she'd even show up for this. There needs to be something for her to gain by coming."

Travis smiled and reached over to squeeze Maya's hand. "Ahh, you were listening to me. You're exactly right. We need a two-pronged approach, sharing the meaning of the Hungry Mother Creek property while also showing our support for her retreat center. Now how could we do that?"

"I have no idea."

"We need someone to buy the land from her and leave it undeveloped," Travis said, sighing.

Travis suddenly stood and walked through the living room to look out the creek-side windows. He ran his fingers through his hair. Maya watched him. She tried to keep her mind on ideas for saving the Mother Tree but had trouble concentrating because of the handsome distraction in front of her. She piled up the dishes and took them to the kitchen, letting Travis continue to think. She set the dishes in the sink and Travis strode into the kitchen.

"Maya, I have it," he said. "It would be hard to find one person to afford the property, but maybe we could find several people to invest, including the city and county. I have no idea if it would work, but maybe a mixture of public and private funds could buy the land and then we'd create a community park."

Travis was pacing back and forth in the kitchen, full of enthusiasm. Maya leaned back against the counter and smiled. She'd never seen him this fired up about something. Actually, she'd never seen any man like this. Her father got passionate only when he was lubricated with red wine and, in the end, the only strong emotion Steven had was anger.

Travis continued, "I'll write a sermon about our responsibility to care for Mother Earth. Maybe that will plant a seed and inspire folks to help. We can ask for partners to buy the land at the rally. What do you think?" Travis asked, picking up a towel to dry the dishes Maya had washed.

"They're all good ideas, but a little overwhelming," Maya said slowly, avoiding eye contact by staring at the sudsy water in the sink. "When this started, it was only my circle trying to save our sacred spot and now it involves the county government, your church, practically the whole town. I don't know. The Mother Tree is where I've shared intimate parts of my life. It's hard to think of all these other people there too." She turned to face him. "I know it's selfish, but that's how I feel."

Travis put down the towel and considered what she'd said. "No, not really," he said thoughtfully. "But what would be selfish is not letting others know what's going on so they can help. Maya, nature comes from an infinite source. The Hungry Mother Creek property has more than enough energy to provide for us all, as long as we are present and allow it to."

"I know," Maya said. She felt her chest tighten and her eyes filled with tears. What was wrong with her? What was she crying about? Maybe she was emotionally drained from the day. Then she knew and began crying in earnest. She, Hazel, and the others had been vulnerable around the Mother Tree, sharing their personal struggles. She'd spread Steven's ashes there off the beach. She didn't want random people tromping through their circle, picnicking on the beach. It felt disrespectful.

Maya turned away from Travis, embarrassed by her tears, but he stopped her and pulled her to him. Travis never said a word. He held her until the front of his T-shirt was damp from her tears. After a few minutes, Maya's sadness subsided and she felt a sense of calm. She was amazed at the value of a good cry. She'd rarely allowed herself to do this before living in Oriental, but was learning to deal with her emotions in the present rather than bottling things up.

"Feel better?" Travis asked. He loosened his grip and she looked up at him.

"Yes. Thanks." Maya smiled and then laughed. "Travis, do you even know why I was crying?"

"Well, kind of, but I've learned it's better to stay quiet and not ask questions when a woman is crying," he said, teasing her.

Travis continued to keep one hand firmly in the small of her back. With his other hand he pushed back a piece of her hair that'd slipped out of her headband. She was acutely aware of the pressure of his body against hers. She should step away. They were just friends now. But she couldn't. Travis reached down and took her chin in his hand, angling her face toward him. Instinctively she reached her hand behind his head and he leaned in to kiss her. Any lingering thoughts about the Mother Tree disappeared and she was only aware of his lips and the warmth of his body against hers.

CHAPTER 7

Sloan didn't need to look at the clock. She knew what time it was. This morning she awoke not to flashbacks from childhood, but to her mind swirling with thoughts about her meeting with the women's circle yesterday. She regretted how she behaved with them, especially when they brought up GG. Well, she couldn't change what'd already happened.

Sloan turned on her right side, away from Peter. Why was she even trying to go back to sleep? She slipped out of bed and quietly walked to the door, avoiding the creaky floorboards she'd identified on other early-morning awakenings. She almost walked straight into the bedroom door. Why was it closed? She distinctly remembered leaving it open last night. She turned to see if the thud of her foot against the closed door woke Peter, but he was still and breathing deeply. Sloan turned the doorknob. It was locked. She was almost prepared for this and didn't have nearly the reaction she'd had the first time, but she still felt a sense of dread. This was the fourth time in the past two weeks that she'd awoken early and found the door closed and locked. She could only think of two explanations for this: either she was going crazy, or Peter was playing tricks on her. She quickly discounted Peter as the reason. He understood her phobia of locked doors and would never intentionally do anything to cause her anxiety. Maybe she was going crazy. Her emotions had been erratic over the past month. She unlocked the door and quietly closed it behind her.

In the kitchen, Sloan put on the tea kettle. While she waited for the water to boil she looked outside, hoping to see Nellie. There was no moon and it was hard to see the end of the dock, so after she made her Earl Grey tea, she walked outside with her mug. Sloan moved away from the glow of the kitchen lights and her night vision improved. She took a few steps out onto the dock but Nellie was nowhere in sight.

Back in the kitchen, Sloan sat at the table with her tea. The map the women had left yesterday stared up at her. Part of her wanted to throw it away and not think about the Mother Tree again, but another part wanted to know more. Sloan spread the map out and saw a red X about one-third of the way down. This marked the location of the Mother Tree where the women's circle gathered. That one red X meant nothing to her compared with the money she'd get from logging, but maybe the Mother Tree had been important to GG. Sloan racked her brain trying to produce a memory of GG talking about the women's circle or the Mother Tree but came up empty.

Why hadn't GG told her about the circle? Sloan stood and circled the kitchen with the map still in her hand. Her agitation needed an outlet and she decided to walk over to her great-grandmother's house. Maybe being in the place where she'd spent time with GG would help her memory and she needed to check on the property anyway. She'd promised her mother she'd do a walk-through and find any maintenance work that needed to be done. Today was as good a day as any. Sloan folded the map, put her mug in the kitchen sink, and went upstairs to change.

Sloan walked briskly to dissipate the effects of the locked door and the red X where the Mother Tree stood. She tried to focus on her breath and the sound of her footfalls on the pavement. She watched the stars being absorbed by the sky as dawn broke. Sloan slowed her pace and wiped the sweat from her forehead with a bandana. She turned and walked down the dirt driveway to her family's home. The tire tracks were still bare but the grass between them and in the yard was knee high. She'd check with her mother to find out who mowed the grass. She rounded the bend of the driveway and paused when GG's house came into view. The square house, two rooms by two rooms, had a small front porch and was set on a cinderblock foundation only a couple feet above the ground.

The house was enveloped in morning shadows and looked exactly as Sloan remembered. She walked toward the front porch, like Ebenezer Scrooge with the ghost of Christmas past. She wondered if she looked in the windows whether she would see her grandparents and GG in their morning routines. Her grandmother would be in the kitchen by now, making coffee and starting biscuits. Her grandfather would be shaving in the bathroom, and GG would still be asleep. Sloan felt the opposing tug of gratitude and grief as she reminisced. She took in a deep breath and smelled the sulphuric, earthy aroma of the pluff mud in the creek behind the house. She instantly knew the wind was out of the southwest, pushing water out of the creek and exposing the mud. She heard the morning insects, a kingfisher calling, and a squirrel scurrying in the leaves, sounds and smells from her summers in Oriental.

Sloan walked around the left side of the house to the screened porch. A screen was torn and would need repair, but otherwise it looked OK. She sat on the back step and watched the woods awaken. She'd done this many times, waiting for breakfast as a child. Sloan realized she'd rarely paused long enough to appreciate the morning for most of her adult life. She was always busy getting the kids ready for school, squeezing in an early-morning aerobics class, getting to the office by 7. Even on the weekends she was moving, busy, scheduled. Sloan felt a pang of regret at what she may have missed in her pursuit of achievement and financial success. But had she only been in pursuit? Had she used her busyness to run away from her abuse?

Sloan stood and walked back to the creek—actually it was more of a gully—a 10-foot-wide channel of water that fed into a wider creek which then met up with Dawson's Creek. A small john boat or kayak was all that could be used in these shallow waters, the best waterfront property a black family could buy in GG's generation. The path her family had worn down to the creek was now overgrown. She did the math and calculated it'd been over 15 years since her grandmother died and anyone had lived here. She pulled away vines and briars, stepped over logs, and crouched under low-hanging branches.

Sloan paused in a clearing near the creek to wipe the sweat from her eyes. To her right was a huge magnolia tree. She turned to face it. She remembered this tree. Its trunk and lower branches were much thicker and its height had doubled since she'd last been here, but it was definitely the same tree. Now that she was in front of it, Sloan couldn't believe she'd forgotten coming here with GG. When she'd gotten her first period the summer she was 12, GG brought her to sit and talk by this tree. At least two or three times a summer after that, they would wake before dawn and walk down here to sit and talk as the sun rose. She remembered these conversations being different. Her great-grandmother treated her like a grown up when they talked under the magnolia, and she gave Sloan her full attention. It was here that Sloan shared the middle-of-the-night visits by her white uncle and here where she came alone to comfort herself. How could she have forgotten this?

The weight of these memories pulled Sloan to the ground. She leaned back against the magnolia and cried. She cried for her younger self and the suffering she'd endured. She cried for GG, wishing she was here with her now. She cried for her relationship with her mother, stunted by her not speaking and her mother not asking. Sloan never allowed herself to cry like this, but sitting under the tree that had borne witness to her pain before allowed her to be vulnerable.

After several minutes her sobs subsided and she heard the rustling, chirping, 'croaking, buzzing morning song of the woods. A mullet splashed out in the water. She was still here. The memories and intense emotion hadn't swallowed her. Sloan used her bandana to wipe her eyes, face and neck, wet with sweat and tears. She felt the tree supporting her from behind, its branches shading her from the morning sun now dappling the forest floor. She closed her eyes and visualized GG sitting under the tree with her. Just her imagined presence provided Sloan with comfort. She knew that GG had never told her about the Mother Tree circle but realized she'd shared the essence of it with her when they sat together here. Sloan picked up a shiny magnolia leaf the length of her hand and stood to finish her walk to the creek.

Sloan watched the water bugs skiing across the surface and thought of the map on her kitchen table. Did the tree on Hungry Mother Creek provide the same sense of comfort and healing she'd experienced sitting by the magnolia? How would she react if someone cut down all the trees in the woods behind her great-grandmother's house?

Suddenly contractor's quotes, Deidre's rehab bills, and the reality that she had to have an income from her retreat center crowded out the thoughts of trees and women's circles. There was no other way. She had to log the land to get the money she needed. Sloan threw the magnolia leaf into the creek and slashed at the vines and briars to get out of the woods.

THE MOTHER TREE

CHAPTER 8

Maya woke up before her alarm and lay on her back. Doodle Bug was still breathing heavily on the floor beside her. If she was going to run her 6-mile route this morning she needed to get moving, but she couldn't. She had no motivation and her body was pinned to the bed like an insect pinned to a Styrofoam board. What was wrong with her? She usually got up without hesitation or any internal dialogue. Get up, run, go to work. That'd been her routine since college. For fifteen years she'd worked 40 hours a week, done exactly what was asked, and stayed under the radar, never calling attention to herself by speaking up, creating conflict, or even excelling.

She turned on her stomach and dropped her left arm over the side of the bed to pet Doodle Bug. The room lit up for an instant and Doodle Bug lifted her head and perked her ears at the low rumble that followed. Good, an excuse to stay in bed a little longer, she thought, and the rain began a gentle rhythm on the roof. A rainy Monday. Now I need a reason to not go to work. Can you take a sick day if you're mentally ill or on the brink of being bored to death? And in that question, she found an answer. Boredom was pinning her to the bed. Her routine had provided comfort in times of transition, a touchstone in the midst of a tumultuous relationship, but now her personal life was stable and she didn't need the same old boring routine to keep her sane. In fact, it was now the cause of her distress.

Maya swung her legs out of bed and picked up her cell phone. Before she lost her nerve, she called the office and left Dr. Allan a message that she wasn't feeling well and wouldn't be in today. She patted the bed, giving Doodle Bug permission to jump up. "Doodle Bug, I'm staying home with you today. No co-pays, medical charts or discourses on back pain. I'll make pancakes, read, and kayak later, when the rain stops." Maya glanced at her clock—6:20 and the whole day was before her, a gift in shiny foil paper.

She lingered in bed a bit longer and enjoyed the hum of rain on the roof. Wonder what Travis was doing today, she thought. Since their dinner last Wednesday, she'd replayed their kiss a hundred times, trying to analyze what it meant. What did she want it to mean? This was probably the better question. Maya turned on her side and rubbed Doodle Bug's stomach. Was she ready to make herself vulnerable again? Was Travis even interested in a relationship? Maybe their kiss had just been a heat-of-the-moment reaction.

Thinking about it would never answer her questions, but the way her stomach flipped in anticipation of seeing Travis Sunday provided feedback about her own feelings. Maya and her women's circle were going to the Baptist church to hear Travis' sermon on the divinity of nature and his announcement about the rally to save the Hungry Mother Creek property. That was still six days away. A long time to wait, but, she didn't have to wait to make pancakes.

Maya dried the griddle, put it away, and then wiped down the countertop where the pancake batter had spilled. She leaned against the sink, cradling her coffee cup, and stared out the window. Pancakes on a Monday. Calling in sick when she wasn't. Wow, what a rebel. Breaking all the rules. Maya laughed out loud, and said, "If making pancakes on a Monday is my idea of a rebellion, I think I need a more interesting life." Doodle Bug looked at her nonchalantly and lay down beside the air conditioning vent. She rested her head on her paws as if to say, "I'm perfectly content. Don't know what your problem is."

Maya dumped the rest of her coffee in the sink and rinsed her mug. The red tail lights of Bay's car caught her eye. She must be heading to her 9:00 class, Maya thought. She felt a pang of envy. Bay had a dream she was following and here she was, stuck in a routine with no idea of what she wanted to do with her life.

Maya picked up her phone and quickly texted Bay, inviting her to lunch. Her classes were done at noon and Marsha's Cottage was closed today, so she'd be free. Well, at least Maya had a purpose for the morning. She'd run to the store shortly and get ingredients for chicken salad.

Maya left Doodle Bug snoring by the vent and walked down the hall to the back porch to check on the weather. She wanted to get on the water if she could. The sun was streaming down the hall and Maya's heart filled. "Yea. I'm going to change and go kayak," she said to no one in particular.

Before she reached the bottom of the staircase, something caught her eye. The sunlight at this angle revealed an irregularity in the wood paneling under the staircase. There was a rectangular section from her waist to the floor cut into the wood. She knelt down to look more closely. Why hadn't she noticed this before? Of course, until she cleaned out the house, the hallway was lined with boxes and you'd never notice this subtle irregularity. She guessed she was always looking out the back door toward the water and never paid much attention.

Maya ran her hands over the wood, following the rectangular seam. What was this? Maybe a door? She applied pressure with her palms and when she got to the middle of the right side she felt the wall give a little. She pressed harder, heard a click, and then the wall swung open, almost hitting her in the nose.

"Oh, my," Maya said in surprise. She felt another presence, flinched, and lost her balance. It was only Doodle Bug meandering down the hall to check out the commotion. Maya got on her hands and knees and peered into the darkness under the staircase. Doodle Bug was right beside her, sniffing the musty air. The hair on the back of her neck stood up.

"It's OK," Maya said, but felt trepidation about the empty space before her. Maya stood. "Wait a minute, girl," she said. "I'm going to get a flashlight from the laundry room."

Maya hurried back, flashlight in hand, and knelt again beside Doodle Bug, who hadn't moved. She turned the flashlight on and aimed it into the blackness. Maya still couldn't see anything and crawled past the threshold. The air was thick and smelled like her grandmother's attic. She moved the light from right to left. The room was about 8 feet long and 4 feet wide and the ceiling sloped down on the left as it followed the contour of the staircase.

As her eyes adjusted, she made out a collection of household items, but not something you'd pick up at Target. Maya felt like she was looking into a museum display case. Everything must've been at least 50 years old. She wondered if Hazel knew this existed. From the smell and thick coating of dust on everything, it didn't seem like anyone'd been in here for a long time. Maya looked back at Doodle Bug who'd lain down in the hallway, intuiting this could take a while.

"Good girl. Keep your eye out for any mice that may be hiding in here," Maya instructed. Doodle Bug lifted one eyebrow and then closed her eyes to begin her morning nap, seemingly unconcerned with the threat of mice.

Before she moved anything, Maya looked closer at the contents of the hidden room. It seemed well organized, the outdoor tools to the far right where there was more vertical height, then the household things—a stand-up mixer, old phonograph, a large aluminum Dutch oven. There were four boxes that lined the wall where the ceiling began to slope. The boxes were bloated from the years of humidity and looked like they would disintegrate if picked up. Tucked where the slope of the staircase met the floor were children's toys. There was a red barn made out of pulp wood, a doll house, and a sock monkey lying on top of a stack of board games.

Maya crawled closer and found, at the very back, a doll's bed with two aged dolls lying on it in their yellowed night gowns. Beside the bed was a white wicker doll-sized rocking chair with a faded brown teddy bear in it. The chair was an exact replica of the one in her bedroom. The one she sat in for hours while caring for Hazel.

Maya laid the flashlight on the floor and gently pushed the chair. She watched it silently move back and forth, its rockers making tracks through the dust on the floor. She wondered who had last played with these toys. She sat back on her heels and thought. It must have been Hazel. She was the last child who'd lived in the house. Maya's eyes filled with tears, thinking of Hazel as a child. She ducked lower and picked one of the dolls off the bed, hugging it to her chest.

"What did Hazel call you?" She held the doll out in front of her and the head flopped back, causing the porcelain eyelids to open.

"Oh," Maya said, startled to suddenly be staring into blue eyes almost the same color as Hazel's. She looked at the doll as if she would introduce herself. "Lord, I'm losing it. Expecting a doll to talk. I must be running out of oxygen in here," Maya said aloud. She put the doll back on the bed and picked up the flashlight to leave when something shiny caught her eye. It was the gold hinge on some sort of box peeking out from under the bed. She slid the box out and tucked it under her arm. She crawled backwards out of the room and when she passed the stack of board games, she picked up the vintage version of Monopoly.

She used to love playing this with her sister. It'd be fun to compare her childhood game to this one.

Maya scooted past Doodle Bug into the hallway, where the sunlight and cool, fresh air made it feel like she'd broken the surface after swimming underwater. She sat with her back against the wall with the box that had been under the doll's bed in her lap and the Monopoly game beside her. She picked up the rectangular box first. It was about 10 inches long and 2 inches deep and made of brown leather. There were two gold hinges on the backside and a gold latch on the front. Embossed on the top in dark brown stitching was a monogram with the initials GRW.

Maya ran her hand over the initials. They definitely weren't Hazel's. It must've belonged to Hazel's mother. Maya racked her brain. Did she even know Hazel's mother's name? Suddenly the name came to her from the list of executors on the paperwork she'd signed for the philanthropic fund: Goldie. Yes, Goldie Waters. How could she forget that name? She'd have to go back to the paperwork to find out what the R stood for.

This box belonged to Hazel's mother. Maya leaned her head against the wall and watched the dust floating lazily in the sunlight streaming down the hall. Doodle Bug jerked in her sleep, chasing a squirrel in her dream. She noticed her anticipation but didn't rush to open the box. She thought about who may have touched this last and why it was hidden under a doll's bed in a secret storage area.

Maya flipped the clasp on the box. She lifted the lid and the hinges creaked. The interior was lined in cloth and contained a satin drawstring bag. Maya guessed this must have been a jewelry box to hold something special. She opened the bag and emptied it onto the cloth lining. Not exactly what she'd expected. With the monogram, lining, and satin bag, Maya'd imagined something a bit more ostentatious with diamonds and other precious stones. She didn't understand what it contained, but her intuition told her it was important.

Her reverie was broken when her cell phone beeped in the kitchen with a text message. It must be Bay. She ran and looked at her phone. Bay couldn't come for lunch and asked if they could make a kayaking date later that afternoon instead.

Since Bay wasn't coming, Maya decided to go for a short run. She needed to stretch her legs after crouching under the staircase for an hour. On her way to change into her running clothes, Maya knelt in the hallway by the monogrammed box. She returned the contents to the satin bag and then closed the lid. She put the monogrammed box back in the room under the stairs and set the Monopoly game on the coffee table in the living room. She wondered if Travis enjoyed board games.

***

"I'm leaving," Sloan said, gently pushing open the door to Peter's studio.

Peter turned away from his canvas and smiled at her. "Ah, my muse. I'm in need of some inspiration." He stood from the stool in front of his painting in progress and pulled Sloan to him. "You look lovely. Where is it you're going again?"

Before Sloan could answer, Peter pulled her closer and kissed her. She leaned into him, returning his kiss. After a minute of this, Sloan stepped away. "If we keep that up, I won't be going anywhere."

"Are you in a hurry?" Peter asked playfully.

Sloan glanced at her watch. 12:15. "Yes. I'm meeting Jana for lunch in town at 12:30. I better leave now to make it on time."

"OK, but I want a raincheck," Peter said. "Now, who's Jana again? Is she the woman you met on the pier?"

"No, that's Nellie. Jana was my great-grandparents' neighbor. Actually, her mother was the neighbor, but now Jana lives there. She heard I moved to Oriental and invited me out to lunch."

"Have you ever met her before?"

"I vaguely remember her. On Sundays she would drive from Havelock to her mother's for lunch and sometimes the two of them would stop over to see Grandma Ruth and GG. I think she's about 15 years older than me and we didn't have much in common then." Sloan looked at her watch again. "I definitely have to leave now."

"Enjoy your lunch and I'll count on cashing in my raincheck later this afternoon." Peter slapped her affectionately on the butt and turned back to his canvas.

Sloan smiled as she walked to the car and appreciated how Peter's playful spirit balanced her intensity. He didn't deserve being on the receiving end of her anger and she was thankful she'd kept that in check the past few weeks.

Sloan pulled her Volvo into Brantley's parking lot and found a spot near the back. She hurried across the parking lot so she wouldn't be late and then slowed by the windows that lined the front of the restaurant. She looked inside and saw the booths along the walls and simple square tables scattered in the dining area. It seemed everything was in the exact same spot as 20 years ago when she'd last been here, before her grandmother died.

Sloan stepped inside and the smell of fried food made her nostalgic. Every summer her family came here to celebrate her birthday. They pushed two tables together to fit the six of them: her grandparents, Uncle Jake and his wife, and she and GG. They'd start with a couple baskets of hushpuppies and Sloan would order her regular—fried chicken, mashed potatoes, and green beans.

Sloan continued into the restaurant, hoping she'd recognize Jana. A quick survey of the room told her that wouldn't be a problem. There was only one black woman there and she was waving to Sloan from one of the booths under the window. Sloan walked that way, aware of the eyes on her. It felt like all conversation paused and a spotlight followed her across the dining room, accentuating the brown woman in a floral dress walking through the room of white people in T-shirts and Columbia fishing wear. Sloan felt like she was in ninth grade again, crossing the cafeteria with her lunch tray. At least this time she knew someone would let her sit with them.

Jana stood, gave her a hug, and they slid into the booth across from one another. Sloan took a sip from the glass of water already at her place. Her hands were shaking. It'd been a long time since she'd been self-conscious about her skin color. Raleigh had a diverse population and most places she went had a mix of colors and ethnicities. Even if she was the only person of color at a business meeting, it never created the reaction she'd just experienced.

Jana smiled at her. "Don't worry, honey. They weren't staring at you because you're black. They're looking at you because you're new, and maybe because you're dressed so nice."

"So people were looking at me and I wasn't imagining it?"

"Yes, but it happens to anyone who's not local," Jana explained. "I find myself doing it, too. If I see someone familiar I don't pay much attention, but I'll do a double take for a new face. Oriental's a small town and we can be nosy, but we also look out for each other. But enough about that. Welcome!" she smiled warmly. "I'm happy you're back in Pamlico County, and right down the road from Sadie's, where you spent your summers."

"That's right," Sloan said. "When you were growing up, my great-grandparents were your neighbors. You were living in Havelock by the time Grandma Ruth and Papa moved back to care for GG, weren't you?"

"Yes," Jana nodded thoughtfully. "Henry and I came back to live in Momma's when we retired six years ago. I miss having your family for neighbors but it's good to be home and by the water. But enough about me. What made you come to Oriental and buy Magnolia Bend, no less, the oldest home in the county? Last I heard, you were in real estate in Raleigh."

Before Sloan could answer, the waitress came. For old time's sake, Sloan requested her usual and then took a minute to study Jana as she ordered. She looked like she was in her late 50s but Sloan knew she was at least 15 years older than that. Her hair was cut close to her head, almost half of it white, the only indicator of her age besides a thickness around her waist.

After she ordered, Jana leaned back, put her napkin in her lap and said, "So, you were about to tell my why you came back."

Sloan tried to formulate an explanation of something she wasn't even sure of. "A few years ago, I came down in the fall to check on GG's house for Mom. It was the first time I'd been back in 15 years. Something about being here and close to the water resonated with me. I felt more relaxed that weekend than I'd felt in years, and when I got back to Raleigh, I felt homesick for Oriental. After that, I kept a close watch on the real-estate market. I didn't have a specific plan and told myself I was looking for investment property. I couldn't admit I wanted to live here because it didn't fit into my five-year career plan."

"Lord, Honey. You had a five-year plan?" Jana waved her hand, half respectfully and half admonishingly. "I admire your organization but sometimes it's good to be spontaneous and react to what we're feeling in the moment, even if it doesn't coordinate with our plans."

"I know," Sloan said, acknowledging both sides, "and that's what happened when I saw Magnolia Bend come up for sale. It's a beautiful property with an interesting history. I remembered sneaking around there peeking in the windows when I was young. It felt surreal to be in the position to buy it. I went to look at it out of curiosity but then fell in love with it."

Sloan and Jana sat back to let the waitress serve their food. Sloan salivated as she anticipated the taste of the fried chicken. They were silent for a minute as they started their meals.

After having a taste of everything, Sloan said, "Wow. This tastes exactly as I remember. Mom can cook wonderful gourmet food but she never did get the hang of fried chicken."

"So how is your Mom?" Jana asked, lifting her napkin to dab her mouth. "I'll always remember that amazing meal she cooked one Sunday when she was here to visit. Now I imagine she's retired? Do you think she and your Dad will move here?"

"Yes. Mom's retired but is a guest lecturer at the culinary arts program at Wake Tech. Dad sold the restaurant and plays a lot of golf. I don't see them moving here. I'll be lucky if they can fit a visit into their social calendar." Sloan hoped Jana didn't notice the hint of sarcasm that'd crept into her voice. Her mother rarely had time for her when they were only 20 minutes apart. She doubted her mother would make regular trips to see her in Oriental.

"I'm glad they're doing well. And how about your children?" Jana asked. "I remember your grandmother saying you had a son and daughter."

Sloan took a bite of her mashed potatoes to gather her thoughts. "They're doing well. Anthony lives in Chapel Hill and works at a newspaper and Deidre's in the mountains right now, in between jobs." Sloan left it at that, hoping Jana wouldn't ask any follow-up questions, fearing judgment if she was honest about Deidre.

"They grow up fast, don't they? It doesn't seem possible that my oldest is in his 40s because in my mind I'm still 25. So anyway, you looked at the house and then ended up buying it?"

Sloan's shoulders relaxed when Jana didn't question her about her children. "Yes. That's the gist of it. I couldn't stop thinking about Magnolia Bend. My boyfriend Peter was supportive, so I decided to make an offer. It's a huge change from living in Raleigh and my fast-paced real-estate job, but so far I think I made the right decision." Sloan looked away, knowing she was leaving out her financial stress and feelings of doubt.

"Are you retired, or will you go into real estate here in Oriental?" Jana asked.

"I haven't made a decision about pursuing real estate yet. My focus is on updating and renovating the east wing of Magnolia Bend to create a retreat center."

Jana leaned across the table with interest. "That's a wonderful idea. What kinds of retreats do you plan on having?"

They finished their lunch and Sloan shared her plans for the retreat center and the hope it would be up and running by the following spring.

"This is exciting," Jana said, clapping her hands together. "Your retreats will bring in visitors and help Oriental's economy. Let me know if you ever need an administrative assistant to help you out. I wouldn't mind having some part-time work to keep me busy."

The waitress came and cleared away their lunch dishes. Before she could ask them about dessert, Jana said, "And we'd like two slices of Miss Sil's lemon pie."

Sloan started to protest, not used to eating this heavily at lunch.

"No, no," Jana insisted. "We're celebrating today, and you should never pass up the opportunity for a piece of pie. As you can see," Jana said, patting her stomach, "I never do."

"Well, OK. I read about her lemon pie in *Our State* magazine. They said it was the one thing you shouldn't miss if you were in Pamlico County." Jana nodded silently in agreement. "This will be research. I may want her to supply pies for the retreat center meals."

The waitress returned quickly and set a slice of pie in front of both of them. The meringue was thick and airy, like fog settling over the firm lemon layer. Sloan savored her first bite, having learned from her mother that this is when the flavor of a dish is most intense. The crust was flaky with a buttery flavor and the lemon had just the right amount of bite. She put her fork on her plate and looked across the table. Jana's head was down and she focused intently on her slice that was already halfway gone. "Don't worry. I'm not going to steal your pie," Sloan said, smiling.

Jana looked up and saw Sloan's plate. She put her fork down and leaned back. "Gracious. Sorry for my bad manners. It's a habit from growing up with three brothers. I had to eat Momma's dessert fast, or else they'd be stealing it off my plate."

"That's OK." Sloan laughed. "I was the only child with food nerds for parents and would get in trouble if I ate too quickly, so that habit is hardwired into me."

"Isn't it strange how things from our childhood can still impact us today?"

Sloan nodded and took her second bite of pie. She knew this all too well.

"Did you ever get to talk with a woman named Lilith?" Jana asked. "She's gathering information about women who were in a circle that Mom and Sadie were a part of. Did your great-grandmother ever talk about it?" Jana paused but Sloan didn't respond, focusing on her piece of pie.

Jana continued. "I remember Mom leaving early in the mornings for her meetings and I always wanted to go. It seemed mysterious to me when I was a child. Anyway, I enjoyed talking with Lilith about Mom. When we were done she showed me a list of names of women who'd been in the circle and I saw Sadie's name. I gave Lilith your contact information so she could interview you about your great-grandmother. I hope you don't mind."

Sloan took a sip of water to wash down the pie stuck in her throat. She quickly ran through different versions of what she could say. What would Jana think if she told her she'd met with Lilith, but it was because she was planning to log the land where the circle met?

"No. I haven't heard from her yet," Sloan lied and her intestines coiled like a snake.

"That's surprising. Lilith was thrilled to learn that you were Sadie's great-granddaughter."

Yes. I bet she was, Sloan thought.

"I'm sure you'll hear from her soon," Jana said.

Sloan didn't respond and busied herself with the check and getting her wallet out of her purse.

"Sloan? Are you OK? You've gotten quiet. Hope my bad manners didn't offend you?"

"Oh no. Sorry," Sloan said quickly. "I was thinking about GG and it made me a little sad."

Jana reached across the table and covered Sloan's hand with her hers. "I'm sorry, sweetie," she said. "I bet it's hard being here in Oriental without them." Jana paused. "But I've learned that returning can make the memories stronger. I sense Momma's presence more, now that I'm back here."

"Yea. You're right. I went by the house a couple days ago and I expected them all to walk out the front door."

"Well anytime you want to talk you just call. Maybe one Sunday you and your friend—" she hesitated.

"Peter," Sloan said.

"Yes. Peter can come over to have Sunday lunch with me and Henry."

"We'd love that. Thank you."

"And if after you talk with Lilith you're interested in the circle I can show you where they meet. Momma took me there several times."

Sloan thought of the map with the red X in her kitchen drawer. She knew where it was.

Sloan and Jana hugged goodbye outside the restaurant and made tentative plans to meet again for lunch in a couple weeks.

The heat, along with the fried chicken and bitter untruthfulness in her belly, slowed Sloan's progress to the car. Her eyes were damp and she blinked hard and slow. Sloan slid into her front seat and stared straight ahead at the speedometer. Sweat trickled down the back of her neck and then tears slid down her check and added more salty water to her neck.

What am I doing, she thought. I want to be friends with Jana, but I wasn't truthful about Deidre, my finances, or the logging. Lying is not the way start to a friendship. Maybe if I told her the truth, she'd be able to help me. If I'd been totally transparent with the women's circle about needing the money maybe we could have worked together instead of becoming adversaries.

Sloan's hands tightened around the steering wheel. If others knew the truth they could use it against her. Sweat continued to roll down her back. She slowly backed up and steered out of the parking lot, continuing her internal debate. She wanted to be authentic and truthful, but something always stopped her. Why couldn't she trust other people? She turned left and picked up speed. The car locks automatically engaged, giving her the answer.

***

Maya and Bay pushed away from the river bank and paddled down Beards Creek toward the Neuse River. There was barely any wind, so they'd decided to head out to the bigger water in hope of finding some dolphin feeding in the late afternoon.

"Maya, what's the occasion? Why are you off on a Monday?" Bay asked.

Maya slowed down so their kayaks were side by side. "No special reason. I just needed a mental health day." Maya took a breath and continued, "I think I'm bored. Now that the office is organized, I do the same thing every day: file, bill, talk with insurance companies, listen to the patients complain. It's weird. I've always done this type of work and it's never bothered me before but now I want something different."

"What do you want to do instead?" Bay asked while rhythmically paddling.

"I don't know," Maya said. "That's the other half of the problem. I don't have any sense of what type of work I'd enjoy. You're lucky. You have something you're passionate about and have a natural talent for."

"With a 20-page sociology paper due next week, I'm not feeling lucky right now. But I see your point. From the moment I began dressing my Barbies, I knew I loved fashion."

Maya started laughing. "I haven't thought about Barbies in ages. My sister Kate and I had them. She was more like you, dressing them up and sending them on dates. Me, on the other hand, I took them outside. I would build them a house of mushrooms, leaves, and branches and take them swimming in the stream behind our house."

"Ah. I see a theme," Bay said. "Being outside and active, some of the things you enjoy now."

Maya stopped paddling and coasted for a moment. "You have a point. Being outside and moving around in some way has always been a passion but I'm not sure how I could make a living doing that, except for being a forest ranger."

Maya was silent as they headed north out onto the Neuse. Why had she gone into medical records and office management? She thought back to her first job at UVa. The income motivated her then, as, like any recent grad, she tried to avoid moving back in with her parents. It had a decent salary and benefits, and she was good at it. After a year, it was comfortable and didn't require much effort. It made sense to stay in that field when she moved to Bay St. Louis, then Raleigh, and now Oriental. The more medical record jobs on her resume, the easier it became to get a job in that field.

Maya picked up her pace, digging her paddles deeply in the water as an outlet for her frustration. What was the matter with her? Her career was based on convenience and comfort. She'd always taken the path of least resistance and hadn't realized it. At the time it never even felt like she'd had a choice.

"Hey! Wait up!" Bay called out.

Maya realized how fast she was paddling and slowed down to let Bay catch up. "Sorry. Didn't mean to go so fast."

"Don't forget I'm still a newbie," Bay said, slightly out of breath. "It'll take a while for me to build up my paddle muscles."

"You'll be there in no time," Maya reassured her, slowing her cadence to match Bay's. "How have you been? How did your meeting go with the professor at N.C. State on Friday?" Maya asked.

Now Bay stopped paddling and drifted a minute in the light breeze. "It was a hard day."

"I'm sorry. I know you were looking forward to it," Maya said, remembering her quick conversation with Bay that morning as Bay left for Raleigh and Maya was cooling down from her run.

"Oh," Bay said, brightening, "that part was great. Dr. Engle said as long as I keep my grades where they are, I shouldn't have a problem getting accepted to the school of design."

"That's wonderful."

"The hard part was that I saw Holden."

"Oh, Bay. I didn't know you were planning on seeing him. That's the first time you've seen him since Laura got custody, isn't it? How'd it go?" Maya watched Bay staring off at the water. A tear slid down her cheek. Maya waited, giving Bay time to compose herself.

"I didn't plan it, but as I was driving downtown I passed his nursing home and on the spot decided to visit. I saw him for a few minutes while Laura waited outside the room. He hasn't improved at all and had another small stroke. Now he can't eat and needs a feeding tube. I sat beside his bed and held his hand. It's probably the last time I'll see him."

If Maya'd been on land, she would have hugged Bay, but instead she held onto the side of Bay's kayak and gave her her full attention. She knew Bay was trying to cope with conflicting emotions.

"It's complicated, isn't it?" Maya said. "When I was dealing with Steven's death I felt sadness, anger, love, and guilt practically all at the same time and it was hard to know what to focus on. Let go of the guilt first. You couldn't have prevented Holden's stroke and putting off your dreams won't change his situation. It will only leave you with regrets."

"Thanks, Maya," Bay said, wiping her eyes. "You're right. I need to focus on what I have control over and not be so hard on myself."

Bay had barely finished her sentence when Maya heard one of her favorite sounds, "Phew."

"Dolphins!" Maya yelled and paddled her kayak away from shore into the sound.

"Come on, Bay! Looks like there's about 10 of them. Let's try and get in the middle."

For the next 15 minutes they followed the pod, watching them circle to trap the fish and occasionally leap out of the water. One even swam directly under Maya's kayak. Finally, Maya and Bay turned back toward Beards Creek. The dolphins worked their usual magic and Maya felt more peaceful than she had before. She hoped they'd done the same for Bay and kept her silence to avoid breaking the spell the dolphins had cast.

***

Sloan dried her cereal bowl and put it away. Peter was cloistered in his studio and she was still full from lunch, so Raisin Bran sufficed for dinner. She went to her study to work on a brochure for the retreat center, but before she'd even turned on the computer, she stood, too antsy to sit in one place.

Since lunch with Jana, Sloan had been questioning not just whether she should log the Hungry Mother Creek property, but if moving to Oriental had been the right decision. She loved her home, being by the water and more time with Peter, but felt more unsettled than she ever had in Raleigh. Through omission or flat-out lies, she was keeping potential friends at a distance, even making them adversaries in the case of the women's circle. One of her strengths in real estate was keeping emotional distance with her negotiations and not putting all her cards on the table. This was not helping her now.

Sloan sat in the wingback chair in the corner of her office and rubbed the back of her neck. Deidre's weekly call this afternoon made things more complicated. She was happy Deidre was making progress but overwhelmed with the thought of paying for the additional month the facility recommended. And then there'd be the cost of supporting Deidre until she could find a job.

Sloan fidgeted, racking her brain for options to get capital besides logging. At 50, she couldn't risk liquidating her retirement and with

Magnolia Bend's mortgage and the fact she had no income, a loan would be out of the question, too. She took a few steps out into the hall and looked up the stairs but Peter's studio door was still shut. She needed to talk with someone.

She picked up her phone to call her mother and then put it down. Maybe she could find Nellie. It'd been almost a month since she'd seen her. She'd driven up and down Magnolia Bend Road several times, hoping she'd see Nellie out in her yard or walking, but never had. She didn't even know Nellie's last name, so looking at the mailboxes hadn't been any help, either.

Sloan walked back to the kitchen and slipped on her flip-flops by the patio doors. Before she went outside, she wrote her phone number on a sticky note and put it in her pocket. The sun had almost set and the west sky was pink and orange. Sloan headed east to the pier. She didn't see Nellie there and decided to walk the circumference of her property and then down Magnolia Bend Road to try again to figure out which house was Nellie's.

The movement of her body helped slow the pace of her brain and Sloan focused on the most important thing: that Deidre was in recovery and would be home in a couple months. She reached the northeast corner of her property and turned toward the road when the old well caught her attention. The realtor had mentioned it, but Sloan had almost forgotten it was there. It must be almost 200 years old, like the house, she thought. She changed directions and walked over to inspect it.

The top of the well was surrounded by large stones. She leaned over the edge, smoothed by years of others doing the same, and peered down. It was too dark to see if the well was covered or if water was still accessible. She kept staring down, wondering about the people who'd used it long ago. Did slaves retrieve water for the plantation owner?

Sloan shuddered and then felt another presence. Nellie had appeared beside her.

"Nellie, you startled me," Sloan said, feeling the momentary jolt of adrenaline in her chest.

"Sorry, you were deep in thought."

Sloan turned to look at Nellie and instinctively examined her neck but didn't see a bruise on the right side. She wondered if there was one on the other side, like there usually was.

"It's good to see you," Sloan said. "I was about to walk down the road to look for you." She took the sticky note out of her pocket. "Let me give this to you before I forget. That's my cell phone. When you get home, call me, and then I'll have your number."

Nellie took the paper from Sloan. "Thank you." Nellie pointed down the shaft of the well. "Can you still get water from it?"

"I don't know," Sloan said. "I'll have to look when there's more light. I was just thinking about the people who may have used this well. Do you know anything about the history of Magnolia Bend and who lived here? Seems like I remember you saying something about that once."

Nellie tensed and stepped back. She slid her hand in the pocket of her low-waisted, pleated skirt and looked up at the house. Her white sweater glowed against the coal-gray eastern sky.

"It's OK if you don't know anything," Sloan added. "I thought since you've lived here a while you may have heard stories about my house."

Nellie looked up toward the house again and this time Sloan saw the blue-black edges of a bruise on the left side of her neck. She needed to ask about it, but before she could, Nellie began to speak.

"I've only heard sad stories about this house," she said quietly. "I'm sure you know Magnolia Bend started as a plantation. Supposedly the owners shackled the slaves down in the basement while having elegant parties upstairs."

Sloan leaned back against the stones of the well. She remembered the glint of iron when she'd peeked in the basement windows years ago and instinctively rubbed her wrists. She couldn't imagine the physical sensation of being shackled and acid burned her stomach with the thought of it. She hadn't found the courage yet to go to the basement and see if they were still there.

Nellie continued, never taking her eyes off the house. "I also heard there was a young family who lived here in the early 1900s. The husband had a successful lumber business and was active in local politics, but people rarely saw his wife and son. They say he wouldn't let them leave the property except for an occasional trip to church." Nellie paused, and kept her eyes on the house. "I heard the wife would lock herself and her son in her bedroom so he couldn't hurt them in a drunken rage."

"What? She would lock herself in the bedroom to stay safe?" Sloan asked incredulously. She thought about her locked bedroom door a few mornings ago and the panic it created. Before Sloan could ask more questions, Nellie continued.

"A housekeeper who worked for them said she saw bruises on the wife and the son, but people thought she was exaggerating. The actions of a wealthy white man were rarely questioned then."

"Hmmph," Sloan said, "Unfortunately that's still true today."

"And the story gets worse." Nellie paused. "Are you sure you want to hear it? After all, it happened where you're living."

"Yes," Sloan said firmly, though the answer tightened her throat. "It can't be worse than the shackles and I need to understand the history of Magnolia Bend—the good and bad."

"The wife and the son died on your property," Nellie said, still gazing at the house. "It was the weekend right after Valentine's Day in 1924. The husband said his 10-year-old son had a fatal accident playing with a sickle and his wife died of heartbreak within hours."

For a moment, no words passed between them. The air was filled with the sounds of dusk falling, the peaceful song of crickets now made ominous with Nellie's reveal.

"Nellie, that's horrible," Sloan spoke first. "Are you sure it's true and not just an urban myth?"

"I haven't met anyone who disputes it," Nellie said, her voice serious and level. "That's why I told you the first time we met that this house needs to see happiness."

Sloan looked at Nellie in the dimming light. She imagined an abusive husband's hand tightening around Nellie's pale neck and wondered if she identified with the woman who lived here long ago. Sloan tried to formulate a tactful way to ask Nellie if she needed help.

"Speaking of bringing happiness to the house," Nellie asked before Sloan could say anything, "how are things progressing with your retreat center?"

Sloan tucked her question to Nellie away, promising to ask it before they parted. "OK, I guess," she said, shrugging. "In a couple weeks the contractor's coming to get an idea of what supplies to order. We're starting with installing a handicapped bathroom and ramp and then creating pocket doors so the ballroom can be made into two meeting spaces. The loggers are scheduled and will begin the first of September." Sloan paused and took a breath. "I'm having some doubts though, Nellie. It seems the property I'm planning to log is meaningful to people in the community."

"Meaningful? Why is that?" Nellie asked. "Is there a cemetery there or something?"

"No, I don't think so," Sloan said. "There's this tree there. People call it the Mother Tree." Sloan described the details of the women's circle, her great-grandmother's involvement, and her conversation with Jana at lunch. "It's even more urgent that I get the money because Deidre needs another month of rehab. There's no other way. I'm worried that logging the property won't start my business off on a positive note, but what can I do?"

"Have you asked anyone else for ideas?" Nellie crossed her arms across her chest and took a step away from the well. Sloan wondered if it was an instinctively protective gesture. "Maybe there's someone who could loan you the money. I wish I could be more help. I'll let you know if I think of anything."

"You've been a big help just by listening. I'm glad we ran into each other."

"Me too." Nellie looked at her watch and moved toward the road. "I guess I better get home."

Sloan took a couple steps toward Nellie, the underbrush crunching beneath her feet. "Nellie, wait. There's something else I want to talk about." Nellie paused for Sloan to catch up to her.

"Sloan. Sloan. Are you out here?" Peter's voice called out. Sloan stopped when she heard it and looked back to the front porch.

"I'll be right there," she shouted in reply.

Sloan turned and saw that Nellie had started walking down the road. Nellie looked over her shoulder and said, "I'll call you tomorrow so you'll have my number. We can talk then."

"OK," Sloan said, and waved goodbye. She stood there a minute and watched Nellie walk away. Nellie always seemed anxious when she headed home and Sloan worried about what happened when she got there. She understood the fear and isolation Nellie must be experiencing and desperately wanted to help. She resolved to immediately offer help the next time she saw Nellie and not give her a chance to slip away.

Sloan turned and walked back to her front porch. Peter's voice brought her out of thought.

"There you are, my love," he said. He handed her a glass of chardonnay and put his arm around her waist. "What were you doing out here?"

"I went for a walk to clear my mind and ran into Nellie beside the old well," Sloan said.

Peter looked over her shoulder. "Is she already gone? Maybe she'd like to come in for a glass of wine. I'd like to meet her, too."

Sloan looked back but didn't see Nellie. "She's probably almost home by now. She lives somewhere down Magnolia Bend Road but she's never told me exactly where or given me her phone number."

"That's a little strange," Peter said.

"I know," Sloan agreed. "But I think it's because her husband is controlling and even physically hurts her."

Peter removed his arm from Sloan's waist and took a step away to look at her directly. "What?" His voice was filled with concern. "How do you know that? Does she need our help?"

"I've seen a bruise on her neck every time we've been together," Sloan said. "She also gets nervous when it's time for her to leave, like she'll get in trouble if she's late."

"Is there anything we can do?"

"Not right now," Sloan said, though it pained her to admit it. "I haven't felt comfortable enough to talk with her about it, but I gave her my phone number tonight."

"Let me know if I can do anything," Peter said.

"I will. I plan to talk to her about this the next time we're together."

Peter put his arm back around Sloan. "I love you," he said, and kissed the top of her head. "Now come see what I've been working on today."

Sloan and Peter stepped inside, and Sloan gently closed the door behind her. She followed Peter up to his studio, grateful that she could feel safe in her home, something she knew Nellie couldn't.

CHAPTER 9

Maya walked to the end of the pew and Violet, Ella, and Lilith followed. They sat on thick, burgundy cushions, a sharp contrast to the camping chairs and hard ground at their circle. The small sanctuary held about 150 people and was filling quickly, so Maya was glad they'd gotten there early. She leaned forward and whispered to them, "This is where Hazel always sat."

From the other end of the pew, Lilith said, "Then there'll be a bit of her spirit with us this morning." Lilith folded the church bulletin and continued, "I don't know about you guys, but I feel a bit awkward. Flip-flops and sitting outside are way more comfortable to me." Lilith emphasized her point by crossing her legs and wiggling her left foot at them, accidentally throwing her Birkenstock sandal off.

Maya let a giggle escape and then covered her mouth. Why was everything funnier in church? Violet and Ella smiled, too. Lilith slipped her foot back into her sandal and smoothed her tie-dye skirt.

Maya looked toward the front of the church. The morning sun came through the stained-glass window and threw purple, blue, and green streamers on the white carpet. She glanced down at the bulletin and saw Travis had titled his sermon, "Our Sacred Contract." He was going to preach on the role Christians have in protecting the environment and she and the other women were here to support him. The hope was that after the sermon and telling the congregation about the plans to log the Hungry Mother Creek property, folks would be inspired to come to the rally in a few weeks. Maybe someone would even have an idea about how to stop the logging. Maya still had mixed emotions about bringing in people other than the circle, but everyone had agreed it was the only way.

Travis walked in from the left in his black robe. Maya smiled when she saw the splash of green in his stole. He'd told her that a friend from seminary had made it, but he'd never felt comfortable wearing it until today. It had an oak tree on either side with roots reaching down and limbs extending up toward his neck.

Travis stood at the pulpit for the Call to Worship. "Psalm 118, verse 24," he began. "This is the day the Lord hath made. Let us rejoice and be glad in it." He sat down to the right and the choir rose. Maya looked at her program, found "For the Beauty of the Earth" in the hymnal, and stood to sing.

At the conclusion of the hymn, Travis returned to the pulpit. His eyes searched the congregation and stopped on her. Maya smiled up at him and he gave a slight nod. The thump of her heart drowned out Travis' welcome. Blood flushed her face, neck, and chest. Why did she always have such a strong reaction to him? She shifted in the pew and saw Lilith looking her way. She smiled knowingly at Maya and Maya's blush deepened. She turned her attention back to Travis, who reminded the congregation about vacation Bible school next week.

Travis paused and then said, "There's one more thing I want to share. It's not directly related to church activities, but is something that will impact most of us." Maya sat up straighter and leaned forward. "It's been brought to my attention that the property at the back of Hungry Mother Creek, where the beach area is, is going to be logged for timber in September." There was an audible intake of air from the congregation. Maya looked around and noticed wide eyes and frowns. Heads leaned together and people whispered. Travis was right. The Hungry Mother Creek property did mean something to others.

Travis elevated his volume over the hum. "Now, I know this property is important to many of us and we don't want to see it damaged by logging. With God's grace, and the community pulling together, we hope to save this sacred land so future generations can enjoy it. I want you to know that there will be a rally to save the Hungry Mother Creek property on Saturday, August 16, at Lou Mac Park. It will be at 9 in the morning and I hope you'll be able to attend. I'll have more details in the coming weeks." Travis neatened his notes on the lectern and opened the large Bible to his right. "And today's sermon was inspired by the Hungry Mother Creek property."

Travis took a breath and began. "Romans 1, verse 20-22: 'Ever since the creation of the world his eternal power and divine nature, invisible though they are, have been understood and seen through the things he has made. So they are without excuse; for though they knew God, they did not honor him as God or give thanks to him, but they became futile in their thinking, and their senseless minds were darkened. Claiming to be wise, they became fools;' So people, us," Travis emphasized his point and spread his hands in both directions across the congregation, "we have no excuse for not knowing God's power and divinity because we have all his creations as evidence, proof, inspiration. We can walk down to the waterfront at first light and watch the sun, 864,000 miles in diameter and 93 million miles away from us, rising from the Pamlico Sound, a part of the Atlantic Ocean that covers 41 million square miles, the immenseness and beauty of the sun and water a testament to God's life-giving power. Without light and water, we would not survive. And how many of us find solace just being by the water? The peace and comfort it offers is another manifestation of God's character. Other times we may go to the woods and sit under a tree in search of wisdom to understand life."

Travis paused and looked at Maya and the other women. Violet reached over and held Maya's hand.

"The strength, perseverance and majesty of trees, again, a reflection of our creator. We're lucky to have live oaks here hundreds of years old. Their roots reach down in the dark, loamy soil and their limbs reach up in the sun-drenched sky, receiving nourishment from both directions that girds them to withstand hurricanes and drought. Leaning against the trunk of one of these trees, especially in times of uncertainty, can ground us, help us discern the best direction for our life. But is all the natural world here to serve us? Provide us with food, water, comfort, beauty? I think not. In healthy relationships, the love and care flow in both directions."

And Travis continued elaborating on the role humans have protecting God's creations. Maya watched him and could tell he loved what he was doing. He was engaged and enthusiastic. She hadn't been able to appreciate any of this eight months ago when she was here with Hazel. She'd been shocked to find out Travis was a minister and not just a kayak guide and handyman, and hurt that after all the time they'd spent together, he hadn't told her. Now she'd forgiven him for that omission.

She looked at him now and it almost felt like it'd never happened. Maya tried to remember the moment she forgave Travis but couldn't. It slowly came to be, the product of time and learning to forgive herself for staying in an unhealthy marriage. Maya noticed that since she'd become more accepting of her own mistakes, her compassion for others had increased. Well, except for Sloan. She needed to keep working on that.

Maya realized Travis was finishing his sermon. "Verse 22 warns us not to claim to be wise and think we know what is best for creation," he said, "and then become fools by not honoring God as she is manifested in our natural world. When you leave here today, pay attention to how you treat our natural world—the plants, living creatures, and water—and look for ways to honor these gifts that have been bestowed upon us." Travis gathered his notes and stepped away from the pulpit and the choir stood, prompting the congregation to do the same. Maya opened the hymnal, to "All Things Bright and Beautiful." She moved her lips, but in her mind, she was on the ground in front of the Mother Tree, listening to the call of the osprey as it fished for breakfast.

Travis finished the benediction and Maya and the other women filed out of their pew, following the other parishioners to the front door. They bypassed the receiving line and stood together on the sidewalk, off to the side. Maya watched the end of the Baptist, Sunday ritual, people greeting one another, shaking hands and hugging, conversing about their lives—not that different from what they did at their circle, she thought. She overheard comments about the Hungry Mother Creek property as people reacted to Travis' announcement about the logging.

"First camping trip was there."

"Mom and I gather pinecones there every Christmas for our decorations."

"Lay on that beach for hours reading and swimming when I was young."

Lilith said, "You hear that? It seems like everyone has a memory of spending time on Hungry Mother Creek. I hope they all come to the rally and show Sloan that more than four women and a tree will be affected if she logs that property." She clasped her hands together, the urgency in her tone growing. "We should have made flyers about the rally to pass out so people wouldn't forget. What are we going to do there, anyway?"

"Let's not discuss that now," Violet said, putting an arm around

Lilith's shoulder.

"I'm meeting with Travis in a couple days to begin planning for the rally and will have a better idea of how it will flow after that," Maya said.

"Let us know how we can help," Ella said. Suddenly she giggled and covered her mouth.

"Do tell," Lilith said. "What's so funny?"

"Nothing about that. For some reason I had the vision of me camping out in the top limbs of the Mother Tree, refusing to come down like that woman, Butterfly something, did in the giant redwood in California. Now that'd be a sight."

Lilith grabbed Ella's arm. "Ella, that's a brilliant idea. If things don't go well with the rally, I'm going to do that and you're welcome to join me."

Ella looked at Lilith in shock. "I was only kidding. I don't think my boss would understand a sabbatical to live in a tree." Ella began laughing again.

Maya stepped closer to Lilith. "Let's keep that idea in our back pocket and use it if nothing else works. But I have faith that together with Travis and these folks," Maya pointed to the parishioners now heading to their cars, "we can figure something out."

Lilith squeezed Maya's hand. "You're right, but I'm more than willing if we need to," she said with a mischievous twinkle in her eyes.

"What are you ladies laughing at over here?" Travis said, walking up to their group.

"Ella and Lilith may set up camp in the limbs of the Mother Tree if the rally doesn't convince Sloan to stop the logging," Maya said, smiling. "Travis, you know Violet, but I don't think you've ever met Lilith and Ella," Maya said, gesturing to each one. Travis shook their hands. Maya watched his reaction to Ella, knowing her beauty was not easily overlooked, but his gaze didn't linger.

"It's nice to meet you all. Lilith," Travis said and paused. "Oh, you're the one who makes bread. I had some over at Maya's and it was delicious." Travis put his arm lightly around Maya's waist. "Yes. Maya loves it too. Even my dynamic personality couldn't keep her attention away from your bread that night," Travis said.

Maya blushed, both at his teasing and his physical display of affection. She glanced at him out of the corner of her eye. He appeared relaxed, like having his arm around her was the most natural thing in the world. In her awkwardness, Maya couldn't think of anything to say, but Lilith saved her.

"I know all about her love affair with my bread. I may hit retirement a year earlier because of all I've sold to her," Lilith said, smiling widely.

Travis released Maya and she stepped away, thankful for the chance to regain her composure. Lilith winked at her and then continued her conversation with Travis. "Travis, thanks for your beautiful sermon. It's not often I sit in a church for worship but you made this trip worthwhile."

"I agree," Violet said. "Your grandmother would be proud. From listening to the conversations out here, it seems your sermon and the announcement about the logging has gotten folks fired up. Hopefully it will result in a solution to save the Hungry Mother Creek property."

"That's the plan," Travis said. Someone called to him from the front steps of the church. "I better go. Thanks for coming." Travis looked directly at Maya. "I'll call you later so we can figure out a time to get together and talk more about the rally." He hurried off toward the church before Maya could answer him. A gust of wind blew one side of his stole behind him. He reached back to retrieve it, caught Maya looking at him and gave her a smile. Never in her wildest dreams had she ever thought a minister would be flirting with her, and that she'd be happy about it.

***

Maya threw her sundress on the bedroom floor and put on some running shorts and a T-shirt. She pulled her hair into a ponytail and laughed at Doodle Bug tap dancing behind her in anticipation of going outside.

"Come on, girl. Buster's out there waiting for us."

Maya and Doodle Bug ran down the steps, out the back door, and across the yard to the pier. Doodle Bug jumped in the water and swam along the pier and Maya walked to the end to talk with Buster.

"Hey there, Maya Lou! You trying to give an old man heat stroke out here in the sun at high noon?" Buster said jokingly.

Maya laughed. "You could have gone home any time you'd like and called me on the phone for an update. You've only yourself to blame if you fall out from the heat."

Buster maneuvered his skiff closer to shore and in the shade of a live oak leaning out over the creek. "Well, you got me there. I wanted to see you in person and hear how things went at church."

Maya leaned against the rail even with Buster's skiff. "You know you could have come and sat in the air conditioning with four pretty women and heard for yourself."

"I know. I appreciate you inviting me." Buster paused and watched Doodle Bug swimming. "The last time I was in that church was for Eleanor's funeral five years ago." Buster's voice thickened. "I couldn't bring myself to go. Her absence still permeates every moment of my day and . . ." Buster turned his head away and took a bandana from his pocket. He wiped the sweat from his forehead, catching some tears on his cheek in the process.

Maya was silent for a moment and the only sound was Doodle Bug shaking off water and then the jingle of her collar as she ran toward them.

"I'm sorry, Buster," Maya said. "I can't imagine the emptiness you must feel without your partner of 50 plus years." Maya sighed. She quickly did the math and realized she'd have to get married in the next year and live to at least 90 if she was going to make it to 50 years of marriage. Damn. She was doing it again, focusing on her own issues. She took a breath and put her attention back to Buster.

"Thanks Maya," he said. "The greatest gift of my life was my marriage to Eleanor. Of course, I wish we'd had more time together but as you well know, life doesn't always go according to plan."

"That's true," Maya acknowledged, watching the skiff sway gently. "But sometimes it's still good to have a plan. I realized the other day that I've never really had one for my life. I made choices based on options that were right in front of me but never went out and created opportunities for myself. I always took the path of least resistance."

"You mean how you stayed with Steven even though you knew it wasn't good for you?"

Maya winced at the truth, but knew Buster only had her best interest at heart. That was why she'd felt comfortable telling him the truth about her marriage.

"Yes," she admitted. "That and my career. My first job was in medical records, and from then on, I never sought out anything different. I never enjoyed the work. It's just what I knew how to do." Maya plopped herself on the pier and let her feet dangle over the edge.

Buster reeled in his line and leaned against the center console. "I've always known how to fish, but thankfully I love it. Still do. Sounds like you're trying to figure out what you want to be when you grow up."

Maya started to laugh, "Yeah. That about sums it up. I thought 39 was grown up but maybe I'm wrong."

"Maya Lou, we're never done growing up. As long as the sun rises we have the option to reinvent ourselves. Now seems as good a time as any to figure out what you want to do." Buster started laughing.

"What's so funny?"

"Maybe we need some dolphin to show up and tell you the career you're destined for," Buster said, knowing how she looked for signs from the dolphins.

Maya kicked her foot toward Buster's skiff, sending a spray of water in his direction. "You never know. Well, enough about that," she said, waving it off. "Let me tell you about Travis' sermon."

Maya and Buster spent the next 30 minutes talking about the Hungry Mother Creek property and the rally. Buster said he'd contact his hunting and fishing buddies so they could support the cause.

Buster rubbed his stomach. "I haven't died by heat stroke yet but am about to die of hunger. Want to hop in and I'll drive us to Toucan's for lunch?"

Maya stood up. "That'd be fantastic. I'm hungry, too." Maya put Doodle Bug inside and the dog immediately lay by the air conditioning vent. Maya grabbed a baseball cap and some money from her wallet and hurried back out to Buster's skiff.

CHAPTER 10

Sloan's hand shook as she put her cell phone on the counter. She walked over to the kitchen table and sat with her head in her hands. A ball of emotion hit her in the chest, making her gulp for air, and then rose through her throat and came out as a sob. She wrapped her arms around her stomach and rocked back and forth, willing herself not to cry.

What was wrong with her? She'd become an emotional wreck since moving to Oriental. She could count on one hand the times she'd cried in her adult life, but she'd had several breakdowns in the past month. She heard Peter's study door open and his bare feet moving quickly down the steps. She stood and grabbed a tissue to blow her nose and wipe her eyes, but before she could finish, he had pulled her into his chest.

"What in the world is wrong, sweetheart?" he asked, rubbing her back. "Did something happen with Deidre?"

Safe in Peter's embrace, Sloan relaxed into his body and cried softly, her tears dampening his paint-splattered white T-shirt. "No," she said, her voice muffled. "As far as I know, she's fine. I should be mad about this, not sad and crying. I don't know what's happened to me since we've moved here."

Peter released her and poured her a glass of water. "Let's sit," he said, pulling out one of the kitchen table chairs. "Now tell me what's going on."

Sloan sat down and took a sip of water. "I just got off the phone with Jana."

"The woman who lives next door to your great-grandmother's house?"

"Yes. The one I had lunch with a couple weeks ago. She called to ask me if I was really planning to log the Hungry Mother Creek property."

"I didn't think you'd told her yet."

"I haven't. She said the headline in today's *Pamlico News* is about my plan to log the property."

"How did the paper find out and why is it even a news story?" Peter asked. "People log land for timber all the time."

"Jana said the paper reported that on Sunday the minister at the First Baptist Church announced it, and then gave a sermon on the sanctity of nature. She even said a rally is scheduled soon." Sloan's voice caught in her throat.

"A rally? Like a protest?" Peter asked incredulously.

"Yes." Sloan paused and Peter was quiet and rubbed her hand. "I guess I should go buy the paper and read if for myself. It seems ridiculous. The small trees will be left and the logging company will plant new ones to replace what they cut. It's not like I'm going to cut down every tree and put a parking lot there."

"Have you walked the property yet?" Peter asked gently.

And that simple question ignited Sloan's anger. She jerked her hand out from under Peter's and stood. "Why do you keep asking me that?" she yelled. "What difference will it make? I know what trees and bushes look like. You think I'm making a mistake, don't you? Well there isn't any other way. Deidre's rehab fees are due in a couple weeks and if I don't have the retreat center making money by the spring, I won't be able to pay my part of the mortgage."

Peter stood to face Sloan. "I never said I thought you were making a mistake, he said. "Only that it would be wise to look at the property before you log it."

"Easy for you to say," Sloan spat, her voice growing louder. "You don't have anything to worry about. You get your check from N.C. State, pay your part of the mortgage and watch the balance of your retirement account grow."

Sloan saw Peter's jaw tense and knew she was overreacting, but it was too late to pull herself back now.

"You are in this situation because you chose to buy this house," Peter said in an even, firm tone. "You chose to use all your savings to make it happen. Don't take your anger out on me when I've done nothing but try to support you through this."

Sloan started to speak, wanting to defend herself, but Peter held up his hand. "I'm going out to kayak," he said, deflecting her with his palm. "We can finish this discussion once you've calmed down and can speak rationally."

Peter walked out the patio doors and down to his kayak pulled up on the river bank. Sloan slammed a fist into the table and then held her head in her hands and stared at a knot hole in the hardwood floor. She'd done it again.

The headline read, "Magnolia Bend's Owner to Log Beach Property on Hungry Mother Creek." Sloan had driven to The Bean and bought the paper. She'd read it three times already and actually felt a little better. The article wasn't focused on her, but more an homage to the property and what it meant to the community. She'd learned that for generations people were drawn to the land because of the trees, beach area, and abundance of deer and turkey. They'd even interviewed Lilith from the women's circle, who talked about the history of the circle and its connection to the Mother Tree.

Sloan threw the paper into the passenger seat and stared out the window. It didn't appear from the article that anyone interviewed had ever owned the land, nor had their families. She couldn't understand how people who'd been trespassing for over 100 years felt as if they had some claim to the land, and the right to decide what happened to it.

The rising temperature in the car forced Sloan out. She put the map the women's circle had left in the pocket of her Bermuda shorts, and locked the car. She was standing at the edge of her property that bordered Hungry Mother Creek. Peter was right. She should at least walk it. Her guilt would ease after seeing it and confirming it wasn't anything that couldn't be replaced.

Sloan stepped into the shade of the woods and immediately felt relief from the summer heat. She realized she wouldn't need the map and followed the well-worn trail. She placed her feet carefully and kept alert for snakes that may be passing through. It'd been years since she'd hiked in the woods, maybe even decades. Paved greenway trails and a couple short walks to scenic overlooks while on vacation had been the extent of her time in nature.

After a few minutes of walking, Sloan paused and looked up. The leaves, needles, and branches wove a thick tapestry overhead. It glowed in a hundred shades of green from the late afternoon sun, but here and there the branches and sky provided threads of brown and blue. The resilient rays made it through the weave and created puddles of light on the forest floor.

Sloan heard a heron call and figured she must be close to the water. She took the map from her back pocket to see where the Mother Tree was in relation to the water. If she kept following the path, she should find it easily.

Her pace slowed as she neared the water, but her inner conflict gained momentum. What if she felt something special when she saw the Mother Tree? What if it reminded her of GG? What would she do then? She sped up and thought, that's ridiculous. I don't need to change my plans. I can always ask the loggers to leave the Mother Tree. It may be too old and big to use anyway.

Suddenly the path opened up into a clearing and she saw the water off to the right. Inside the clearing there were rocks that formed a circle. They began and ended on either side of a huge live oak, the Mother Tree, Sloan thought. She stepped inside the stone circle and stood across from the tree. There were several fat candles at its base, melted from use, like ice cream left in the summer sun.

This must be where the circle meets, Sloan thought. OK. Well, I've seen it. She tried to stay in her head, analytical. I'll tell the loggers to leave this tree and let the circle continue to meet. She looked at her watch. 5:45. She should leave. Peter would be worried. But her feet wouldn't move.

Sloan took a breath and smelled the pluff mud, the same smell as behind her great-grandmother's house. She sank to the ground and sat on the worn dirt in front of the Mother Tree. She wondered where GG sat when she was a part of the circle. What had she shared? Did she have wounds that needed to heal? Sloan wished her great-grandmother were here to share her wisdom and guidance, but Sloan also wanted to learn more about her life, things she'd never thought to ask as a teenager.

Sloan took a breath and repositioned herself on the hard ground. She raised her eyes and took in the Mother Tree for the first time. What she saw in the trunk caught her off guard. She could make out the faint outline of a face in the undulations of the bark: two eyes, a bump for a nose, gently curved lips. No one had mentioned the face. Was she really losing it? Sloan blinked to refocus and confirmed that there was a feminine face in the trunk. Maybe that's where the name Mother Tree came from.

The sun was lower, making the temperature bearable. A light breeze blew off the water and created a clicking noise behind her as the fans of the huge palmettos bumped one another. Sloan closed her eyes and took a few breaths. Her senses were heightened and she was aware of smells and sounds that she rarely took the time to notice. She hated to admit it, but there was something special about this place, the water behind her, the Mother Tree in front of her, the birds, insects, squirrels, and other small animals living their lives around her and all of this covered in a protective canopy of green. Maybe she felt this way only because the setting reminded her of the special times under the magnolia with GG. Surely there were hundreds of places like this all over Pamlico County. Her heart knew the answer her head didn't want to accept. She started a list of rationalizations for logging the land when the hair on the back of her neck stood up.

Sloan quickly looked behind her to the water but didn't see anything. Her heart rate picked up. Why was she anxious when she'd been relaxed a moment ago? She got to her feet and then heard the pop of a stick under someone's foot. She turned in the direction of the noise and saw a white man emerge from the woods. He had a fishing pole and small cooler with him.

Sloan stepped back beside the Mother Tree, hoping he wouldn't see her and she could sneak down the trail once he started fishing. He was her height but probably 300 pounds. His belly was so large his Salt Life T-shirt couldn't cover it and a white band of flesh was visible above the waistband of his jeans. Hanging from his belt was a leather sheath containing a knife. His belt buckle was the Confederate flag. The combination of the white flesh and Confederate flag made Sloan gasp. She covered her mouth and tried to conceal it, but her sound and movement caught his attention. The man took a few steps into the circle.

"Well. What do we have here? I've never seen you here before," he said, and set the cooler and fishing pole down.

Sloan instinctively recoiled from him. Her chest was tight and it was difficult to breathe. In her best effort to hide her fear, she put her shoulders back and, making full use her 6-foot height, stepped forward. "That makes two of us," she said, surprised by the evenness of her own voice. "I've never seen you here, either. I'm here on a hike."

The man smiled and Sloan's stomach turned as she felt his eyes traveling up and down her body. "I'm here to fish," he said, pointing at his fishing rod and continuing to stare at her. "You here alone?"

Sloan's heart was in her throat. She wasn't sure how to answer. "No. My husband is here somewhere." She looked in the woods behind her. "He's checking on a deer stand he left here." Sloan waited, hoping her lie would work.

The man took a pinch of chewing tobacco and put it between his lip and gum. He looked into the woods behind her and then back at Sloan. He smiled a lopsided smile and spit a stream of tobacco juice on the ground. "Is that so?" he said sarcastically.

"Yes. I'll leave you to your fishing," Sloan said and inched her way toward the trail.

"What's your hurry?" he asked. He opened his cooler and took out a Budweiser. The sound of the pop top echoed in the woods. "Here," he said, holding out the beer, "have a beer with me."

"No, thanks," Sloan said, slowly getting closer to the trail. "I'm going to find my husband."

"What? You're too good to drink with a white man?"

Sloan froze at the edge of the circle. There was no way to answer this that would satisfy him. She didn't want to continue talking to him as the longer she was near him the greater the chance something could happen. He took a step toward her. In an instant she calculated her

153

mass and fitness versus his mass, mouthful of tobacco and open beer. Her body flooded with adrenaline and she turned and ran.

Briars caught her ankles and branches lashed at her arms, but she kept running. Her feet instinctively stayed on the trail. She could tell he wasn't following her but heard the beer can hit a tree and him yelling. Her breath and footfalls drowned out the cussing and racial slurs she imagined he was saying. In less than half the time it took her to hike in, she was back at her car beside the road. She leaned into the side of her gray Volvo to catch her breath. She noticed red welts on her arms and tiny drops of blood around her lower legs, but otherwise she was fine.

Now that she was safe, Sloan's fear curdled into anger. She hit the roof of her car. She was the owner of this property, a strong woman. Why did this overweight, white redneck have the power to make her afraid? The slash of white flesh above his waistband burned in her mind. She heard her uncle unbuckle his belt. He put his hand on her shoulder and forced her to turn toward him. His pungent musk nauseated her. She kept her eyes on the white skin of his stomach, avoiding what was below for as long as possible.

Sloan leaned down and threw up beside the car. She looked back toward the woods in disgust. She'd never go back there again. She'd log the whole damn thing and put a fence around it just to keep that bastard out.

***

Maya climbed the steps to the dining room at The Silos, which lived up to its name by being inside a grain silo. The place was packed, probably because of the open mic night she'd seen advertised on the sign outside. She'd been here a couple times but never when it was this busy. Maya scanned the crowd for Lilith, hoping she'd already gotten a table. A hand went up in the back left corner, and Maya weaved her way through the tables and sat down.

Lilith pushed a draft beer toward her. "I took the liberty of ordering you an IPA," she said. "I got here a little early because I knew it would be crowded."

"Thanks," Maya said, taking a swig of her beer. "I've lived here almost a year and never knew there was so much action on a Wednesday night," she laughed.

"We better get our talking done before the music starts," Lilith said. She reached into her backpack on the floor and pulled out a newspaper. "Here's the article I told you about on the phone." She laid *The Pamlico News* in the middle of the table.

Maya read the article quickly, struck again by how many people the Hungry Mother Creek property impacted. She was also taken aback that Lilith had been interviewed and talked about their circle. "Lilith, you didn't tell us you were interviewed for this article. I wish you'd checked with us before telling everyone about the circle," Maya said.

Lilith put her hand on Maya's left arm. "I know the circle is new to you, but remember, it's been a part of Oriental for over 100 years. A lot of people are familiar with it and many had women from their family participate. The story of our circle exemplifies how sacred this land has been over the years and we need to capitalize on that."

Maya took a breath. "You're right. I've got to stop being possessive of the Mother Tree. Everyone has the right to enjoy that land."

"And the more people who want to protect it, the better chance we have of success," Lilith said. Maya and Lilith paused to give the waiter their pizza order.

"You know, if I'm possessive of the land," Maya said, "I wonder how Sloan feels? She's actually the one who owns it."

"She may be feeling the same way but for different reasons," Lilith said, sipping her beer, "She's thinking of the money she'll make, not the nature."

"Yeah. That's what it seemed like when we met with her," Maya agreed. "Wonder if she's thought more about her great-grandmother's involvement or even gone to see the Mother Tree?"

"I don't know," Lilith said. "She certainly didn't seem open to anything at our meeting but logging the land."

"Maybe this article will make her re-think things?"

"I doubt it," Lilith said. "The only thing that would stop her from logging would be to find another way to get the money."

"I know," Maya said. "That's really the bottom line. We need to come up with a plan to help Sloan get the money she needs so she can leave the property around our Mother Tree alone."

"I like your thinking, Maya," Lilith said, nodding. "We're probably more likely to solve this by figuring out a way for all our needs to be met and not just fighting Sloan. I wonder if there are any town loans or grants she could use to help start her retreat center?"

"I don't know. We could ask when we go to the town for the permit. Travis is hoping we could raise the money to purchase the land from her, but that's a long shot."

"Now that would be perfect," Lilith said. "If I camped out in the Mother Tree, that would give us some publicity and help raise money, don't you think?" Lilith asked playfully. The waiter arrived and Lilith put the newspaper away so he could set the pizza in the middle of the table.

"Sounds like you and Travis have been talking a lot," Lilith said, reaching for a piece of pizza. "How are things going there? He sure seemed into you on Sunday." Lilith took a bite and watched Maya closely.

"Things? There are no things," Maya said. "We're just friends working together to save the Mother Tree." She felt a blush creep up her neck as she remembered their kiss in her kitchen.

"I'm teasing," Lilith reassured her, raising an eyebrow. "You can give me more details whenever you're ready because I know there're more. But you do need to write up your interview with him about his grandmother for our circle history. I've continued to interview folks. Monday I met with the granddaughter of Abagail Jenkins. She was in the circle in the early 1940s."

Maya did the math, aligning that date to Hazel's life. "Hazel would have been about 14 then. I wonder if Abagail was in the circle with Hazel's mother?"

"Well, we can find out," Lilith said, pulling a manila folder out of her backpack. "Abagail's granddaughter was very helpful and had gone through family albums and paperwork to find as much information about her grandmother as possible. And look what she found."

Lilith opened the folder, revealing several black-and-white photos that had browned with age. She slid the first one in front of Maya. There were five women on the beach of Hungry Mother Creek. Two of them had on one-piece playsuits and the other three had on cropped pants with untucked blouses. Maya smiled at the contrast of their clothes to how women currently dressed. Today, she would wear something like that to work, not for spending time in the woods. They all were barefoot, so the picture must have been taken in the late spring or summer. The trees were smaller and the undergrowth less dense, but the Mother Tree was clearly visible behind them. They had their arms around each other's waists.

Maya's eyes filled with tears. Without even knowing them, she felt a connection to these women because of their shared experience in the circle around the Mother Tree. "Lilith, what a gift to have these pictures. Do we have to give them back?"

"No," Lilith said. "She made copies and said I could keep the originals to put in our book."

Maya slid the first picture away and examined the other two. In one, the women were standing in ankle-deep water. The tallest woman at the far left was kicking her foot, sending a spray of water toward the others, who were laughing. The last picture showed the women's backs as they walked away from the water to the circle. "I wonder who took these," Maya asked aloud and then answered herself. "Maybe someone's husband dropped her off, like Ben used to do for Violet."

Lilith pointed to the tall one splashing. "That's Abagail," she said. "Her granddaughter said she was 25 when this picture was taken. And this one is Florence," Lilith said, pointing to the black woman in the middle. "I need to make sure to show this to Jana, her daughter. Do you recognize Hazel's mother?"

Maya picked up the first picture and studied the women. "I don't know for sure, but my guess would be this one," Maya said, pointing to the small woman on the right side. "I think her mother would have been in her early 30s about this time and this woman definitely has the same stature as Hazel. May I take one of these home? Maybe I can find a picture of Goldie—that was Hazel's mother—and confirm which one is her." Maya had another reason for wanting to take the picture home but wasn't ready to share it with Lilith yet.

"Sure. Take them all," Lilith said, closing the folder and pushing it her way. "You may want to show it to Travis, too, in case one of these women is his grandmother." Lilith flashed Maya a knowing smile.

"Check. Check. Check, one, two," a voice rang out with some static feedback. Chris, the restaurant owner, was adjusting the microphones, and then introduced the first act for open mic night. Lilith had been right. There was no way to talk with the music. Maya sat back and tapped her foot to "Mustang Sally," but her thoughts were of Travis.

Her heart caught in her throat when a younger man walked past the stage, but it wasn't him. Then she remembered it was Wednesday and he was probably at church. What was she thinking? They could never be a couple. Here she was, drinking a beer, listening to Southern rock, and he was probably leading a prayer right now. Maya glanced at her watch. She was ready to go now.

***

Sloan slammed the car door and walked to the back of GG's house. She'd instinctively pulled into their driveway on the way home from her property on Hungry Mother Creek. She hadn't meant to, but now that she was here, she figured it would be good to take time and decompress before she talked to Peter.

Sunset was still 30 minutes away and there was enough daylight for her to walk back to the creek. She approached the magnolia tree where she'd sat with GG and felt its energy pulling her toward it. With every step closer, rubber bands tightened around her throat and heart, making it difficult to breathe. She leaned with her back against the trunk and the rubber bands broke, releasing her emotions.

Instead of tears, Sloan raised her hands to the sky and unleashed a deep, anguished scream, surprising herself with the volume and intensity. She did it again, this time intentionally, pulling up the anger her 11-year-old self had never expressed. Was she yelling at God for allowing the abuse to happen, at her uncle for committing it, or at her mother for not protecting her? She didn't know. Maybe she was angry at herself for not dealing with this sooner and letting it take a huge toll on her life. Sloan fell on her hands and knees after the second scream and then slumped back against the magnolia, her energy spent. Her right hand absently picked up a magnolia cone.

The sun lowered, the shadows grew, and the frogs continued their croaky conversation. Nature absorbed her sound into the evening, nonchalant to her anger. Sloan knew it was time. Her nightmares, difficulty trusting others, and reaction to the man by the Mother Tree all highlighted the fact she hadn't coped with her abuse. Obviously, staying busy and overscheduled, trying not to think about it, hadn't worked. But what would? She didn't have time for this. She needed to get the retreat center opened. Maybe she should throw herself into renovations and marketing. Sloan started making a list of what to do tomorrow and then caught herself. This was her old way of coping, and it hadn't worked. She needed to do something different. Maybe telling her mother was the place to start.

Sloan took some deep breaths and turned the magnolia cone over in her hands. The evening breeze rustled the river grass. A whippoorwill sang to Venus, the first star, now visible between the tree tops. She reviewed the intense emotions she'd experienced since leaving home this afternoon. Now, by the water and under this tree, she'd found peace. Sloan thought of the Mother Tree and Hungry Mother Creek. GG and women over the last century must have found peace there, too, and she was going to ruin their sanctuary. She held her guilt at bay. She'd think about that tomorrow, but now she needed to get home and talk with Peter and apologize for her outburst this morning.

There was a faint glow of light on the western horizon when Sloan pulled in her driveway. She saw the light on in Peter's studio and rehearsed what she would say to him. She headed toward the front door when a movement by the well caught her eye. She turned and peered into the fading light and saw Nellie raise her arm. Sloan hesitated. She needed to talk to Peter but hadn't seen Nellie in over a week and didn't want to miss this opportunity. Sloan changed direction and jogged over to the well. Nellie leaned on the rock wall surrounding it.

"Nellie, it's good to see you," Sloan said. "Don't forget to call me so I have your phone number. Then we won't have to depend on our chance meetings to see each other. How've you been?"

"I'm fine, Nellie said, not meeting Sloan's eyes with her own. "Sorry I forgot to call you. How are things with you? Have you come up with another way to raise the money you need without logging your land?"

Sloan was ready for Nellie to focus the conversation on her and didn't bite. "I'm still working on that but there's something I need to talk to you about," she said. Nellie stiffened and took a step away from the wall. Sloan took a step closer to her. She glanced toward Nellie's neck but it was too dark to see if a bruise was there. Sloan's mouth went dry and she tried to find the most compassionate way to confront her. "Nellie, I realize we're new friends, but I want you to know that if you ever need help, I'm here." Sloan paused and Nellie stared over her head to the house. "I've seen your bruises and am worried your husband is hurting you. If you need a safe place to go, you're more than welcome here."

Nellie wrapped her arms around her waist and studied the ground between them. She remained silent.

"I know this is hard to talk about, but I couldn't keep ignoring it," Sloan said.

Nellie raised her eyes to meet Sloan's and then she quickly looked away. "Please don't worry about me. I'll be fine," she said in a voice even softer than usual. "He promised it wouldn't happen again and I'm being careful not to make him mad." Nellie took another step back. "I better get home."

Sloan searched for the right words. "Nellie, it's not your fault." She took a step toward Nellie and realized these words also applied to her. "You can tell me the truth. I understand better than you may think."

Nellie's head snapped up and now she looked Sloan square in the eyes. "Does Peter hurt you?"

Sloan looked away. She swallowed the half-truth that surfaced by reflex. "No. No. Peter is wonderful. This happened a long time ago." Sloan paused. "My uncle molested me when I was young." Sloan exhaled and held onto the well for support.

Nellie's posture visibly relaxed and her eyes filled with compassion. "You do understand," she said quietly. Sloan nodded. Nellie continued, "I'm sorry you had to go through that. How old were you? What did your parents do?"

"It happened when I was 10 and 11. My parents didn't know. They still don't," Sloan said. "I never told anyone while it was going on. When I was 18, I told my great-grandmother but swore her to secrecy. I didn't want to throw my family into a turmoil or go through the humiliation of a court trial."

"I know," Nellie said. "Keeping quiet is easier but it's unfair that we do nothing wrong and live with this pain while your uncle and my husband carry on with no consequences."

"But Nellie, you don't have to stay," Sloan said, her voice bordering on pleading. "Even if you don't want to press charges, you can still leave. Peter and I will help you. I've talked to a women's shelter in New Bern and they'll guide you through the whole process."

Nellie tucked a stray hair back into her bun. "Sloan, I appreciate your offer more than you know, but I'm not ready. I'm more afraid to leave and figure out how to live on my own than I am to stay and hope things get better."

Sloan took a breath to calm herself. She couldn't imagine how Nellie could refuse help to stop her abuse. It had been what Sloan had wished for the entire time her uncle had lived with them. But Nellie was an adult and Sloan couldn't force her.

"OK," Sloan said. "But the minute you're ready, you call or just show up at my door."

"I will, but he said this was the last time," Nellie said.

Sloan took a few steps toward Nellie, wanting to hug her, but then resisted, remembering that they had never touched.

Nellie looked over her shoulder, down Magnolia Bend Road. "I better get going. Thanks again, Sloan." She turned and walked away.

"Bye, Nellie, and don't forget my offer. Any time day or night," Sloan called after her. Nellie turned back to wave and then continued walking. Every nerve ending in Sloan's body wanted to run after Nellie and prevent her from going home. Tears pooled in Sloan's eyes. Abuse at any age takes away your power and self-worth, she thought. Sloan could only hope that talking about her experience, and her offer of help, would give Nellie courage to leave her husband.

Sloan quickly realized she was in no place to judge Nellie for staying with her husband. She wasn't even brave enough to tell her mother about her abuse, which seemed to be an easier task than Nellie's. As she watched Nellie walk away, Sloan made the decision to invite her mother for a visit and have the conversation that should have happened years ago.

Sloan turned and followed the glow from Peter's studio window back to the house and replayed her conversation with Nellie. Nellie was only the third person she'd told about her abuse, but it hadn't been that difficult. Maybe because she felt safe with Nellie and that her story could help her. And maybe opening the box where she'd locked away her abuse, and experiencing the feelings she'd repressed, like she'd done under the magnolia tree, was the way to release the power it had over her.

Sloan stepped inside and left her sneakers by the door. She took a breath and went upstairs to Peter's studio to apologize and tell him about her decision to invite her mother for a visit.

THE MOTHER TREE

CHAPTER 11

Maya looked at herself in the long mirror. Bay had definitely done her magic. She'd taken Maya's sundress and accented it with a scarf and earrings of hers. The outfit, a light touch of makeup, and her shoulder-length hair loose from its normal ponytail made her feel pretty. She twirled across the bedroom. "Doodle Bug. What do you think?"

Doodle Bug, feeding off Maya's excitement, circled around her and then began chasing her tail. Maya took some deep breaths and walked downstairs. She needed to relax. She was treating this like a date but wasn't 100% sure that's how Travis meant it. They were originally going to meet at The Bean to discuss the rally but last night Travis called and said he had something come up with the church for the morning. He asked if they could go to dinner in New Bern instead.

Saturday night. Dinner in New Bern. The last time they were together he kissed her. All of that seemed to support tonight being a date. Maya let Doodle Bug out and stood on the back porch. She watched her running from spot to spot, sniffing the grass, the edge of the water, and then the trunk of a tree. Finally, she chose her spot to relieve herself.

"Doodle Bug. Come! It's time for dinner," Maya called.

Doodle Bug raced up the back steps and through the door Maya held open. As soon as Maya finished feeding her, Travis drove up. Doodle Bug started into her happy dance.

"Sorry, girl," Maya said, reaching down and rubbing behind an ear.

"You have to stay here. I'll be back in a little while. You be good."

Doodle Bug understood and went to lie down on her pillow in the corner.

Not wanting to disturb Doodle Bug with Travis' entrance, Maya exited through the office door to the driveway. She turned after locking the door and caught Travis' reaction. He stopped walking and put his hands on his hips, watching her come toward him. He let out a low whistle.

"You look gorgeous," he said, not taking his eyes off her.

Maya hoped she was far enough away that he couldn't see her blush. It'd been a long time since she'd been appreciated like this. When she reached Travis, he took both her hands in his and leaned down to kiss her on the lips. He held onto one of her hands and walked her back to his Jeep. "Where would you like to eat dinner tonight?"

The kiss had taken all her oxygen and Maya couldn't speak. Thankfully Travis continued.

"We could go to The Chelsea, Persimmons—it's on the water. Or if you like Indian, The Bay Leaf is good."

Maya regained her composure enough to answer. "Let's go to Persimmons. Maybe we can eat outside on the deck."

"Sounds good to me," Travis said and opened the passenger side door for her. He walked around the front of the car to his side and Maya smiled. This was definitely a date.

Seated outside next to the river at Persimmons, much of their dinner conversation focused on the rally. Travis had already gotten the permit for Lou Mac Park. They brainstormed how to publicize the rally and other community groups to include like the Boy Scouts, fishing clubs, and other churches.

"What about Sloan?" Travis asked.

"What about her?"

"Should we go talk with her and personally invite her to the rally?"

Maya crossed her arms over her chest. "I don't know what that would do. She doesn't have any reason to come unless we've got a check ready to pay her for the property."

"No. I disagree," Travis said. "If she came, she'd hear what her land means to the community. She'd see that although we want to stop the logging, we also want to raise money and purchase her land so she can complete her retreat center," Travis said.

Maya sighed. He was too damn diplomatic. "You're right. It would have more impact if she were actually at the rally, but we don't know if she's willing to sell it even if we raise the money."

"And that would be the reason to talk with her personally before the rally," Travis said, smiling.

Maya held up her hands in front of her. "OK. You're right."

"Now, enough about that. Come sit beside me and watch the sunset."

Maya lifted her wine glass and slipped around the table to sit next to Travis. He immediately put his arm around her and clasped her bare shoulder. His hand radiated heat through her body.

Maya relaxed and leaned into him. "This is perfect. Sunsets are better on the water."

"I kind of think it's better because I'm here with you," Travis said, rubbing her shoulder and upper arm.

"You do?" Maya said and then immediately regretted it. After years of feeling like Steven did everything in his power to avoid her, it was hard to believe Travis' words.

"Yes," Travis said without hesitating. "I'm glad we've been spending more time together the last few weeks."

"Me too," Maya said, and finally allowed herself to believe it was true.

They continued to stare straight ahead. The sun slid beneath the water and the sky glowed orange, pink, and violet. Maya's instinct was to sit quietly and swallow the questions running through her mind, but she wanted to do things differently than how Steven had conditioned her.

"Travis?" Maya asked.

"Yes," he answered, turning toward her.

"What is happening here? Are we picking up where we left off in November?"

Travis searched her eyes for a moment. "Yes," he said. "It feels like that to me. I think taking some time apart was good, but I missed you. I'd like us to keep spending time together."

Maya bumped her shoulder against his, "Are you asking me to go steady, Travis?"

Travis laughed. "I guess I am." He leaned down and kissed her deeply. "I'll take that as a yes."

Maya could only nod and smile. She hadn't felt this happy in a long time.

An hour later, Travis parked beside Maya's Saturn. They sat silently for a moment. Maya didn't know if she should kiss him and get out of the car or invite him in. Without the air conditioning, the car was heating up and Maya felt a drop of sweat slide between her shoulder blades. She made a choice, fully aware of what it could lead to. "Would you like to come in for a minute?"

Travis turned toward her and took her face in his hands. He gently kissed her. It felt like every nerve ending in her body was connected to her lips and she filled with desire. Before she was ready, he pulled back. "Now it's really hot in here," he said and opened the car door. Maya followed him to the porch steps and fumbled through her purse to find the keys. She heard Doodle Bug's toenails on the hard wood floor as she made her way to the door. Travis pulled her to him before she found her keys. He held her tight and rested his chin on top of her head. He took a breath. "This feels good," he said. His voice was husky and low. He held her tighter and rubbed the small of her back. "Believe me. There is nothing more I'd rather do than come inside, but it's already 11 and I need my sleep. Remember, tomorrow is Sunday."

That reality was like a cold shower. "Oh. I forgot," Maya said, deflated.

Doodle Bug whined on the other side of the door. Maya opened it and she bounded out, weaving between them, her tail wagging furiously.

Maya bent down to pet her and when she stood up Travis said, "Sorry I have to cut our evening short."

"That's OK," Maya said. "It gives us something to look forward to." She looked away from Travis, surprised by her own boldness.

Travis laughed. "Yes, it does," he said. He kissed her again. "I'll be done with church stuff about 3 tomorrow and will give you a call then."

Maya watched him drive away and then sat down on the steps to let Doodle Bug run around. Her mind was racing. She and Travis were a couple. If he'd come inside she'd been ready to make love to him. Was she moving too fast? Was it the right thing to do? Could she be in a relationship with a minister? This was too much to consider all alone. She looked toward the boathouse and saw the front porch light was on.

"Come on, girl. Let's see if Bay is up," Maya said, rising to her feet and patting her thigh to gesture for Doodle Bug to follow.

Maya saw the living room light on and gently knocked on the door. Doodle Bug sat patiently beside her, her tail swishing back and forth on the porch in anticipation of seeing Bay.

Bay opened the door and Doodle Bug bounded in. Bay didn't seem surprised to see them. She grabbed Maya's arm and pulled her inside. "How did it go?" She stepped back and looked at Maya. "Flushed cheeks. Sparkling eyes. I'd say things must have gone well. Sit down and tell me about it."

They sat facing each other with their backs against the arm rests of the couch and their feet curled under them. Bay leaned slightly forward in anticipation of Maya's story. Maya wasn't sure where to start.

"It was an official date, wasn't it?" Bay asked, giving Maya a place to begin.

Maya smiled. "Yes. It was definitely a date. I guess I knew all along but was scared to admit it. I didn't want to be disappointed." She paused. "We're going to keep seeing each other."

"You mean you're dating again?" Bay asked.

"Yes," Maya said, blushing. "It's only been six months since we broke up, but this time things are different. We have a deeper connection than we had in the fall. I don't know if it's because we're being more honest with one another or that we have the common goal of saving the Mother Tree."

Bay interrupted Maya by leaning forward and hugging her. "I'm so happy for you," she said, squeezing Maya's shoulders. "I don't know what Travis has done, but I know you've worked hard to heal from your marriage and Steven's death. I bet that's why you're more connected. The past isn't coming between you two like before. But enough about that. Did he kiss you?"

Maya started to laugh and nodded her head yes. Doodle Bug sensed Maya's mood and jumped up on the couch and licked her face. "Down, Doodle Bug," Maya laughed, dodging Doodle Bug's kisses like a boxer.

Bay laughed and said, "Looks like Doodle Bug is happy for you, too." The dog settled down and lay between them.

"Actually, he kissed me right away when he picked me up," Maya confided. "Then again at the restaurant and of course when he brought me home."

"And . . . ?" Bay asked.

"There is no 'and," Maya sighed. "I invited him in but he needed to get to bed early. Remember, he's a minister and tomorrow is Sunday."

"Damn. But if he'd come in, would you have had sex?" Bay didn't mince words.

Maya blushed again. She'd never talked this openly before about her sex life. "You sure are inquisitive," she said. Bay just waited expectantly. "If you have to know, yes. I didn't invite him in to admire the antiques." She and Bay laughed for a minute and then Maya got serious. "Do you think I'm making a mistake?"

"What?" Bay asked. "Where did that come from? Of course you're not making a mistake. You agreed to date him, not marry him, so there's nothing to lose and I've never seen you happier. What could be wrong with that?"

"Nothing, I guess. It's just—" Maya hesitated. "He's a minister. Am I good enough or spiritual enough to be with him? And what if things progress? How can I be a minister's wife if I don't even go to church?"

She'd said out loud what'd been bothering her the past few weeks. Tears welled in Maya's eyes and she swallowed hard. She rubbed Doodle Bug's head for comfort.

"Shouldn't Travis be part of that decision, Maya? If he doesn't think you're right for him, why is he taking you out to dinner and putting in all those hours to help you with the Mother Tree?"

Maya stared at Bay and let that sink in. "You do have a point." She hadn't thought about it like that before.

"Yeah. Easy for me to say, but I had the same doubts when I was with Holden," Bay said. "In fact, I never really felt smart enough or cultured enough to be married to him, only pretty enough, I guess."

"And here I am not feeling spiritual enough. What's wrong with us?" Maya asked.

"Hopefully nothing that can't be fixed," Bay said.

"Well, enough about me," Maya said. "How's everything with you? It won't be long until you leave for Raleigh."

"Two weeks from today I'll be moving into my apartment there," Bay said. "Classes start on August 20."

Hearing that date made Bay's departure a reality. Maya's throat tightened. She leaned forward and embraced Bay again. "I'm going to miss you," she said into Bay's blond hair. "Who's going to dress me when I have a special date? Who's going to help me figure out my life?"

"We'll talk, email, text and I definitely want you to come visit," Bay reassured her. "There's no way I'm going to lose touch with you. You've been a life saver for me."

Maya drew back from their hug and saw Bay's eyes glistening. "OK. Enough of this," Maya said. "We've still got two weeks together before we really have to cry."

Bay smiled. "That's right. Hey, how about next weekend I help you organize your closet and put together some outfits for you? If there's some staple items you're missing, we can shop at Marsha's Cottage with my employee discount."

"That would be super," Maya said. Doodle Bug's snores prompted Maya to look at her watch. "It's getting late. We better get to bed. Thanks for listening."

"No problem," Bay said. "It's a pleasure and I hope Travis gets to see your antiques soon."

Maya laughed and swatted playfully at Bay. "Don't worry. I'll keep you updated. Come on, Doodle Bug. Let's go home." Doodle Bug hopped off the couch and ambled to the door.

Maya smiled all the way back to her house, overwhelmed with gratitude for her special evening with Travis, her friendship with Bay, and of course for Doodle Bug.

***

Sloan and her mother walked slowly from the car to the front porch. They'd been to Sunday worship at the church her mother grew up in, and now the noontime heat was intense. Her mother stopped at the bottom of the steps, and despite the temperature, looked elegant with her close-cropped gray hair and pearl earrings that matched the buttons in her pale blue two-piece suit.

"It was hard for me to understand why you wanted to settle here in Pamlico County," her mother said. "I wouldn't want to give up my life in Raleigh to live way down here, but now that I've seen Magnolia Bend and heard about your plans, it makes more sense. When will you have your first retreat?"

Sloan didn't want to tell her mother about the financial strain of Deidre's rehab delaying her opening. She knew her parents would offer to help and, at 50 years old, that was the last thing she wanted. "I hope to open it this spring," she said. "I need the fall and winter to complete renovations to get it ready."

"Before I go, will you show me what you're going to do?"

"Sure," Sloan said and opened the front door. Peter had made himself scarce so she could be alone with her mother and the house was quiet.

"Feels good in here," her mother said. "I don't know how folks managed before air conditioning. I'm going upstairs to change and pack and will be right down."

"OK. I'll start getting lunch ready," Sloan said.

Sloan put the bowls in the fridge to chill for the cucumber soup and arranged lettuce on the plates, ready to receive the curried chicken salad. Yesterday, after her mother arrived and they'd surveyed her grandmother's place for what needed to be done, they spent the afternoon preparing today's lunch. It was a comfortable way to be together and gave them a chance to get reacquainted after several months apart.

Sloan heard her mother's suitcase thump at the front door and then her steps in the hall. Her heart beat faster in anticipation of her revelation.

Her mother swooped into the kitchen, ready to take charge, like she always did. "What a perfect day for a chilled soup. Do you have any fresh dill for garnish?"

Sloan, who knew her mother well, had bought some on her Friday shopping trip to New Bern. "There's some in the fridge, in the vegetable drawer," she said over her shoulder while ladling the soup into the chilled bowls.

"Perfect," her mother said, retrieving it. "But you do know it's better to put it in a glass of water."

Sloan rolled her eyes and didn't say anything. She knew she wouldn't be able to serve a meal without at least one critique.

Sloan watched her mother trim the stems and break the sprigs of dill into the perfect garnish size. Her mother's hands moved deftly. Sloan held the soup bowls and her mother sprinkled the dill. Sloan looked at their hands, black and brown. As a child, Sloan had wished that she and her parents had one skin color instead of three. When they went out as a family, people would stare and give them second looks, but this didn't happen when it was just her and her mother. She'd come to learn that brown and black went together better than brown and white.

"That looks perfect," her mother said, bringing Sloan out of her thoughts. Sloan put the soup and salad on the table and filled their glasses with iced tea.

Before she took her first bite, Sloan's mother took a moment, like she always did, to appreciate the presentation of the meal. "I'm happy we can share a meal. It's been a long time," she said.

"I know," Sloan answered.

"We rarely did this, even when you lived in Raleigh, because you were always busy," her mother said.

"Mom, you were busy, too."

"I know." Sloan's mother paused. "Now that I'm older and look back on my life, I regret not making more time for you."

Sloan's mother put her head down to take a spoonful of soup but not before Sloan saw tears in her eyes. She'd rarely seen her mother cry—and never over her.

"I know, Mom," Sloan said. "Since being here I've realized I did the same thing. Always working late and on weekends to get ahead, and before I knew it, the kids were gone. Sometimes I blame myself for Deidre's addiction. If I'd been more attentive, maybe she wouldn't have turned to drugs."

"Oh, don't do that," her mother broke in quickly. "You provided love, support, discipline, and look, Anthony is doing fine. Deidre's always had a rebellious streak in her and been more like her father."

Sloan hadn't thought of her ex-husband Jerry in a long time. He'd been an alcoholic for over 20 years but the last time they'd talked, he'd been sober for five years.

"Thanks, Mom," Sloan said. "I try not to dwell on that and be the best mother that I can right now."

"That's right. No mother is perfect. We just do the best we can."

Sloan and her mother ate silently for a minute. Sloan looked across at her mother. She'd always been smaller than Sloan but now was beginning to look frail. Her mother's hair was totally gray and the lines around her eyes and mouth were multiplying. How would the news about Sloan's abuse impact her? Would she spend the last years of her life filled with guilt? Would she tell Sloan's father, and how would he handle it? Her uncle was still alive and her father occasionally saw him.

Sloan thought about what her mother had said: mothers do the best they can. Sloan reflected on her own inadequacies as a mother. She hadn't been able to protect her children from everything, just like her mother hadn't been able to protect her. That was the reality of being a parent.

"Sloan, are you all right? You've gotten awfully quiet," her mother asked.

Sloan couldn't do it. She couldn't tell her mother knowing how much it would hurt her. She would focus on making their relationship in this moment as good as it could be.

"Everything's fine," Sloan said. She reached across the table and covered her mother's hand with her own. "I'm glad you're here."

CHAPTER 12

Maya wished Bay was there to help but she didn't want to bother her. Bay was leaving for Raleigh in three days and busy packing. Maya stared into her closet. She didn't need to be dressed up but wanted to look more put together than shorts and a T-shirt. It was hard enough to figure out what to wear four days a week to work and now she had to dress up on her day off, too. Maya's thumb released her frustration into her spinner ring and she stepped back for a better view of her closet.

Last Saturday, when the circle met to discuss the rally, Maya had shared Travis' suggestion that someone meet with Sloan to invite her and ask about her willingness to sell the property. Everyone agreed Maya was the best one to do it. Ella was traveling for work, Violet didn't think she would be assertive enough, and Lilith thought she'd be too assertive.

How can I convince Sloan of anything if I can't even convince myself of what to wear, Maya thought. Finally she grabbed a pair of black capris and a sleeveless, white linen shirt. You couldn't go wrong with black and white, she thought, and it was a sure bet because Bay helped her put this outfit together last weekend when they did her closet makeover.

Maya let Doodle Bug out and picked up her phone from the kitchen counter to put in her purse. She saw a text from Travis. "You'll be great. Can't wait to C U tonight." Suddenly Maya forgot all about Sloan and broke into a smile. She was taken by surprise that Travis was thinking of her today.

Maya took a deep breath and walked to her car. She'd do her very best for Travis, her circle, and to help save the Mother Tree. She didn't think she'd convince Sloan on the spot to stop the logging, but at the very least get her to come to the rally and agree to sell the property if they raised the money. Maya put a flyer for the rally on the passenger seat and steered down the driveway.

***

Sloan sat down at the desk in her office and pulled a stack of envelopes and her checkbook from the drawer. She should have done this over the weekend but had kept putting it off. She couldn't wait any longer. Deidre's rehab fees were due in less than a week. She didn't have to subtract the $10,000 for Deidre, her part of the mortgage payment, and the electric and water bills to know it would only leave $5,000 in her checking account. When she was working in real estate she'd have twice that in her checking and 3-4 times that in her savings, not including her investments. Of course, they were gone now, liquidated to purchase Magnolia Bend.

The muscles in the back of her neck tightened when she looked at the balance of her accounts. She should have $50,000 more, plenty to cover the renovations and tide her over until the retreat center was making money, but Deidre's hospital bills after her overdose and her rehab had changed that.

Sloan tore the checks out and stuffed them in their respective envelopes. She slapped stamps on each one and stomped out the front door to the mailbox. God, it was unfair. She'd finally taken a risk to do something to make her happy and it backfired. She was as stressed as she'd ever been and now less financially stable.

She slammed the mailbox shut and decided to walk for a bit to calm down. She walked 10 minutes down Magnolia Bend Road all the while looking out for Nellie, but never saw her. Her pace slowed on the way back. She thought of Deidre and felt guilty for being angry. That's what was most important. As long as Deidre was sober, Sloan would figure out the rest, even if it meant cutting down the Mother Tree. There were lots of beautiful live oaks in Pamlico County but only one Deidre. Sloan needed to save her daughter more than that tree.

Sloan went inside to the kitchen and poured another cup of coffee. She stared out the window at the water. She'd done the right thing using her money to get Deidre the best help possible. It was unfortunate she had to log part of her land to compensate, but it's what she had to do.

Sloan went back to the computer in her office and opened the file with the brochure for the retreat center. In a few more weeks it would be ready for real estate colleagues in Raleigh to review. A knock on the door startled her. She'd been focused on the spacing and layout for the brochure and hadn't even noticed that someone had driven up. She leaned over and looked out the window. She saw a red Saturn. It looked familiar—she remembered it was the car the women's circle had come in. There was a second knock at the door and she stood to answer it. Why would they be coming back, and without even calling ahead? She was relieved when she only saw one woman through the narrow window beside the door. She couldn't remember her name, but at least it wasn't Lilith, who'd been the more belligerent one.

Sloan opened the door. Before she could speak, the woman in front of her said, "Sloan, I'm Maya, from the women's circle."

"I know. I remember you." Sloan stood in the doorway with one hand on the doorknob.

"I should have called to let you know I was coming, but I was worried you wouldn't agree to meet," Maya said.

Sloan didn't respond, waiting for Maya to explain why she was here. Maya thrust a piece of paper at her. "I wanted to invite you to come to the rally to save the property on Hungry Mother Creek," she said.

Sloan didn't even look at the paper in her hand, keeping eye contact with Maya. "You mean my property on Hungry Mother Creek." Her voice was firm and unwavering. "You've wasted your time driving all the way out here. There's no reason for me to go. I've made my decision and in a few weeks, they'll begin logging. Nothing that happens Saturday will change my mind."

"But what if we could raise the money to buy it from you? Would you be willing to sell it?"

So that was the reason she came. Sloan stared at Maya, who wiped a bead of sweat from her forehead and shifted from one foot to the other. Sloan realized she was nervous about talking with her and burning up in the mid-morning sun.

She stepped out of the door frame and waved Maya inside. "Come in out of the heat and we can talk in my office."

Sloan led Maya directly off the foyer and motioned for her to sit on the couch across from her desk. Sloan took a breath and reminded herself of her vow to be more open and trusting of others. The least she could do was hear Maya out.

"Maya, buying my land is an interesting proposition and could solve both our problems, but it doesn't seem realistic," Sloan began, gazing down at her clasped palms and the flyer sitting in front of her on her desk. She noticed a prominent vein running down the back of her left hand. "I thought of trying to sell it, but my realtor said there was an eight-year supply of land already on the market and that it would take a while to sell. I couldn't afford to wait. I don't see how you could find an investor or raise the money before I start the logging." She glanced up at Maya, who looked more composed now that she was sitting down and cool.

"We know it's a long shot, but have to try," Maya replied. She pointed to the flyer. "We're going to give people a chance to share what the property means to them. There are plenty of wealthy people here in town, and you never know who may be moved by the stories and donate. We've invited the mayor and some county commissioners to come, too, in hopes they may have some funds available to contribute since the goal is to make it into a park."

Sloan took a minute and examined the flyer. They were going to have bands playing, a poetry reading, children singing, and the rotary was even selling hot dogs and drinks. She had to admire their efforts and optimism. "Looks like you're making this quite an event."

"I've only been here a year, but Travis, the minister at the Baptist church, told me Oriental loves to celebrate. We thought having different groups involved and making it festive would help with attendance," Maya said.

"How do you plan to raise the money?" Sloan asked. "My realtor told me the value for that 50 acres is between $200,000 and $300,000. That seems like an awful lot of money to raise by passing the hat at a rally." Sloan immediately felt badly for saying this when she saw Maya blush and look toward the floor.

"I know."

They sat in silence and Sloan let this scenario play out. If, somehow, they did raise the money, she would end up with more than enough for the retreat center and could use the rest to pay down the mortgage on Magnolia Bend, and she wouldn't feel guilty for destroying something that was a part of her great-grandmother's history. But who was she kidding? There was no way they could raise that much money in three or four weeks.

"Maya, I certainly appreciate you coming out to talk with me about this," Sloan paused, "especially after how things ended at our last meeting. I'm sorry I was abrupt." Now it was Sloan's turn to be nervous. Her neck muscles tensed as she contemplated sharing more with Maya. "The last few months have been stressful. I had money set aside to start the retreat center but right after I closed on this house, I had a family emergency that depleted those funds." She watched Maya taking this in and continued. "So, if you could raise the money, I'd be open to selling the property to you."

Maya's whole body seemed to exhale in relief. "Oh, thank you!" she exclaimed quickly, before Sloan could change her mind. "We'll do our best." She paused, as if afraid to press her luck. "If we only raise half the money, would you be willing to divide the property and sell the 25 acres closest to the Mother Tree?"

Sloan smiled, knowing it was next to impossible for them to even raise half. "Sure. I'd be willing to discuss that."

"Wonderful." Maya stood. "I won't take any more of your time. The rally starts at 9 on Saturday morning over at Lou Mac Park. I hope you decide to come."

Sloan stood as well and walked Maya to the door. "We'll see. Keep in touch about the fund raising but unless I hear different, the logging will begin as planned."

"Yes. I'll let you know." Maya put her hand out and they shook.

Sloan watched her drive away. What a different interaction from a month ago. She appreciated the circle for respecting her need for the money and not making her the villain for logging the land.

Sloan sat back down at her computer but had lost her focus. They were going to all this trouble and the Hungry Mother Creek property would still be logged. Once the retreat center was thriving and bringing money into the town, and the trees were growing back, hopefully the community would move on. Sloan looked at her watch. She'd finish the brochure later. It was time for her to head into town to meet the yoga instructor to discuss how they could work together.

***

Maya drove away from Magnolia Bend with the windows down to breathe in the fresh air. She may have stumbled over a few words, but overall, she was proud of how she handled her meeting with Sloan. She'd been nervous about a confrontation but it had all worked out. She felt something new tugging strongly at her heart—compassion for Sloan and her reasons for logging the property. Despite the fact the meeting went well, Maya still felt discouraged. Sloan was right. There was little chance they'd raise the money they needed in such a short amount of time. She would call Travis and Lilith and give them an update when she got home, Maya thought. They were both optimists and would lift her spirits.

She crossed the bridge into Oriental and when she drove past the Baptist church, she noticed Travis' Jeep out front. Maybe she should stop and talk with him in person. But he was working and in the church. Would it be appropriate for her to talk to him there? Would he be embarrassed if she showed up? She remembered her conversation with Bay about not being good enough. She was being ridiculous. These thoughts were her insecurities and had nothing to do with Travis. He'd probably be happy to see her. By now she'd spent so much time debating herself that she was already on the outskirts of town. She pulled into the Dollar General and turned around.

Maya wasn't sure where Travis' office was but couldn't imagine it would be hard to find. She let herself in a side door that led to the Sunday school classrooms. The thick carpeting muffled her footsteps but she still felt the urge to tip-toe. The smell in the hall reminded her of vacation Bible school she'd attended with friends when she was a child. It contained a mixture of crayons, the musty smell of old books, and the leftover fragrance from Sunday's flowers. Instantaneously, the smell brought on the unease and confusion she felt when visiting church all those years ago. With no guidance from her non-church-going parents, she didn't know if she should clap after the choir sang, when to sit or stand, or whether she should say she believed something if she wasn't sure. Her 12-year-old mind couldn't grasp the conflicting messages of death, judgment, sin, and hell with the love, grace, mercy, and eternal life that was also espoused. By the time she was in high school, she stopped accepting invitations to church and tried to make sense of the world by reading books like *Siddhartha*, *The Alchemist*, *Walden*, and *The Essays of Ralph Waldo Emerson*.

She reached the end of the hallway and hadn't seen anything but classrooms, so she turned around. She followed the hall to the church sanctuary and walked across it, feeling like a trespasser. As soon as she exited the sanctuary, she heard Travis' voice.

Maya immediately smiled and headed in that direction, forgetting her discomfort. He was talking with the church secretary about his phone messages and someone who was in the hospital. Travis had his back to her. She gently knocked on the open door. He turned around and the way his face lit up made Maya warm all over. She couldn't remember the last time someone had looked at her that way. Even at the beginning of their relationship, Steven was never this unguarded with his emotions.

"Maya, I'm so glad you stopped by. How did the meeting with Sloan go?" Travis closed the distance between them and gave her a big hug. Maya hugged him back cautiously and made eye contact across his shoulder with his secretary, a fit, tan woman probably in her mid-60s.

She was smiling broadly. Before Maya could say anything, Travis said, "Linda, this is Maya. Maya, Linda is my assistant and lifesaver. She keeps me and the church organized and running smoothly."

Linda and Maya shook hands and Linda said, "It's nice to meet you. I've heard a lot about you."

"You have?" Maya asked incredulously.

"Of course. Travis talks about you all the time."

"Linda's my second mother and we talk about everything. I told her that we are seeing each other." Travis blushed, a contrast to his usual composure.

Linda stood. "I think it's about time for me to take lunch. I'll leave you two. Travis, I'll be back by 1:00."

"No problem. Take as long as you'd like."

Maya and Travis were silent for a moment while Linda took her purse from a file cabinet and left. Travis took Maya's hand and said, "Come on back to my office and you can update me about your meeting."

They walked through the door behind Linda's desk into Travis' office. There was a large oak desk covered with books and stacks of papers at the back of the room. To the right of the door were a couch, coffee table, and wingback chair. This area was bright with sunlight streaming in the double windows that faced the lawn behind the church. Maya guessed this is where he counseled his church members. Travis sat in the chair and she sat on the couch, which put too much distance between them. She wanted to climb into his lap and kiss him but figured that wasn't appropriate behavior for church. Instead, Maya gave Travis the synopsis of her visit with Sloan.

"Awesome. Sounds like it went as well as it could," Travis said after listening carefully, without interrupting.

"It was definitely better than our last meeting, but nothing significant has changed," Maya said. "She only said she was logging the Hungry

Mother Creek property in a nicer way."

"I know, but at least there's an open dialogue happening. That gives us a better chance of something changing than if no one is talking."

Maya smiled. "How do you do it? You always find a bright side."

"I guess you could say it's part of the job description," Travis said. "Every week I talk with church members struggling with challenges, sit by the sick and dying, and preach at funerals. If I lose sight of life's blessings, how can I bring others hope?"

Maya was quiet a minute, letting this soak in. "I should learn to do that."

"Once you look long enough for things to be grateful for, it becomes a habit and you see them everywhere," Travis said. Light shadows danced across his face as a tree branch bounced in the breeze outside the window. Maya looked at him, ignoring the spark of longing for him in her stomach, and noticed he looked completely at peace and confident in his words.

"When I was with Steven, I lost sight of that," Maya said. "Most of my focus was on dealing with his mood and trying not to do or say anything that would send him into a rage." She paused and stared over the top of Travis' head at the bookshelves lining the back wall. Travis was silent. She looked back at Travis. "During that time, running provided the opportunity for me to be grateful; grateful for time alone, the sunrise, the animals I saw, the strength to complete a long run."

Maya's eyes filled with tears and for the first time since Steven's death, she felt deep compassion for herself. She'd endured an abusive marriage but had survived. She was healing and creating a new life for herself. Now she filled with gratitude and tears spilled down her cheeks.

Travis immediately moved to the couch to hug her. He held her close and gently rubbed her back. Maya pressed her head into the crook of his neck, the smell of his skin, another reason for gratitude. Travis held her and didn't say anything trite to comfort her.

Maya kissed his neck and slid away from him, but he kept his hand on her knee.

"You've come a long way since then, haven't you?" Travis said.

Maya nodded. "You're such a good listener. Does that come naturally or was that part of your training in seminary?"

"A little of both, I guess, and lots of practice."

"What made you want to be a minister?"

Travis leaned back against the couch. "I can't believe I haven't told you already."

Maya smiled at how men's memories worked. "How could you have told me when we broke up the day I found out you were a minister?"

Travis smiled. "It seems like we've been together longer and you should already know. I'll try to give you the abridged version. A few months after college, Sharon and I got married. I bounced between entry-level jobs at a bank, and in retail and insurance, but nothing satisfied me. I ended up working in construction and enjoyed the physical labor and a tangible outcome from a day's work."

"Ah," Maya interjected. "That's why you could renovate Hazel's boathouse into an apartment."

"Yup," Travis nodded. "And while I was trying to figure out what I wanted to do with my life, Sharon and I were trying to make our marriage work. We shouldn't have married right out of college, now that I look back." He paused. "That was a difficult time. I thought I would graduate college, get married, find a decent job, have two children and be happy. It didn't work that way for me."

"Yeah. Me either," Maya said, and Travis squeezed her knee.

"Finally, after five years of trying, Sharon and I split. I took my part of the money from the sale of our house and traveled around the country for almost a year, mostly west of the Mississippi. I was alone with my thoughts, trying to figure out what to do with my life. I worked odd jobs to make money, I read, prayed, and began journaling. I visited different types of churches across the country. Little by little my spirituality deepened and my connection to God grew stronger."

Maya interrupted. "How did you know that your connection to God was stronger?" she asked, wondering how he measured the strength of a relationship that felt inaccessible to her.

Travis paused and looked over her head out the windows. He looked backed at her and smiled. "Now that is a good question. I think God is more available, at least to me, when there is quiet, time, and emptiness. A few weeks into the trip, my mind stopped analyzing my marriage, what job I needed, where I had to be, and I was more in the moment. This, and long periods of time alone, quieted the chatter in my mind and allowed me to hear God, or maybe someone else would call it their higher self. Either way, I felt more at peace than I ever had and like I was a part of something greater than my own life and its struggles."

Travis ran his hands through his hair. "Am I making any sense? It's something that you have to experience before you can truly understand."

Maya had leaned forward, her eyebrows knitted together in thought. "I think I understand a little. What you're describing sounds like how I felt the first time I sat in front of the Mother Tree."

Travis sat up straighter and said, "Exactly! Now imagine that feeling for the better part of three months. My life became more centered and purposeful. I began to think about the ministry as a way to help others do that same thing. It started as a niggling at the back of my mind that at first I tried to ignore."

Maya laughed. "What the heck is a niggling?"

"You know. That voice telling you the right thing to do. Usually it's the more difficult path so you try to pretend it's not there."

Maya nodded, knowing exactly what he meant. She'd heard that voice for over a year telling her to leave Steven.

"At some point, I couldn't ignore it anymore and went back to Greensboro, my hometown. I talked with family and close friends and spent time with the minister at the church where I'd grown up. He's probably the reason I ended up going to a Baptist seminary. That and it's part of my heritage. Now here I am, a minister at the church my mother and grandmother attended."

Maya leaned forward and took Travis' hand. "Looks like we've both come a long way."

"Yeah, and I'm glad our long ways ended up in the same place," Travis said.

Maya's stomach growled loudly and she covered it with her hand. "Sorry. I'm getting hungry."

Travis looked at his watch. "It's already 12:30. Want to grab some lunch?"

"Sure. Maybe while we're eating we can figure out how to raise all that money to buy Sloan's property."

Travis stood and threw one of the pillows from the couch down at her. "We should have that done before the food arrives."

THE MOTHER TREE

CHAPTER 13

Maya, Lilith, and Ella sat in folding chairs under the live oak in the middle of Lou Mac Park. The word "park" made it sound like a large space, when actually it was only a small expanse of grass beside the river. The women hoped it would soon be filled with people in support of the Hungry Mother Creek property. They'd moved the two picnic tables and Adirondack chairs off to the side in preparation.

It was 8:30 and everything was in place for the rally. There was a podium, sound system, chairs, and a mobile chalk board so folks could write their thoughts about the Hungry Mother Creek property on it. The Pamlico Community Band and was setting up in the lot across the street from the park and the rotary club had just pulled up with their hot dog stand. A few people had already arrived by foot and bicycle, and they milled around with coffee in hand. A low hum of conversation filled the air, occasionally punctuated with the call of "Good morning!" A couple of children were chasing one another, clutching the song lyrics they'd be singing shortly.

Maya watched all this with gratitude. The community, her community, was coming together to save the land on Hungry Mother Creek. No matter how futile their efforts might turn out to be, everyone seemed to be upbeat. She hoped she would absorb the mood of the crowd.

"Everyone seems enthusiastic," Maya said to Ella and Lilith. "Do you think we even have a chance of raising the money we need?"

"I don't know. $250,000 is a lot of money," Ella said. "I want this to work so we can save the Mother Tree, but the business side of me can't imagine how we can be successful."

"You guys, don't give up before we even get started," Lilith said. "You have to believe in the possibility of success. This town is full of people who believe in the seemingly impossible. Circumnavigating the world, the entire planet, in a sailboat seems impossible, but I bet we've got at least 30 sailors here who've done that. If any town can achieve the impossible, it's Oriental." Lilith stood while she talked to emphasize her point.

Maya stood too and gave Lilith a quick hug. "Thanks, Lilith. You're right. Until the first tree is cut, we have to hold onto the belief we can save the property," Maya said, trying to stay positive. "I hope what you just said is part of your speech today."

"It's not, but maybe I'll add it to the end."

"Looks like the crowd is starting to gather," Ella said. "And here comes Violet."

Maya reached into a box at her feet and handed each woman a stack of papers. "We better start handing out the programs."

Violet arrived and quickly hugged each woman.

"Here's your stack of programs, Violet," Maya said.

"Thank you, dear. These look great," Violet said, scanning the paper.

"I know," Maya said. "The Oriental Women's Club printed them, and look," Maya said, turning the program over. "On the back it tells people how they can donate."

Maya walked toward some people arriving to give them a program when arms encircled her from behind. Travis. She broke into a huge smile and leaned back into him. He kissed her on the neck and spun her around for a kiss on the lips.

"Don't you look beautiful," Travis said.

Maya tucked her hair behind her ear, grateful she'd chosen to wear a jersey dress that skimmed her athletic figure rather than her standby of shorts and a T-shirt. It had the desired effect.

"Travis, look at all the people," Maya said, pausing and looking behind her to the street. "And more are arriving. You did a great job with publicity."

"Thanks," Travis said, smoothing a flyaway wisp of hair behind her ear. "But that's not hard in a town this small and it was easy to get support because people care about the land." He took the rest of Maya's flyers. "I'll finish handing these out. Will you go over to the chalk board and encourage people to write about the property?" He looked at his watch. "We still have about 10 minutes before we start." As Travis finished his sentence, the band started its set with "Hands Across the Sea" by John Phillip Sousa.

"No problem," Maya said loudly over the music.

"Great. See you when it's over." Travis squeezed her hand before they separated to complete their tasks.

Maya walked to the chalk board set up to the right of the speaker's podium. Linda, Travis' secretary, had written at the top of the board, "Reflections on Hungry Mother Creek" with a sketch of some trees by a creek. No one had written on it yet. Maya thought she could start and then pull others over to do the same. She picked up a piece of green chalk and held it in mid-air, thinking. She dropped her arm by her side. How could she put her feelings about that land into a few sentences?

Maya felt another presence and saw a young girl, probably about 6 or 7, beside her. Her curly brown hair was pulled into two small pig tails on either side of her head and tied with thick, white grosgrain ribbon. She looked up at Maya and smiled. "Can we draw on the board?"

"No," Maya said. "But you can write about your memories on the land by Hungry Mother Creek. What do you do when you go there?"

Maya assumed she'd been there.

The little girl looked away from Maya and thought. "My Mom and I go there and build fairy gardens. We make boats out of leaves and sticks and race them. We tell each other stories and eat peanut butter sandwiches."

Maya smiled. "That sounds like a perfect day. How do you feel when you're there?"

"Like magic," the little girl said and twirled around to emphasize her point, her pink skirt flaring.

"Then maybe that's what you should write on the board."

The girl immediately grabbed a purple piece of chalk and wrote MAGIC in capital letters a few inches from the bottom of the board, the highest point she could reach. "Thank you," she said, and ran off to pet a dog that was meandering through the crowd.

She didn't have difficulty thinking of what to write, Maya thought. Maybe I should ask myself the same question. How do I feel when I'm at the Mother Tree? Immediately, Maya knew the answer and wrote in green chalk, "Connected to something greater than myself." After she wrote it, she realized she'd used almost the same words that Travis had when he described his relationship to God the other day. Maybe they weren't as far apart spiritually as she'd thought.

Satisfied, she replaced the chalk in the tray and invited others over to the board. Soon three people were writing. One took the little girl's lead and wrote PEACE in capital letters, and the other two wrote more, sharing their memories. Maya heard static from the sound system and knew Travis was about to start the program. She left the chalk board and found Lilith, Ella, and Violet. They sat on the back row of chairs, letting Lilith have the end since she'd be getting up to speak. The band behind them finished their last song, "America the Beautiful."

Travis walked to the podium. The lower branch of the live oak stretched over his head, reaching a hand to the Neuse River directly behind him. Maya wondered if Buster had made it here. She scanned the crowd and saw him with several men his age off to the right side of the park. Buster must have felt her gaze and waved.

"Welcome, everyone," Travis said. The sound of his voice automatically got Maya's attention. "Thank you for being here to help save the land on Hungry Mother Creek." He scanned the crowd and Maya thought he looked completely composed, like public speaking was a breeze. She admired his confidence and her heart swelled. "For hundreds of years, this land has provided our community with a place to hunt deer and have picnics, to climb trees and lie on the beach to read, to sleep under the stars and hike upon her ground. It's been a sanctuary offering peace, comfort, and a place to reflect on our lives. Part of what makes the land special are the trees there, the loblolly pine, cypress, white cedar, magnolia, sweet gum and of course, the huge live oak off the beach, fondly called the Mother Tree by the generations of women who have gathered there."

Travis caught Maya's eye when he mentioned the Mother Tree. He looked handsome in his fitted khakis, flip-flops, and sea green Columbia fishing shirt. Maya appreciated how his shoulders and chest tapered into his waist, how when he used his hands to talk, his biceps strained against the fabric of his shirt. She remembered the pressure of his arms around her waist 30 minutes ago and anticipated the next time he would hold her.

Maya felt Lilith's hand on her left thigh. She smiled and leaned in to whisper to Maya, "I'm jealous. You're looking at him with more adoration than my bread."

Maya blushed, embarrassed that her eyes had revealed her longing. She'd missed Travis' last few sentences and now he stepped away from the podium and a group of about 10 children between the ages of 5 and

9 came up. The woman accompanying them said, "The Heart Works after-school program would like to sing 'The Tree Song' in honor of the trees on the Hungry Mother Creek property. For the past two weeks in summer camp, these young people have been learning about trees, and practicing this song. It's called 'Mr. R's Tree Song.'"

"Do you know that one tree makes 260 pounds of oxygen? That's enough for me and my brother to breathe all year!" shouted one of the boys in the group. He was dancing from one foot to the other and looked like he wanted to share everything he'd ever learned about trees. The audience laughed, and Maya smiled at his exuberance.

The woman with them leaned down and whispered something to him and then said, "I think we have a future biologist in our midst." She turned back to the children. "OK. Everyone ready?" The children's faces got serious and they nodded. The teacher stepped away from the microphone and they formed a semi-circle around it, each one gripping a piece of paper with the lyrics. The band started behind Maya and she tapped her foot to the simple, jazzy rhythm. The tallest child in the middle began and the others quickly followed.

"Trees, trees, trees have roots and trunks and leaves," they sang in unison. "Trees, trees, trees have buds and fruits and seeds."

They began quietly, every so often looking out at the audience as they must have been instructed. The only one not fully participating was the little girl from the chalk board. She'd stopped singing and was watching a butterfly fluttering near her head. As the song continued, the children gained confidence and danced to the beat while increasing their volume. They repeated the refrain for the last time at the top of their lungs: "We all need our trees, trees, trees!"

The audience laughed and clapped their approval.

Maya wondered if Sloan was here. Surely this jubilant song about trees would have touched her. She looked at the edges of the park and then turned around in her seat but didn't see her. Did she really expect Sloan to come? Her disappointment told her that she did.

Travis was back at the podium. For the next part of the program, speakers were sharing what the Hungry Mother Creek property meant to them. A boy scout would start off, followed by an 86-year-old woman who'd lived in Oriental all her life. She was going to share memories of Hungry Mother Creek from her childhood all the way to the present. Buster had convinced one of his buddies to talk about the hunting and fishing, and Lilith would finish, sharing the history of the women's circle.

Thankfully, the southeast breeze picked up to counteract the heat of the climbing sun. Maya was familiar with what the speakers were saying because she and Travis had worked with them to keep their reflections to five minutes. She let her mind wander. Maya watched the sunlight reflecting on the water and two sailboats leaving Whitaker Creek, their white sails the only clouds in the blue sky. She was aware of Lilith, Ella, and Violet surrounding her, Travis up front, Buster off to her right, and familiar faces from The Bean and grocery store scattered in the crowd.

Without warning, Maya got a lump in her throat. Hazel was missing. She was deeply grateful for the sense of community and belonging she felt in Oriental, but there was definitely a void without Hazel, the first person here that she'd allowed herself to trust. Maya reminisced about Hazel and her uniform of button-down Oxford shirts, rolled at the sleeves, a string of pearls around her neck. She noticed several fins out in the water, about 50 feet off shore. Maya watched closely and counted five dolphins. They were done feeding and were swimming without pause toward the sound. Five. That was how many women there'd been in the circle when Hazel was alive. Maya smiled. She'd have to tell Buster that Hazel had sent her a sign through the dolphins.

Lilith stood and walked to the podium. Maya's heartrate quickened. She was proud to be a member of the circle and have Lilith share some of the history, but part of her felt exposed. She held her experiences in the circle close and didn't discuss the details with anyone. Now Lilith was going to talk about the circle in front of all these people. Maya exhaled to release her discomfort. She knew the circle was an important part of the history of Hungry Mother Creek and it needed to be included.

Violet took Maya's and Ella's hands and they all instinctively moved to the edge of their seats to listen. Lilith began with the story Hazel had told at Maya's first circle, how the circle started with Native American women meeting at the Mother Tree and slowly evolved into its current form. Lilith shared the essence of what occurred and left out details to maintain the sanctity of their circle.

"People may argue that we could meet anywhere to sit in a circle and find another tree should we lose the Mother Tree." Lilith's voice faltered, and she paused to take a breath. "And we could, but it wouldn't be the same. Sweat and tears from women before us have been deposited in the ground that contains the Mother Tree's roots—bits of DNA connecting us to the past. We inhale the oxygen the Mother Tree releases and she absorbs our carbon dioxide, an energy exchange repeated thousands of times between the Mother Tree and the women encircling her trunk. The sweat, tears, and breath have infused the Mother Tree and ground beneath her with the wisdom and love shared there for over 100 years. We cannot replace that."

Maya, Ella, and Violet released hands to clap for Lilith. Maya hugged her when she slid in her seat. "You were amazing. Thanks for being our spokeswoman," Maya said.

"I hope Sloan is here somewhere," Lilith whispered back.

"Me too, but I haven't seen her yet."

Travis returned to the podium to share details about fundraising to purchase the land. Maya searched the crowd again for Sloan.

**

Sloan's hands ached, and she realized they were clenched in fists while she listened to Lilith. She opened them and noticed deep crescent moons in her palms where her fingernails had dug in. She hadn't planned to come to the rally. She'd made peace with her decision to log her land once she'd clarified that helping Deidre was her priority. But this morning, after she and Peter finished breakfast, she'd been restless. She told Peter she was going to The Bean for coffee and to get the *News and Observer* but they both knew that was an excuse. Even though she wasn't going to change her mind, if the town was holding a rally to honor her land, she felt she should be there.

Until Lilith spoke, Sloan had been unmoved by the speakers and the writing on the chalkboard. She was more curious than anything else. It was difficult to understand the connection all these people felt to her land. She'd never looked at a piece of property as having intrinsic value and only saw the value in what it could become. As a child, she had no special place outside. She was always in school, the dance studio, or her parents' restaurant. Hearing people talk about the role the Hungry Mother Creek property played in their lives made no sense to her. How could trees, water, and dirt influence your life?

And then Lilith talked about the circle and Sloan thought of GG sitting under the Mother Tree. Soon this image morphed into she and GG sitting under the magnolia. What if she'd grown up here and played by the creek behind her great-grandmother's every day? What if she'd watched the land change with the seasons year in and year out? What if she and GG had sat under the magnolia hundreds of times instead of a handful?

The guilt knotted her shoulders and Sloan massaged her temples to ward off the tension headache that was building. She shouldn't have come, because nothing was going to change. Talking about how special the property is was not going to pay for Deidre's rehab or the renovations. She turned and walked toward her car with Travis' voice in the background talking about an account at the bank for donations.

Despite the heat and her sandals, Sloan picked up her pace to a jog, her mind full of doubts again. Maybe she should forget it. Sell Magnolia Bend and move back to Raleigh. She opened her car door and sat down. She thought of leaving the river, her house, her dream of the retreat center and knew she couldn't do it. She couldn't leave. She felt connected to this place. And with that thought, the stories that had confounded her 30 minutes ago resonated. She closed the door and started her car. She had to get home quickly because a migraine was starting.

***

Doodle Bug was spread eagle across the air conditioning vent, supervising Maya as she cleaned up. Violet and Ben, Lilith, her husband Paul, Buster, Ella, and Travis had all come over late that afternoon to debrief from the rally. Maya had made roasted potatoes and Travis grilled hamburgers. Violet brought a salad, Buster some fresh shrimp, and of course Lilith brought her bread. They finished their meal with peach cobbler that Ella had made. Maya put the last of the dishes away and left the roasting pan in the sink to soak.

She reached down and scratched Doodle Bug's ears. "Come on, girl. Let's go outside and see if Travis is done cleaning the grill."

Maya stepped out onto the back porch. It was only a little after 8 and the sky glowed mandarin orange. The fireflies weren't as plentiful as in June but a few created sparks amongst the river grass. Doodle Bug bounded down the steps to chase Elvis, Travis' dog.

Travis closed the grill. "OK. That's all done. Can I help with anything inside?"

"No." Maya shook her head. "I'm finished, too."

"Perfect. Now I can spend the evening with you," Travis said.

"Well, me and the dogs," Maya said, laughing. Elvis and Doodle Bug ran past the porch and then Elvis turned to Doodle Bug and they wrestled playfully.

Maya walked down the steps and Travis met her at the bottom. All day she'd anticipated this moment. She'd enjoyed having her friends for the cookout but had been aching to touch Travis. She stepped off the last step and he put his arms around her waist and pulled her close. She laced her arm around his neck and they kissed deeply.

"That was worth waiting for," Travis said.

Maya shook her head in agreement and pulled him toward her again. On cue, the dogs ran over and circled their legs.

Travis laughed. "Lord. It's worse than having chaperones." He bent to pet Elvis and then led Maya to the top step of the porch. He put his arm around her and she leaned in. The dogs, finally tired from their play, lay in the grass at the bottom of the steps.

"Maya, how do you feel about the day? Did it turn out like you'd expected?"

"No. It was better. I never imagined we'd have that much support."

"Are you OK with Lilith talking about the circle to so many people? I know that was bothering you."

Maya thought for a moment. The fireflies blinked silently. "Yeah. I realize that people knowing about the circle won't change anything about my time there. The memories others shared on the chalk board and in their talks made me see they have their own special connection to the land. I'm glad everyone wants to help, but I still think it would take a miracle to get the money we need." While she spoke, Travis traced her upper arm with his index finger, making it difficult to concentrate.

"We got $10,000 right off the bat from a couple of civic clubs and individuals," Travis said. "We haven't heard yet from the city and county and there'll be an article in the paper Wednesday. You never know."

"Maybe Nicholas Sparks up in New Bern will read about it and donate the rest," Maya said.

"Hey. That's a great idea," Travis replied. "I'll contact his foundation to see if he's interested."

Maya laughed. "I was being sarcastic."

"I know, but it's worth a try. The worst that can happen is he says no."

Maya smiled. She wished she could think more like Travis. He always saw the opportunity while she saw the obstacle. They sat quietly and the first stars appeared. Maya's left shoulder, hip, and thigh were pressed tightly against Travis' body and she felt like she was plugged into an electric socket. She slid her bare foot over his and this additional skin contact intensified her desire.

Travis took her chin in his hand and turned her head to him. He kissed her again, with more urgency than ever before. He caressed the curve of her neck with his left hand.

Maya was dizzy and the usual evening sounds of frogs and crickets were muffled by her heart. She was aware of Travis' lips and tongue, his breath in her ear. She slid a hand under his shirt and pressed it into his skin. There was more of him she wanted to touch. Travis took her other hand and kissed her palm, wrist, and forearm. Now that her lips were free she whispered, "Would you like to come inside?"

Travis didn't answer, but stood, pulling her up with him. Inside, he followed her upstairs to her bedroom.

***

Maya heard someone whispering her name. Was she dreaming? She felt the warmth of a body behind her. For a millisecond she was confused, and then the fog of her sleep lifted. Travis. She and Travis had made love and he'd spent the night. She smiled and slid back to better mold into the curve of his body.

"Maya," he whispered again.

"Hmmm?"

He kissed her shoulder. "I have to leave."

Maya opened her eyes. It was still dark. "What time is it?"

"5:15. I have to go home and get changed. I need to be at church by 8:30."

Maya was awake now. She turned over to face Travis. "Church?"

Travis laughed gently. "Yes. Today's Sunday and I am a minister."

Suddenly she felt guilty about being naked in bed with a minster on a Sunday morning. "Travis, I'm sorry. I totally forgot about that. I should have never invited you in."

Travis leaned down and kissed her gently. "I have absolutely no regrets. Last night was amazing."

"You don't?"

"No. Do you?" Travis asked.

"Of course not. I guess I'm feeling guilty because—"

"I'm a minister and we aren't married," Travis finished for her. He pulled her to him. "I can fall in love and desire a beautiful woman like anyone else. That's not off limits to me because I'm a minister."

Fall in love. Did she hear him right? Did he say love? Her heart soared. "That makes sense," she said.

"Of course it does, and it's not like either of us is sleeping around. Last night was nothing to be guilty about." Travis looked at his watch.

"I really have to leave. Go back to sleep and I'll call this afternoon when I'm done."

Travis moved to get out of bed, waking Elvis and Doodle Bug who were sleeping on the floor beside their respective owners. "Come on, Elvis. We need to go," Travis said as he retrieved his clothes strewn between the door and the bed.

Maya patted the bed and Doodle Bug jumped up. She circled several times and then lay in the warm spot Travis had vacated.

Travis walked back to Maya. He rubbed Doodle Bug's head. "Don't get too comfy. I plan to be back in that spot again."

"I'm glad to hear that," Maya said, smiling up at him.

Travis leaned down and kissed her, and their passion quickly escalated. Travis stepped back. "Whew. I definitely need to go now. Hold that thought and we can continue later."

"Will do," Maya said, snuggling back into her pillow.

She listened to Travis going down the stairs, through the kitchen and out through the office door. His footsteps were followed closely by the click clack of Elvis' toenails on the hardwoods. Maya rolled over to pet Doodle Bug. Out the window, the trees across the creek were back lit by the first trace of dawn.

Her body was warm and relaxed from Travis' kiss but her mind was a free for all. Flashes of their lovemaking were interrupted by his words, "fall in love" and "desire a beautiful woman." She needed to talk to someone about all this. Wait. She was meeting Bay in an hour to run. Thank goodness. She was bursting to talk about Travis and it was too early to call anyone. Suddenly Maya's eyes filled with tears and she rubbed Doodle Bug's head for comfort. Today would be her last run with Bay. She was leaving after breakfast for Raleigh to settle in before classes started.

Maya rolled to her side, but it only took a couple minutes to realize she'd never doze off with thoughts of Travis and Bay competing for attention. "Come on, Doodle Bug. Let's get up," she said. "I'll make some coffee and then take you out for a bit." Doodle Bug lifted her ears and eyebrows but otherwise lay still on the bed. Halfway down the steps, Maya heard Doodle Bug following her and smiled to herself, thankful for her loyal companion.

A few minutes before she was to meet Bay, Maya settled Doodle Bug on her bed in the kitchen. It was too hot for a dog to run this morning. She went out the office door to the driveway and saw Bay heading up from the boat house. Her eyes quickly filled with tears and when Bay got closer, she saw her friend's eyes were red. Without saying anything, they hugged each other tightly.

"Good thing we did that now before we are sweaty and gross after our run," Maya said.

Bay stepped away from Maya and held both her hands. "I know." Bay paused and looked closely at Maya. "Wait a minute. You look different. I know it's warm this morning, but you have an extra glow."

Maya looked over Bay's shoulder toward the water and then spontaneously broke out in a smile. "Travis came over last night to look at the antiques," she said, eluding to their earlier joke. "Well, to be honest, he spent the night and only left about an hour ago."

Bay hugged her again and then released her. "That's awesome. I want to hear all about it, well, the G-rated version, anyway," she said playfully. "That will give us something happy to talk about while we run rather than how much we'll miss each other."

Maya and Bay jogged slowly down the driveway and then turned right for their usual 5-mile run. By the time they returned, Maya had shared more details about her night and Bay had shared her fears and expectations about her move and starting school.

"What am I going to do without our runs to keep me sane?" Maya asked as they cooled down in the shady driveway. "I may have to get a therapist." Maya remembered how she initially hesitated to accept Bay's invitation to become running partners, worried that the conversation would be all about Bay, and now, here she was, bereft at the thought of losing their time together.

"I know," Bay agreed, lunging forward to stretch her calf muscle. "It will be lonely running without you, but we'll stay in touch. Let's schedule some road races to do together this fall."

"Definitely," Maya said. "And we'll call and text every week."

"Of course." They stopped at the top of the path that led to the boat house. "Maya, you've helped me through one of the most difficult times in my life and I will never forget it. I'm going to miss you like crazy and you're just going to have to deal with a sweaty hug," Bay said, wrapping her arms around Maya.

Maya stepped back from Bay and Bay turned to walk to the boat house. "Text me when you get there tonight," Maya said.

"Will do," Bay said.

Tears clouded Maya's vision as she walked to the house. It would be strange living here without Bay down in the boathouse. She was always there to talk and kayak with, and provide fashion advice. What would she do without her? And then Maya remembered last night, and Travis, and seeing him again this afternoon, and she smiled through her tears.

CHAPTER 14

Sloan drove down Highway 55 toward Bayboro. She kept glancing at the Pamlico newspaper lying in the passenger seat. The front-page story was about the rally on Saturday. Since spending most of Sunday in bed with a migraine, she'd tried to keep her mind off it by finishing the brochures for the retreat center. Between that task and Peter's support, she'd been able to quiet her ping-ponging thoughts about logging Hungry Mother Creek.

She looked at the paper again. The headline read, "Community Pulls Together to Save Hungry Mother Creek Property." She took a breath and focused on the road. She wasn't going to go there. She'd weighed the options hundreds of times and this was the only way.

Sloan passed the Bayboro post office and slowed down to turn right into the courthouse. She wanted to research the past owners of Magnolia Bend to help her write a brief history of the property. Sloan entered the side door of the courthouse and suddenly felt self-conscious in her capris, T-shirt, and flip-flops. In the past, she'd go to the register of deeds as a part of her real estate practice and would be dressed professionally, but she'd learned the dress code in Oriental was almost always casual.

Sloan walked down the main hall in the courthouse and looked for a directory. The building, built in the late '30s, reminded her of her elementary school. The ceilings were high, with floors made of wide pine boards, and there was a large round clock with faces on both sides attached to the wall above a water fountain. Sloan bent down and drank some water just because she could. The first day of third grade she'd headed for the water fountain when Charlie Hess, the son of the man who managed the Hudson Belk, stood in front of it with his arms crossed. His body language was easy to read, and Sloan immediately changed directions, ignoring him. She had no nostalgia for that time in her life. Being a biracial kid during desegregation was not a memory she wanted to dwell on.

Sloan realized she was gripping the edge of the water fountain. She released it, took a breath and walked slowly down the hall, looking for the register of deeds. After she found the names of previous owners of Magnolia Bend, she'd go to the library and the Oriental history museum to see if she could learn more details about them.

She found the register of deeds at the end of the hall and stepped in to find two women behind an elevated counter. She prayed they hadn't been at the rally and knew who she was.

Good morning," she said. "I'm Sloan Bostwick and would like to research the past owners of my home." She left off the name Magnolia Bend, not wanting to give them enough information that they'd link her to the logging.

"Sure," the younger of the two women said, coming out from behind the counter. The computers and records are right here." She led Sloan into the adjacent room with three computers on one wall and thick red and black books on the other three walls. "The computer has everything until 1963. For dates prior to that, you'll have to use these," the woman said, pointing to the books lining the walls.

Sloan walked to the computer, relieved the woman didn't know who she was.

"Have you done this before?"

"Yes," Sloan answered. "I was a realtor up in Raleigh and did this on many occasions."

"OK. Great. I'll be next door. Don't hesitate to come get me if you need anything."

Sloan nodded and was already typing in the name of the couple she'd bought Magnolia Bend from. She felt a sense of anticipation of what she might find. Of course, the deeds would only give her names, but they were the key to the history.

Real estate documents were familiar turf, and Sloan quickly exhausted the computer. She went to the books and continued to find the previous owners, one deed at a time. She made a chronological list of the owners and how long they'd had the property. Some of the names were familiar because they were still common in Pamlico County. Sloan's stomach growled, and she glanced at her watch. Two and a half hours had flown by. She was at 1932. She'd look up one more deed and then call it a day. She took the name of the person who sold Magnolia Bend in 1932 and found the deed when they'd purchased it in 1924 from Joseph Allegany.

She wrote the name down on her list. She forgot her hunger and decided she had enough time to find one more. Joseph Allegany. She searched for the deed from his purchase. She found it, but it listed Joseph and Nellie Allegany as the buyers in 1912.

"Nellie," Sloan said aloud. That was interesting. She wondered if her Nellie knew that she had the same name as a former owner of Magnolia Bend. She hoped Nellie was OK. It'd been several weeks since her offer of help and Sloan hadn't seen her since. Sloan couldn't call and check on her because Nellie still hadn't called her with her number. Maybe her husband restricted Nellie's access to the phone. She'd drive down Magnolia Bend Road again today to look for her.

Sloan brought her attention back to the deed and transcribed the information from it onto her legal pad. She thanked the women in the office and left.

The landscape passed without Sloan noticing. She thought about all the names on her list and wondered what their lives were like when they'd lived at Magnolia Bend. Was Nellie right, were most of their lives filled with struggle and sadness? Surely, she would find some happy stories associated with Magnolia Bend. And what a coincidence that someone named Nellie had lived there. Except for the mean girl on "Little House on the Prairie," she'd never met anyone named Nellie and now the name appeared for a second time since moving to Oriental. She wished she had time to stop by the library to find out more information about the previous owners, but needed to get home to meet an electrician. He was going to quote her a price for rewiring the ballroom for new lighting, outlets, and wi-fi.

Sloan pulled into her driveway and saw a truck marked Pamlico Electric already parked there. She liked the fact he was early. Sloan waved at the man in the truck and hurried ahead of him to open the front door. She went to her office and retrieved the list of things she wanted to discuss with him.

She'd left the front door open and the electrician was standing in the hallway when she returned. She took a look at him and immediately felt like she was caught in a rip tide pulling her out into the ocean. Her heart was pounding. Her chest was tight. She couldn't breathe. She wanted to call for Peter but her vocal cords were frozen and she wasn't even sure if he was home.

The man walked toward her. "Ma'am. Ma' am. Are you OK?" He reached out to steady her.

Sloan blocked him with her arm. "No. I'm fine," she managed to squeak out with the little oxygen she had. Sloan held onto the banister for support and then sat on the second step.

"Do you want me to call someone?" the man asked.

"No. I feel faint, but it will pass in a minute." Sloan kept her head down, trying to get the courage to look back up at the face that could have been her uncle 40 years ago when he was in his mid-20s. The black hair falling across his forehead, the shape of his face, and his brown eyes were all the same.

She remembered those eyes and how she'd learned to read them. When she saw a certain look, she knew what would happen that night. Why didn't her parents know what that look meant? He had it in front of them, but they never noticed.

Sloan slowed her breath. She studied the grain in the hardwood floor and noticed the hot summer breeze coming in the front door that was still open. She finally lifted her head, keeping him in her peripheral vision and then turning toward him. She saw "Jason" stitched on the corner pocket of his work shirt. She made herself look up and saw the authentic concern on his face.

"Are you OK?" he asked.

She looked at Jason standing awkwardly in the doorway and saw the situation from his perspective. He probably thought she was an old woman on the verge of a stroke. She smiled, grounded now in the present. "Yes. Yes. That feeling has passed." She stood and put her hand out. "Now for a proper introduction. I'm Sloan Bostwick."

***

Maya sang "Whenever I See Your Smiling Face" along with James Taylor as she drove to The Bean. Since Saturday, everything seemed right in the world. Her favorite songs were always on the radio. Her runs were faster, her coffee better. Even Dr. Allan's patients hadn't aggravated her this week.

Travis stayed with her Sunday and Monday nights. They'd cooked together, eaten on the back porch with Elvis and Doodle Bug, talked about their days, and made love before falling asleep. Last night Travis needed to get things done at home and start on his sermon. She missed him, but he was coming over later this afternoon to kayak and then picnic on the beach at Hungry Mother Creek.

Maya's heart swelled like a helium-filled balloon and she thought it might pop out of her chest. She couldn't remember the last time she'd been this happy. Even in the beginning with Steven, she hadn't felt this good.

Maya pulled into a parking spot beside the town dock and across from The Bean. She didn't usually come here, preferring to start her day off from work with coffee on her back porch, but she wanted to pick up a copy of the *Pamlico News*. Lilith had called earlier to let her know that a story about the rally had made the front page. She climbed the steps to The Bean, thinking she'd prefer an iced coffee because of the heat. Through the front door window, she saw the back of Travis' head. Perfect, she thought. We can read the story together. She put her hand on the door knob and then froze.

Travis was seated at one of the tables with a beautiful blond woman. She wore a fitted V-neck T-shirt that accentuated her ample breasts and cleavage. Maya's chest tightened and she couldn't breathe. She stepped back from the door and looked in from the front windows, staying out of the woman's line of sight.

The woman's head bowed toward Travis' and they looked at something on the table. Travis must have made a joke because the woman threw her head back and laughed. Travis laughed, too. He reached out and put his hand on her upper arm and then leaned in to say something else that put them both into fits of laughter. She raised a delicate, well-manicured hand to her eyes to dab at the tears her amusement had created.

Maya felt the stab of jealousy. Why did this woman and Travis seem familiar with one another? Why was he touching her and laughing? The woman neatened the papers on the table and she and Travis pushed back their chairs to leave. Maya didn't want Travis to see her, so she took the steps two at a time and ran to her Saturn. She pulled out of her parking spot and saw the two of them descending the steps from The Bean in her rearview mirror. She slowed down to see how they would part. They hugged and then her view was obstructed by a car behind her that forced her to move. She tried to watch their heads to see if they kissed but couldn't tell.

Maya turned the radio off and drove home in silence. Was Travis involved with this woman? Why hadn't he told her he was meeting someone today? They definitely looked like they knew each other well. Was he sleeping with her, too? Maya knew she was jumping to conclusions, but she couldn't think of another reason Travis would be laughing and touching a woman way more beautiful than she.

Maya held it together until she opened the door and Doodle Bug bounded out, doing her happy dance. Maya burst into tears and sank down to hug the dog who'd stopped her dance and stood quietly to absorb Maya's emotion.

Maya's phone dinged with a text and she took it from her purse. It was from Travis. "Hi, beautiful. Hope you're enjoying your morning. Can't wait to see you tonight." Maya threw the phone back into her purse on the steps. Why was he calling her beautiful when he'd just been with a beautiful woman? Was he feeling guilty?

"Come on, girl. Let's walk to the mail box."

Maya sorted the mail and threw everything away except her water bill and a statement from Trident Investments. She opened the statement, but all the numbers ran together, and she threw it on the kitchen table.

"God, Doodle Bug. Can't I do anything right? I'm letting Hazel down. I haven't done anything with her fund and it's been six months. Travis may be cheating on me and I'm in a dead-end job that's boring me to death."

This line of thought opened the floodgates, and she began reciting the litany of failures in her life. Soon she was joined by Steven's voice. "You're so needy, Maya. No one would put up with you besides me. Can't you fix yourself up sometimes? You always look like you just came back from a run. Sometimes I don't even know why I stay married to you." Maya paced the kitchen floor, fueled by shame, Steven's hurtful words, and her self-criticism. She punched her fist into her hand to keep from breaking something.

Finally, Maya ran out of negative thoughts and leaned back against the counter. Doodle Bug watched her with wary eyes from her spot under the kitchen table. Doodle Bug's gaze made her self-conscious and she realized how crazy she must have looked pacing the floor, pounding her fist into her hand and muttering to herself. Well, she did have half her mother's genetics. God, was she going to end up clinically depressed like her mother?

Maya knew she didn't need to pursue this line of thought and ran upstairs to get the novel she was reading off her bedside table. Doodle Bug waited for her at the bottom of the stairs and then followed her outside to the back porch. Maya scooted one of the wicker rocking chairs into a shady corner and Doodle Bug lay down beside her. Maya opened "The Secret Life of Bees" by Sue Monk Kidd. She was four chapters into the book and mesmerized by the story. She gave herself permission to sit there the rest of the day and finish the book. She hadn't read all day in months, probably not since she'd moved to Oriental. Today it would be the salve for her raw emotions. She positioned the pillow behind her and gently rocked. Quickly she was entranced in the plight of Lily and Rosalyn and her own worries drifted to the back of her mind.

After a couple of hours, she took a break to let Doodle Bug swim and to make a peanut butter and jelly sandwich. She checked her phone and had two more messages from Travis, the last one asking if everything was all right since he hadn't heard from her. She texted him that she was fine and would see him later.

Maya sat down at the dining room table with her sandwich and an apple. The August humidity made it difficult to eat outside. Her time reading calmed her and now she looked back over the morning with a more rational mind. She had overreacted. If Travis was having an affair, he surely wouldn't do it at The Bean, where everyone in town goes. She was hurt and jealous to see him enjoying himself with another woman but figured she must have misread the situation. She would ask him about it tonight.

The bigger question was, why had she immediately assumed he was cheating on her? Would she have felt the same way if the woman hadn't been blond and beautiful? Was her self-esteem that bad? And she thought she'd made peace with her marriage, so why were Steven's words haunting her again? She was thankful she hadn't said or texted anything she'd regret.

Maya took her lunch dishes to the sink. The house needed dusting and she should look over that statement from Trident, but she wanted to keep reading. Lily's longing for a mother resonated with her and she wanted to see how it ended. She got a bottle of water and a couple tissues, anticipating tears, and returned to the book waiting for her in the rocking chair. Doodle Bug resumed her position beside her and Maya dove back into the world of the black Madonna, honey, and the Boatwright sisters.

Maya closed "The Secret Life of Bees" and held it in her lap. The wicker chair creaked with her gentle rocking. She needed time to leave the story of Tiburon, South Carolina, and return to her world. She kept rocking and thought about the similarities between her and Lily. How they'd both been mothered in unconventional ways. Doodle Bug stirred and ambled down the steps to sniff around the trees. Maya rubbed her neck and shoulders, stiff from sitting in the same position. She needed to move.

This reminded her of her kayak date with Travis. He was coming at 6 and she hadn't even thought about what to pack for a picnic. She had no motivation and continued to rock. She needed more time to recover from her reading hangover and wanted to talk with Travis about the woman in The Bean before she could even think about a romantic sunset paddle.

Suddenly Doodle Bug ran across the back yard up toward the driveway. A second later she was running back with Elvis chasing her. Travis was here. The spell of the book was broken and Maya felt her chest burn as she anticipated talking with Travis. What would he say? Would he be angry?

Travis came around the corner from the driveway following the dogs. He picked up his pace to a trot when he saw Maya on the back porch. "Hey, you," he said, slowing to walk up the steps. "Are you OK? I was worried when you didn't answer my texts and my phone call this afternoon." He leaned over and kissed her gently. Her response was lukewarm. "That's not normal. What's wrong?"

Maya watched the dogs playing and then made herself look at Travis, leaning back on the porch railing in front of her. As soon as their gaze met, her eyes filled with tears. Travis kneeled in front of her and took her hands in his. "Babe, what's wrong? Please tell me."

His genuine concern made her cry more openly. She hadn't thought about what to say and blurted out, "I saw you with a beautiful woman at The Bean."

Travis looked confused. "That was Mary Ellen. Why didn't you come in and say hi?"

Maya looked down at the book lying beside her chair. She whispered, "I thought you were cheating on me."

Travis stood up and took a few steps away from her. "What? Why in the hell would you think I would cheat on you?"

"I don't know. She's beautiful and you were laughing and touching her and it seemed like you knew each other well." When Maya was standing outside The Bean in a state of jealously it all made perfect sense. Saying it aloud sounded small and petty.

"We do know each other well and if you'd come in to meet her, I would have told you that. Mary Ellen's lived here all her life. She was my sister's best friend all those summers we spent here with my grandmother. I've known her since she was 8 years old and now she's the director of the preschool at the church."

Doodle Bug ran up on the porch and put her head in Maya's lap. Happy for the distraction, Maya stroked her head. She avoided looking at Travis.

"Maya, Mary Ellen's like a sister. We were laughing at a funny story from our childhood." Travis smiled. "One summer when my sister was about 8 or 9 we were all playing hide and seek. Tracy tried to crawl through the wrought iron railing on my grandmother's front porch to hide in the bushes at the front of the house. She got her head through and that was it. She couldn't get the rest of her body to fit and couldn't pull her head back out. She was stuck and had to sit on a stool with her head through the rails. Grandmother called 911. Some soap on her ears and muscle power finally got her out."

Maya couldn't help herself and smiled. She sat up, keeping one hand on Doodle Bug's head. "Your sister's never lived that one down, has she?"

"No. Pumpkin head is still my favorite nick name for her." Travis took Maya's hands and pulled her to her feet.

Before he could say anything, Maya said, "I'm sorry, Travis. I don't know what got into me. I saw you with a beautiful woman and automatically assumed you'd prefer her."

Travis pulled her to him and kissed the top of her head. "Maya, that makes absolutely no sense. Have I done anything that would make you believe I wanted to be with someone else?"

"No. I guess it's hard for me to accept that someone like you wants to be with me." Speaking that thought out loud immediately decreased its power.

"Well, you better accept it so we don't have to waste anymore of our time on conversations like this." Travis leaned down and kissed her and there was no room for thoughts of Mary Ellen. He released her and said, "Now that's more like it."

Maya put her head on Travis' chest. They stood quietly and their breath synchronized. This only lasted a moment and then Doodle Bug and Elvis were on the porch making semi circles around them and nuzzling their legs.

Maya stepped away from Travis to let them run through. "What is it with them? Do they have a hugging radar?"

"We might need to figure out a way to turn that off," Travis said. Once the dogs got some attention they bounded off the steps. Travis rubbed his stomach and said, "Hey, are we kayaking and having a picnic? I'm starving."

Maya looked at her watch. "Why don't we go in and make some sandwiches and have our picnic out here. We can kayak out to watch the sunset later if we want."

Maya had barely gotten the words out of her mouth before Travis was opening the screened door. "Perfect. I vote for ham and cheese."

Between the two of them it only took a few minutes to make the sandwiches, open a bag of chips, and cut the cantaloupe. Maya took the plates out to the table on the porch and Travis followed with two Fat Tire beers.

Travis dug right in and ate half his sandwich in a couple bites.

"Good gracious. You were hungry," Maya said.

Travis took a sip of beer and leaned back in his chair. "Sorry. I got busy today and didn't take time for lunch."

"That's OK," Maya said and picked up the second half of her sandwich. "Hope you don't mind waiting on me to finish."

"It's my pleasure," Travis said and reached across the table to squeeze her hand. They sat silently a minute while Maya chewed her sandwich and Travis stared out at the water. "Remember the first time we came here together?" he asked.

Maya smiled. "Yes. You took me on the kayak trip when my sister and I were here for a getaway." Maya paused. "It's hard to believe that now I live in this house and am in a relationship with that handsome kayak guide."

"I know," Travis said. "Funny how life works itself out even when it feels tangled beyond repair. Do you feel at home here yet? It's been almost six months since you moved in."

"Yes," Maya nodded. "I'm starting to. Now that I've added my own decorating touches and had friends over, it feels more like mine. But Hazel will always be a part of this house."

"And I'm sure you wouldn't want it any other way," Travis said.

"No. Oh!" Maya exclaimed as a thought popped into her mind. "I can't believe I haven't told you this yet."

Travis leaned forward, "What?"

"I found a secret room under the staircase."

"That's interesting. Why do you say it's a secret?"

"Well, I don't know if it's truly a secret room, but the door was hidden in the grain of the wood and I only noticed it a few weeks ago."

"What's in it? Blackbeard's treasure chest?"

Maya finished her last bite of sandwich and took a sip of her beer. "No. But I did find a jewelry box that belonged to Hazel's mother."

"That could contain a treasure. What was in it?"

"I'll have to show you. I'm still trying to make sense of it and think it may have something to do with the circle."

"That sounds mysterious. What else was in there?"

"A menagerie of things that look like they're from the 1930s and '40s. Some household items, children's toys, and some tools. When I show you the jewelry box, you'll have to look at the tools. Maybe there's something you could use."

"There may be some things in there you could donate to the Pamlico County History Museum, too," Travis said.

"Oh. That's a good idea. Let's take time this weekend to look through everything. Maybe we'll find something valuable that we can sell and then put that money toward the purchase of the Hungry Mother Creek property."

"Hey, you never know. If you ever watch Antiques Roadshow, you'll see that people find valuable things in old homes all the time," Travis said.

"Speaking of money, have we gotten more donations to purchase the land?" Maya asked.

"It's only been three days since the rally. Barely enough time for people to get checks in the mail. Several church members have stopped by, though, and we added another $1,200 to the total."

Maya sighed. "We have $11,200, need at least $250,000 and only have a few weeks left before the logging starts. We're never going to raise that money, are we?" She tried to hide her despair, but it was hard. She imagined the Mother Tree standing alone surrounded by mud, stumps, and tire tracks. The hundred shades of green interwoven with purple and gold wildflowers that circled the Mother Tree like a skirt would be gone. And what about all the creatures who lived there? Maya could hear the scurrying, scratching, and pecking that provided a litany for their circle. Where would the mice, squirrels, opossums, fox, raccoons, deer, bear, osprey, woodpeckers, blue birds, and eagles find food and protection from predators and the weather? Weather. What if there was a hurricane or a tropical storm while the property was stripped of its protection? Without the root systems of the trees, shrubs, and grasses to absorb the water and their physical mass to slow it down, there would be massive erosion. Maya clenched her fists, remembering Katrina and the scoured landscape it created.

"Maya, Maya," Travis said, waving a hand in front of her eyes. "Are you OK?"

"I'm sorry." Maya refocused on Travis. "I was thinking about how the property would look after it was logged and what would happen to all the birds and animals and what if there was a hurricane when everything was bare?"

Travis stood and picked up the plates. "Come on. Let's go kayak and watch the sunset. You need to stop thinking about things you don't have control over. We haven't saved the Hungry Mother Creek property yet, but we can't stop trying. A lot can happen in a short time."

Travis' hands were full with the plates, but Maya managed to wrap her arms around his waist to hug him. She looked up at him and he leaned down and kissed her. "Thanks," she said. She released him and picked up the bag of chips and beer bottles.

"For what?"

"For being here."

"No place I'd rather be."

Maya held the door for Travis and they walked to the kitchen. He deposited the plates in the sink and then went outside to prepare the kayaks. Maya quickly washed the dishes so she could join him. Doodle Bug and Elvis were lying on the porch and Maya leaned down and kissed Doodle Bug on the head. "Be a good girl. We'll be back soon." Doodle Bug licked Maya's hand and then rested her head back on her paws and watched Maya walk to the water.

The west was orange with the sunset and the east a deep navy blue. Travis held Maya's kayak while she got in and then hopped into his kayak to join her. They paddled toward the setting sun without speaking. The only sounds were the dip of their paddles in the water and the occasional splash of a jumping mullet. Maya took a deep breath. She had much to be grateful for, no matter what happened to the property on Hungry Mother Creek.

CHAPTER 15

Sloan knocked gently on the door to Peter's studio. It was on a crack, which meant he could be interrupted.

"Come in," Peter said, and pushed the door open.

"Am I bothering you?"

"No. I'm mixing some paints before I do more work on my latest piece. I'm glad you're here, I wanted to show you this anyway." Peter stepped away from his canvas.

Sloan inhaled, always amazed at Peter's talent. "Peter. It's gorgeous. Why didn't you tell me you were painting Magnolia Bend?" She gave him a hug and they stood with their arms around each other, looking at the painting.

"I wanted to surprise you. I thought we could hang this in the ballroom once the renovations are done."

"Absolutely." Sloan continued to study the painting, imagining it as a focal point in the ballroom. "I love that you included the setting too, the driveway, well, and the river behind it." Sloan saw an 8x10 photo Peter had taken to use as inspiration. She stepped closer to study it. "You could be a photographer, too. I may use this photo for some of my promotional materials if you don't mind. Oh, wait. I don't mean to be picky but there's a glare off our bedroom window."

"I know," Peter removed the picture from the easel to look at it. "I didn't see it in the digital image, only once it was developed. I'll try to

Photoshop it out. The picture on your brochure will be much smaller, anyway. You probably won't notice it."

"OK. If that doesn't work, we can always take another." Sloan stepped back to look at the painting again. "What's left to do? It looks beautiful to me."

"I want to add a few more details like the landscaping, some sea gulls, and maybe a sailboat or two on the water."

Sloan sat down in one of the two director's chairs Peter had in front of his canvas and he took the other. "I've been brainstorming about my first painting retreat here," Peter said. "When do you think things will be ready?"

Sloan immediately tensed and then reminded herself Peter was being supportive and not trying to be critical of how things were progressing. She was the one being critical. She took a breath and relaxed her shoulders. "All the subcontractors have been out to get estimates, and I got the contractor's quote yesterday."

"Great. Then the renovations will begin soon."

Sloan shifted in the chair. "After paying for Deidre's final month of rehab I'll have just enough money to pay the deposit and they should start the beginning of September." Her face flushed, knowing how little would be in her account once she made that deposit. "When I get the money from the logging, I'll have plenty to pay the remainder, purchase furniture, and do my marketing."

"They start logging in a few weeks?"

"Yes. It'll be complete by early October and the renovations will be done by the end of the year."

"Then you'll meet your goal of being ready by spring?" Peter asked.

"Yes." Sloan nodded. "Of course, I have to do my marketing beforehand to actually have a client."

Peter stood and walked to Sloan's chair. He put his hands on the arm rests and leaned in and kissed her on the cheek. "How about I be your first client?"

"What do you mean?"

"What if I have a weekend painting retreat in April? I know I could easily get eight to ten people. That could be your beta test. You can work out the kinks with my group and we'll give them a reduced rate and make sure to get feedback about how we can improve things."

Sloan jumped up and hugged Peter. "That's a perfect idea. You are wonderful. I wish I'd thought of that."

"Two heads are always better than one," Peter said.

"Thanks, Peter. I came up here because I was discouraged and felt like nothing was moving forward and now we have a plan." Sloan's phone rang downstairs in her office. "I'll be right back," she said, turning for the door.

"Hello," Sloan said, out of breath from her dash down the steps. She took the call and then walked back up to Peter's studio.

Peter had his back to her, studying his painting. He didn't turn around and said, "Honey, I really want to start painting."

"OK, but can I tell you one thing?"

Peter turned around with a paintbrush in his hand. "Sure. What's up."

"That call was from Bay River Logging. They've finished a job earlier than expected and can start on my property next Wednesday."

"That's great," Peter said. "That puts you three weeks ahead of schedule. Why don't you look happier?"

"I am happy, but I'm worried about the controversy that may erupt once the logging starts. And now, with less time, there's no way the community can raise the money to buy my land."

"There was no way they'd raise it anyway," Peter said, shrugging. "Once the logging starts, everyone will adjust and move on with their lives."

"You're probably right, but I think I'll call Maya, the woman from the circle who talked with me about buying the land. The least I can do is give her a heads up about the change in the start date," Sloan said.

"Whatever you think is best."

Peter turned back to his canvas and dipped his brush into some paint. Sloan backed out of his studio and gently shut the door. She went downstairs and sat in the wingback chair in her office, holding her phone. She stared out the window at the driveway. Nothing moved in the mid-morning heat. She thought of the Mother Tree and GG sitting by it in her circle and anticipated the disappointment she would hear in Maya's voice when she heard the news. She saw her checkbook lying on her desk and reminded herself of the balance. There was no other way. She dialed Maya's number.

***

Dr. Allan had taken his 11 a.m. patient back and the 11:30 wasn't there yet. Once again, Maya was bored. The scheduling and billing were done online now, and the patient charts were well organized. By this time of day, Maya was mostly done except for answering the phone and checking in patients.

She swiveled her office chair and looked at the UVa diploma on the wall. Written in black, under the picture of Thomas Jefferson, was "Bachelor of Science in Biology, Summa Cum Laude." She had the intelligence and education to do more. For the first time since graduating, she yearned for something other than a safe and predictable job with a reliable paycheck. Maya turned back around, drummed her fingers on her desk, and stared at the computer screen with today's schedule on it. Great, she thought. Now that I'm in Pamlico County with only a handful of jobs, I want to change careers.

She minimized the schedule and opened her internet browser to see what opportunities were out there. She opened monster.com and put in biology for the keyword and New Bern for the location, thinking she might have more luck there. She saw an opening for a biology instructor at Carteret Community College and a lab assistant at East Carolina in Greenville. These were both too far away and required a master's degree. She read through some totally unrelated jobs, like Avon representative, and then saw a job with the North Carolina Coastal Land Trust, and this one was in New Bern. She clicked on it and read the description for the Stewardship Assistant position: "Assists the Stewardship Department with annual monitoring and reports on conservation easement properties, trail work, restoration efforts, and educational activities." Maya sat up straighter and felt the flutter of excitement in her stomach. She skipped over the rest of the description and went to the list of qualifications where she saw it required a bachelor's in biology. She didn't have much of the experience required, but definitely had skills from her current career that would transfer.

She opened another browser page and Googled North Carolina Coastal Land Trust to understand more clearly what the organization did. Maya read the mission statement twice to be sure she'd read it correctly. "The mission of the Coastal Land Trust is to enrich the coastal communities of North Carolina through conservation of natural areas and working landscapes, education, and the promotion of good land stewardship. In short, we save the lands you love along the North Carolina Coast." A bolt of energy propelled Maya to her feet.

Maybe if I work here, she thought, I can save the Hungry Mother Creek property. She quickly realized that wasn't realistic, given the timeline, but this job would give her the opportunity to save and take care of other valuable properties in eastern North Carolina. Maya sat down to read more on the Land Trust web page.

She was interrupted when her cell phone rang. She glanced into the waiting room and it was still empty, so she dug in her purse for the phone. She hoped to see Travis' name on the caller ID and was surprised when it said Sloan Bostwick. Her heart jumped. Maybe she'd changed her mind.

"Hello."

"Hi, Maya. It's Sloan Bostwick."

"Hi, Sloan." Maya stood and nervously walked around her small workspace.

"I'm sorry to bother you at work, but I wanted you to know this information as soon as possible."

Maya stood still and gripped the phone tighter. The tone of Sloan's voice didn't sound good and she released the hope that she'd changed her mind. "No problem," she said, willing her voice to sound calm. "I'm between patients anyway. What's going on?"

There was a moment of silence and then Sloan said, "I got a call today from Bay River Logging." She paused.

Maya stared at the soybean field out the back window of her office and waited.

"They've finished the job before mine sooner than expected and will start on my property next Wednesday."

Maya's heart sank. All hope was gone now. Her eyes filled with tears and she heard the crack of a tree trunk and the sound of leaves and limbs colliding with the ground. She'd heard this all night during Katrina, but that destruction was preceded by wind, not bulldozers and saws. It felt more violent this way.

"I'm sorry, Maya," Sloan continued. "I wish there were another option but there isn't."

There was an awkward silence until Maya found her voice. "Thanks for letting me know."

She'd have to tell the circle. The circle. "Sloan, would it be OK for our women's circle to meet there one more time before they start?"

Without hesitation, Sloan said, "Sure. That'll be fine."

The door chimed and the 11:30 patient walked in. "I have to go now," Maya said.

Maya checked the patient in and dodged his attempts to chat, saying she needed something in the chart room. She rested her forehead on a row of charts. Sloan had said her land was probably worth between $200,000 and $300,000. There was no way now to raise that kind of money. What if Tuesday was the last time the circle met at the Mother Tree? The end of a century-long tradition. She wished Hazel were alive. She'd know what to do.

Suddenly Maya stood up straight and her hand went instinctively to her heart. She rushed back to her desk. After this patient, Dr. Allan had an hour for lunch. There were only four patients scheduled this afternoon since it was Labor Day weekend. He'd be fine without her.

Maya dashed off a quick note saying she had an emergency and needed to leave early. She taped it to her computer and hurried to her car. She dialed Jeff O'Neal's number at Trident as she headed east on 55, praying he hadn't taken the day off and could see her.

Maya reminded herself to slow down when she reached the outskirts of Oriental. Because of her desire to get to Trident as quickly as she could, she'd made it from work to Oriental in record time. On the way she'd left a voicemail for Lilith, telling her about the change in the logging start date and that Sloan had given them permission to meet there one more time. She asked Lilith to call the others to coordinate a meeting there Tuesday at sunset.

Maya pulled into a parking space at the small office complex of Trident, hopeful for the first time in weeks. When she talked with Mr. O'Neal on the phone, she'd asked him to look into the details of the trust to see how much she could donate at once and if the North Carolina Coastal Land trust would meet the criteria to receive the money.

Maya knocked and then let herself into Mr. O'Neal's office. He was seated at his desk at the back of the room staring intently at his computer. When he saw her, he jumped up, pushing his desk chair back with such force that it knocked into the bookcase behind him and then reverberated back and hit him in the knees. He plopped back down into the chair. A blush crept like spilt red wine from his neck to his face.

Maya stifled a laugh.

"Guess I need to move more slowly," he said, and put his hands on the armrests and stood deliberately. By this time, Maya was halfway across the room and it only took Mr. O'Neal four steps and one pull on his waistband to reach her. He took her outstretched hand and pumped it up and down.

"It's good to see you. I've been wondering when you'd be ready to invest in something. It's been almost three months since we met. Not that I'm counting or have the right to judge how you manage your fund." He spoke quickly, keeping cadence with his handshake, and the red wine stain deepened.

Maya managed to extract her hand, worried she'd get tennis elbow if this kept up much longer. "Well, I only found out about this opportunity a few hours ago, but there is a time limit so I'm grateful you could see me today, Mr. O'Neal."

"Jeff. Jeff. Please call me Jeff. No need to be formal." Now that he didn't have her hand to shake, Jeff shifted back and forth on his feet, hiking his pants up at regular intervals. He kept shifting and hiking, all the while staring at Maya.

Finally, Maya asked, "So, were you able to find the answers to my questions?"

Jeff let go of his waistband and threw his hands in the air. "Oh. Yes.

Of course." He scurried back to his desk and bumped his knee on the edge trying to retrieve a file lying there.

Maya laughed out loud this time. "Jeff, I appreciate that you're moving quickly, but please don't hurt yourself on my account."

"That's OK. This is normal for me. I don't do well in the physical realm but I'm a gymnast when it comes to moving around a spreadsheet." He laughed at his own joke and tapped the outside of the file he'd picked up. They walked together to the conference table in the middle of the room.

Maya sat at the edge of the chair, bouncing her heels and twirling her spinner ring. Jeff methodically organized several papers in front of them. He ran his right index finger down a row of numbers and immediately became calm and focused. His anxiety had shifted to her.

"So, what did you find out?" Maya asked. Jeff slid a piece of paper closer to her. Several sentences on it were highlighted in yellow.

"This trust specifies that you can donate up to 5% of the capital every year. Like I told you last time we met, Hazel never donated this much. She rarely gave over 1%. I don't think she understood how much money she had and that as long as she followed these guidelines she'd never exhaust the funds, even with the stock market plummeting like it did this year."

Maya scooted her chair closer. "How is the fund doing and how much is 5%?" Maya tried to remember the balance from her last statement and thought it was somewhere around 4 million. Before she could multiply that by .05 Jeff slid another paper to her.

"The value of the fund is currently $4,374,822. That's down a couple hundred thousand for the year so far, but doing better than the market average."

Maya opened her mouth but before she could ask another question he slid a second paper to her. Jeff pointed to the highlighted number.

"This is how much you can donate this calendar year." Anticipating her next question, he continued, "And yes. The North Carolina Coastal Land Trust is a nonprofit and you can definitely donate to them."

Jeff sat back in his chair, crossed his arms over his chest and smiled. Maya sat there staring at the number. $218,740. Was that enough money to save the property? She had no idea if Sloan would accept this amount. It seemed like a lot and surely more than Sloan would make from logging.

Now it was Jeff's time to prompt her to speak. "So, does this help?"

Maya slumped back in her chair. She had the answers she'd come for but that wasn't enough. "I don't know."

"You don't know? The land trust would be thrilled with a donation this large. What don't you know?"

Maya realized she needed to explain the whole situation to Jeff in order for him to help her. Maybe he would have an idea of the property value on Hungry Mother Creek. "I think I better explain in more detail," she said. "First may I have a bottle of water?"

Jeff jumped up. "Sure." Back in the physical world, his grace evaporated and he did his dance of four steps and a waistband tug over to the refrigerator at his desk.

Maya took a sip of water and then began her story, starting with the history of the women's circle and ending with what she'd learned today about the Coastal Land Trust. Jeff listened attentively, jotting down a couple notes as she spoke. "What I don't know," Maya said, "is whether I can make a donation to them and ask that it be used to buy a specific piece of land."

"And you don't know if the owner is willing to sell it for this amount," he said, pointing to the highlighted number.

Maya shook her head in agreement.

"Hmm. The owner would probably get a tax break by selling it to a nonprofit," Jeff said. "This amount of money plus a tax break might work if the owner has some desire for conservation. She'd definitely have more money in the short term from this deal versus the logging."

Maya clapped her hands together. "Do you think so? Lots of people would be happy if this worked. Can we call the land trust right now and see what they say?" Maya looked at her watch. It was 1:30. "If they think it can work, do we have time to get it all done by Wednesday?"

Jeff shook his head and sat back in his chair. "Moving around this amount of money takes time and a long weekend doesn't help. Even if this works and the owner agrees, it would take several weeks to get all the paperwork drawn up and that's just on my end. I have no idea what the process is at the land trust."

Maya took a breath. She needed to keep her emotions in check. Bouncing between triumph and disappointment was exhausting her. She steadied her voice. "Let's start with calling the land trust, see what they say, and go from there."

Maya drove home replaying the events of the last three hours. She'd gone from despair at hearing the logging would start next week to elation that maybe she could use Hazel's fund to save the property to disappointment that there wasn't enough time for her plan to work.

How would Travis see this? He could always find something positive to focus on. Well, at least she had hope. Now there was a possibility that the land could be saved, whereas this morning there was none. She and Jeff were meeting with the land trust at 9 a.m. on Tuesday to talk further, but they said they needed a commitment from Sloan that she was willing to sell before they could set up a fund for the Hungry Mother Creek property. They also shared some of their current initiatives that her money could support, if this didn't work out. Maya wasn't ready to think about that yet.

She parked her car and heard Doodle Bug barking. She let her out and Doodle Bug immediately ran down to the creek and jumped in. Maya followed and picked up a stick on the way. She spent 10 minutes throwing the stick for Doodle Bug and watching her swim, retrieve, and shake. The repetition helped quiet her mind.

When Doodle Bug was finished, they walked back to the house and Maya made a sandwich to tide her over until her dinner date with Travis. She couldn't wait to see him and tell him what had happened today. Maybe he could come with her on Tuesday.

She had her sandwich midway to her mouth when it hit her. Wait. Should she even tell Travis? Hazel's request was to keep the fund confidential, but she couldn't imagine keeping this from him. Maya took a bite of the peanut butter and banana sandwich. Maybe some food would help her decide what to do before she met Travis later.

***

"Are you done with that?" Thomas, the waiter behind the bar, asked Maya.

"Yes," Maya said and pushed her empty plate toward him.

Thomas put it in a bin under the bar. "Another glass of wine?" he said, reaching for the bottle.

Maya hesitated and then said, "No, but a glass of water with lemon would be great."

Thomas left for her water and Travis said, "You must've been hungry. I've never seen you eat that fast."

They'd both had quesadillas and Travis was starting on his last triangle, oozing with cheese and shrimp. M&M's was full, and Maya and Travis had to sit at the bar. There was no privacy here, so Maya didn't talk about Hazel's fund, but was about to burst to tell Travis everything. It hadn't taken long for her to decide to be honest with him.

She knew Hazel would be pleased about their relationship and would understand her need to share the truth.

Maya leaned forward, putting her head close to Travis. "There's something I'm dying to tell you, but I'm not comfortable talking about it here. Guess I rushed through my meal so we could leave."

Travis cocked his head and said, "Now you've got me curious. What's it about?"

"Something about saving Hungry Mother Creek," she said, and couldn't help but smile.

Travis finished the rest of his quesadilla in two bites and waved to Thomas for the check. He immediately handed over his credit card.

Maya stood and pushed her bar stool under the bar and Travis signed the receipt. When they got outside Travis asked, "Want to walk while we talk?"

"Sure. That'll help get rid of my nervous energy."

"Let's walk over the bridge. It's always nice to look back at town from there."

"Perfect. I've never done that before," Maya said.

"Then come along," Travis said and took her hand. "You're not an official resident of Oriental until you've walked or biked across the bridge." They turned left out of M&M's and then left toward the bridge.

"OK. Spill it," Travis said. "What's going on? Did you talk with Nicholas Sparks about a donation?"

"No. For you to understand everything that's happened today I need to start with Hazel's will."

"Hazel's will?"

"Yes. Remember at the reading of her will when you, her son, and I were all there?"

"Yes. And that's when you found out she'd left you the house."

"Right. And then Mr. Hudson asked you and her son to leave?"

Travis stopped a minute and looked at her. "Yeah. Now I do, and we were going to meet at The Bean afterward but you stood me up."

Maya laughed and squeezed his hand. "I can't believe you remember that."

They were at the peak of the bridge now and leaned against the concrete railing. Travis kept a hold on her hand and said, "There's not much that I forget when it comes to you."

Maya stared at him, still having trouble accepting how important she was to him.

"So, what happened after we left?" Travis said, prompting her to continue.

"Bear with me. I'm going to start with some history, but I promise it will end up about the Hungry Mother Creek property."

"OK. Let's have it," Travis said.

Maya started, "In the late 1800s . . ."

Travis interrupted, "You weren't kidding about the history, were you?"

Maya laughed. "No. As I was saying, in the late 1800s, Hazel's grandmother established a trust, a philanthropic trust. Mr. Hudson said she set it up with the money she'd inherited from her father, who was a blockade runner during the Civil War."

"Whoa. That's interesting. First, that Hazel's great-grandfather did that, and second that her grandmother inherited the money in that day and age and didn't have it controlled by her husband."

"I know. I asked Mr. Hudson about that and he said the trust was started in 1885, about 10 years after women were allowed to control their own finances."

"That's a long time ago. I can't imagine what the fund must be worth now."

"Over $4 million."

Travis let out a long whistle.

"And there's more. The management of the fund has passed through the women of the family from Hazel's grandmother, to her mother, and then to Hazel." Maya paused. Her voice was tight with emotion. She swallowed and continued, "Hazel didn't have a daughter and left me as the executor of the fund."

Travis' eyes widened. "Wow. How come you've never mentioned this?"

"Hazel asked it be kept confidential."

Travis turned his attention down to the water and watched a john boat trawling for shrimp beneath them. He grabbed her hands and said quickly, "Is there a way you can use this money to buy the Hungry Mother Creek property?"

"Yes!" Maya said and then spilled out the details from her day, Sloan's call, how she found the N.C. Coastal Land Trust website, and her epiphany to try to use the fund to save the property. She ended with details about her meeting with Jeff. "Would you come Tuesday when Jeff and I meet with the land trust? It'd be good to have you there since you've been managing the monies we've raised this far, and I'd love the moral support."

"Of course, I'll be there." Travis paused. "But do we even know if Sloan will agree to sell for the amount you have? Do you think it would help if you talked with her again?"

"No, because she can't know where the money's coming from," Maya said. "The land trust will tell her it's an anonymous donor and will do their best to persuade her to sell it for the amount I have. She can't say yes if we don't even ask."

Travis wrapped his arms around her and kissed her gently. "Now look who's being optimistic."

Maya rested her head on his chest. "You've been a good teacher." Her head rose and fell with his breath and she watched the boats fitted with shrimp nets circling in front of the bridge. The brightest stars revealed themselves in the darkening sky. Maya looked up at Travis. "Remember. You can't tell anyone about the fund or my involvement," she said. "If this works, it will be because of an anonymous donation."

"Of course, you have my word," Travis said. He took a breath and pulled her closer. "You also have my heart."

Maya's eyes immediately filled with tears and before she could say anything he leaned down and kissed her. A car illuminated them with headlights and then sped past, ending their interlude. "Come on, my rich heiress. Let's go home," Travis said.

"Oh my. Let's not get dramatic," Maya laughed. "Before we go home, I want to finish walking across the bridge so I can officially claim the status of Oriental resident."

She took his hand and they walked down the incline toward Pecan Grove Marina. Maya was only aware of the pressure of Travis' hand in hers and the light southern breeze on her face. She was not conscious of her feet touching the ground.

CHAPTER 16

Sloan laid the phone on her desk and sat there stunned. She listened to the rain tapping on the roof and after several minutes went into the kitchen and poured herself a glass of iced tea. She stood at the kitchen sink and stared out at the water. The day was gray and it was hard to tell where the clouds stopped and the water started.

She couldn't believe the conversation she'd just had. The North Carolina Coastal Land Trust, who said they were helping the community's effort to save the land on Hungry Mother Creek, wanted to purchase her property and make it a nature preserve. They offered her $225,000 and hoped she'd immediately sign a contract to purchase. They would give her written confirmation that the funds would be available within two weeks. They knew the logging would start tomorrow and were putting pressure on her because of this. She was able to put them off a couple hours.

Sloan had mentally begun listing the pros and cons of the deal but desperately needed to talk it through with someone. Peter was teaching a three-hour seminar class in Raleigh and wouldn't be done until noon. A lightning flash across the river pulled her attention outside. A gentle rumble followed about 15 seconds later. The storm was moving away.

A movement outside caught Sloan's attention. She blinked to focus. It was Nellie! Thank goodness she was OK. Sloan had been worried because she hadn't seen her for a while. She hurried out the patio doors to catch Nellie, who was headed toward the pier. The rain had cooled the air but the humidity was high, creating a light mist. Sloan wished she'd grabbed a jacket.

"Nellie. Nellie," Sloan called. Nellie paused. Sloan jogged the last few steps to reach her. "I'm glad to see you. I've been worried. Is everything OK?"

Nellie shrugged and looked away. "A little bit. Joe's trying to be better."

While Nellie's gaze was directed to the water, Sloan looked at her neck but didn't see any bruises. Maybe things were better.

"I'm glad to hear that. So what made you come out on this dreary day?" Sloan asked.

Nellie fingered the bun at the back of her neck and her eyes filled with tears. "Today is Issac's birthday. I was too restless to stay inside."

"I'm sorry." Sloan left it at that, not sure what else to say and now questioning whether she should even talk about her land. In comparison to what Nellie was dealing with, it didn't seem that important.

"Thanks. I'm glad you're here. Tell me what's going on with your retreat center. I don't feel like talking about Issac."

"Are you sure?" Sloan asked.

Nellie nodded.

"It's damp out here. Why don't we go inside and I'll make us a cup of tea."

Nellie backed away from Sloan and cinched the belt on her rain coat tighter. "No. I don't have much time and I'd rather be outside."

"Oh. OK," Sloan said, noticing Nellie's body language hadn't changed despite her declaration that things were better.

"What's the latest? Has the contractor started yet?" Nellie asked.

"No. He should start in a couple weeks. But you won't believe what happened a few minutes ago. You remember my dilemma about logging my property?"

"Yes. Have you changed your mind?"

"No, but I have an opportunity. The North Carolina Coastal Land Trust called me about 10 minutes ago." Sloan shared the offer from the land trust and together they played out the implications of both accepting and declining the offer.

When they were done Nellie asked, "After talking about this, what does your heart tell you to do?"

"Accept the offer," Sloan said immediately. "I think I knew that on the phone but didn't want to make an emotional decision."

"Like you said, the main risk is the loss of future revenue from the timber and the potential loss if you sold the land at market value," Nellie said.

"I know. The realtor in me is conflicted. It's difficult to let go of the land now that I've seen how valuable it is to others. I could probably sell it for at least 50% more than what the land trust has offered once the real estate market rebounds." There was that conundrum: whether to make a decision based on feelings or the numbers. "What would you do, Nellie?"

"Well, either way, you'll end up with the money to start your retreat center, so you can't make a wrong decision in that respect."

"I know," Sloan said. "I guess I have some more thinking to do." She looked at her watch. She would call Peter after his class. He knew her better than anyone and could help her make the final decision.

"Thanks for listening, Nellie." Sloan didn't want to leave their next meeting to chance. "Hey, are you around this weekend? Would you like to go to lunch on Saturday? My treat. To thank you for all your support the past few months."

"You don't have to do that. I was happy to listen and seeing you made my day better." Nellie smiled and lifted her hand to say goodbye. "I better get home."

Sloan stepped toward her. "So, will you go to lunch with me?"

Sloan watched Nellie think about her offer. She looked down and clenched and unclenched her fists. Sloan wondered if her husband would let her go out for lunch. Nellie swallowed hard and finally answered. "I'll try my best to make it." She avoided Sloan's eyes.

"Great. How about 1 o'clock at M&M's? I haven't eaten there yet and want to check it out."

"OK," Nellie said, starting to turn to walk down the road.

"Can I pick you up?" Sloan asked. She knew the answer before Nellie said it but had to try.

"Oh no. I'll meet you there." She walked away and over her shoulder said, "Good luck with your decision. I know you'll make the right one."

"Thank you," Sloan called after her. Her heart ached as she watched Nellie walk away. She prayed she would come to lunch on Saturday.

The clouds had continued to move east and now the sun broke through, instantly creating sauna-like conditions. Sloan slowly walked across her front yard to the house. Her flip-flops propelled moisture onto the back of her legs. She couldn't worry about Nellie now. She had to make a decision about what to do with her land.

She went inside and sat in the wingback chair in her office. In 10 minutes Peter would be out of his class and they could talk. To pass the time, she took a legal pad from her desk and wrote down the reasons to sell the Hungry Mother Creek property to the land trust, and the reasons to log it and retain ownership. She stared at the list, but it was hard to focus. Thoughts of Nellie cowering in the corner with her arms up to protect herself kept intruding. There had to be something she could do besides wait for Nellie to choose to leave.

Sloan looked at her watch again and it was a few minutes after noon. After she talked with Peter and decided what to do about her property, she would focus on Nellie.

***

Maya looked out the windows into the back yard. The shadows were lengthening and it was almost time for the circle's farewell ritual for the Mother Tree. When she saw Ella paddle by, she picked up her bag by the door.

"Doodle Bug, I have to go. You be good."

Doodle Bug lifted her eyebrows in acknowledgment but never moved from the air-conditioning vent.

Maya headed down to her kayak. The ground was still damp from the earlier rain, but thankfully a northerly breeze had cleared the skies and lowered the humidity. She paddled slowly, careful not to catch up to Ella so she would be the last to arrive.

Maya turned down Hungry Mother Creek and in the distance saw Violet's boat anchored in front of the beach. Ella was pulling her kayak up and Maya assumed Lilith had gotten there first, as usual. Maya got closer and saw Lilith sitting on the beach staring at the water. Violet was immersed in drying her feet and putting on her Keds and Ella sat on the end of her kayak, staring into the woods. No one spoke. Maya paddled faster. When they heard her paddle splashing, they all stood. Lilith helped her pull her kayak up onto the sand. They'd never been this quiet. The somber energy on the beach was palpable. It reminded Maya of the heaviness she'd felt at Hazel's funeral.

"Violet and I came up with a ritual for this evening," Lilith said. "Let's head on back to the Mother Tree so we finish before dark." Lilith's voice cracked and she took the corner of her T-shirt and dabbed at her eyes. Maya had never seen Lilith this somber, not even when Hazel was dying.

Maya took a bag out of her kayak and followed the others who plodded through the sand, past the saw palmettos and into the clearing by the Mother Tree. Violet opened her camping chair and was about to sit down.

"Wait," Maya said. "There's something I'd like to do before we start the ritual."

Maya reached into her bag and brought out four champagne glasses. She handed them out, avoiding everyone's eyes and trying not to smile at their confused expressions. Maya saw that Lilith was about to speak and held her hand up.

"I know it makes no sense that I've brought these glasses, and champagne," Maya pulled out the bottle from her bag, "but it will make sense in about 10 seconds."

All the women's eyes widened. Lilith stepped closer to her and said, "OK, spit it out before we jump to conclusions."

Maya took a breath and almost sang the words, "The Mother Tree is safe. There won't be any logging here tomorrow or ever."

"What?" Ella said.

"This isn't our last time here?" Violet asked and then wiped the tear that rolled down her cheek.

Lilith danced in a circle pumping her fists in the air. "We did it! We did it!" Then she looked at Maya. "How did we actually do this? You and Travis must have worked some super magic to raise all the money we needed."

Everyone's attention was on Maya. "It's a long story," she said, "but an anonymous donor contacted the North Carolina Coastal Land Trust on Friday with enough money to purchase the land. Because of restrictions on the fund they manage, they couldn't buy it directly from Sloan, but could donate to a nonprofit like the Coastal Land Trust. This morning the accountant for the donor, representatives from the land trust, and Travis and I all met. We drew up a proposal for Sloan and called her. After a few hours to think about, it she accepted! It will take a few weeks for all of it to be final, but she and the land trust have signed a preliminary agreement."

Ella interrupted, "So Sloan has sold this property to the land trust. What does that mean for us?"

"That our circle can keep meeting here forever," Maya said. "The land trust will make this land a preserve. It will be protected from development and logging and the community can still use it, with only a few restrictions."

Lilith added, "And besides getting more money than she would from logging, I bet Sloan also gets a nice tax break."

Maya nodded.

"That means everyone is happy," Violet added.

"Yes. And especially us," Maya said and popped the cork on the champagne. She poured some in each of their glasses and then took out a fifth glass and placed it at the base of the Mother Tree. She filled it until it overflowed.

"This one's in honor of Hazel, the women in the circle before us, and the divine. I'm sure they all had a role in this outcome."

The women raised their glasses in a toast, clicking the plastic together. Maya, Ella, and Violet sipped theirs while Lilith drank hers in one swallow. When Lilith was done, she picked up the glass by the Mother Tree and poured the champagne onto her roots. She refilled her glass and then lifted it to the tree, "May you live to inspire women in this circle for hundreds of years to come," she said. Lilith drained her glass again and threw it over her shoulder. She ran to the Mother Tree and wrapped her arms about it. The others watched and then in unison walked over to join her.

Maya felt self-conscious at first, never having hugged a tree before, but soon she relaxed into the trunk. She pressed her cheek into the grooved bark and watched two ants hike its peaks. She breathed in the organic smell of the tree and heard the creaking of the upper limbs through the trunk. A woodpecker high above demanded dinner. Her heart bumped its rhythm into the dense wood and her tears slid into its crevices.

Lilith was beside Maya and reached for her hand. Maya grasped it and then held Violet's with her other. They had enough circumference to stand holding hands with the Mother Tree in the middle. They stood together, silenced by gratitude. The forest dimmed from orange to pink and the fireflies twinkled, decorating the space between the leaves, branches, and blades of grass.

CHAPTER 17

Sloan sat up in bed and pulled the bedspread to her chin. She strained to see if the bedroom door was opening or if she heard her uncle's footsteps. Peter moved beside her, initially startling her and then reorienting her to where she was. In her bedroom in Magnolia Bend. Safe. She released the bedspread, slowed her breath, and repeated silently, "I am safe."

In a few minutes, Sloan's anxiety subsided. She'd hoped her 3:30 wakeup calls were over since she'd gone several weeks without one, but at least she was making progress. Maybe a cup of tea will help me go back to sleep, she thought. She tip-toed across the bedroom, avoiding the creaky boards she'd identified on other mornings. When she got to the bedroom door, she turned the knob slowly, expecting it to be locked. It wasn't. That was strange. She'd almost gotten used to it being locked when she woke early. She opened the door quietly and went downstairs.

Sloan sat at the kitchen table with her tea. Rather than avoiding thoughts of her uncle, she chose to think about him, continuing her endeavor to deal with her abuse. She thought of the last picture she'd seen of him. It was with her father in a restaurant in Denver. Time had taken her uncle's hair and layered his face, neck and waist with flesh. Although he was 11 years younger than her father, he looked older. She held this image in her mind. She was physically more powerful than he.

He was halfway across the country. She was safe.

Sloan wondered if his life was impacted by what he'd done. Was he ashamed? Did he lock that part of his life away and pretend it didn't happen? She would never know, and it didn't matter. She could only create peace for herself.

Sloan stood, turned on the kitchen light and then pushed open the swinging door that connected the kitchen with the ballroom. She stood with her back against the door to provide some light. The floor of the ballroom was covered in plastic and strewn with tools and extension cords. A saw horse stood silently in the shadows.

Sloan smiled at the physical progress toward her dream. The contractor was starting with the addition of a handicapped-accessible bathroom, then adding a ramp and entrance directly from the parking lot. After that the focus would be on wiring for sound, wi-fi, and more outlets. She stared at the room, imagining it complete and filled with people listening to a speaker and then with easels and Peter weaving in and out giving feedback to his students.

Now that she'd sold her property to the land trust, she knew her dream would become reality. On top of that, she had money to help Deidre get re-established once she was discharged.

Sloan put her mug in the sink and turned off the light. She effortlessly navigated the dark hallway to the stairs, lowering her head and lifting her feet in all the right places. After four months, she'd grown accustomed to the heights, widths, and corners of her 19th-century home. Before she got to the stairs, she saw the glow of her computer and went in her office to turn it off. She closed her laptop and stood a minute to let her eyes adjust to the dark. The room came back into focus, dimly lit by the glow of a half moon. A movement outside caught her attention. Maybe it was Nellie.

Sloan walked to the window that looked out on the driveway. She slowly scanned the front yard for shadows or movement. Maybe she'd just seen a deer dart across the yard. She kept looking, and willed Nellie to step out of the shadows. Nellie hadn't shown up for lunch on Saturday and still hadn't called, and Sloan was worried.

She went out the front door and walked barefoot over to the well. Nellie wasn't there. A funnel of cool air came up from the well and Sloan pulled her robe tighter, its hem now dampened from trailing through the dew. The half moon gave Sloan enough light to see the nearby houses but she didn't see Nellie coming through their backyards. She walked around the side of the house and looked down to her pier, but it was empty.

Sloan jogged up to Magnolia Bend Road and looked right and left. She saw nothing but the dark outline of the trees that lined the road. Even though it'd only been a week since she'd seen Nellie, she couldn't shake her sense that something was wrong. The northeast breeze gained strength and ruffled Sloan's hair. It was silent except for the gentle pulse of the waves on the shore and the wind in the tops of the magnolia and pine trees in her front yard.

Sloan chided herself for focusing on her issues and not being more aggressive with helping Nellie. Today she would find her, even if it meant going door to door down Magnolia Bend Road. She needed to introduce herself to her other neighbors anyway. Hopefully she'd find Nellie or someone who knew her. If that didn't work, she'd go back to the register of deeds and put in all the addresses on the road to see which one had Nellie on the deed. Actually, that's where I'll start, Sloan thought. She'd get to the court house as soon as it opened this morning.

Sloan walked down her driveway to the house. When she got inside, she went to her office and turned her computer back on. She was too worried to sleep. She might as well continue her research on the past owners of Magnolia Bend. Hopefully she could finish the history that she'd share with her guests.

***

Doodle Bug lay under the windows facing the creek, keeping a safe distance from Maya and projectile clothing. Maya threw a dress and then a blazer to her left and right and then sat on the bed. She pounded the mattress with her fist. "God. I hate picking out clothes, Doodle Bug. I have no idea what to wear to this interview with the land trust and I have to leave in an hour."

Last week, after things were settled with the Hungry Mother Creek property, she'd spoken with the woman from the Coastal Land Trust about their job opening. She shared a little about her degree and background, which led to her current situation.

Doodle Bug lifted her head and cocked it to one side when she heard her name. "You don't have to worry about things like this do you, girl? You can wear the same thing every day." Maya sighed. "Bay would know exactly what I should wear." Maya looked at her phone. 8:30. Would Bay be in class? It was worth a try. Maya dialed Bay. On the second ring, Bay answered.

"Hey, Maya."

"Oh, Bay. I'm so glad you answered. Is this a good time?"

"Yes. I have a few minutes before I leave for my 10 o'clock class. What's up?"

"I'm having a wardrobe emergency but that can wait a minute. First tell me about school. From your text messages, it sounds like things are going well."

"They are," Bay said. Maya heard her pause to take a gulp of coffee. "I could do without calculus, but otherwise my prerequisites are interesting and not too demanding, but it's only been a couple weeks since classes started."

"Have you made any friends?"

"I talk to the other students in class but Maya, remember, everyone's about 20 years younger than me. I got a part-time job at a boutique downtown and that gives me the opportunity to be around women closer to my age." Bay paused. "I've seen Holden."

"Oh. How was that? Did Laura give you any trouble about visiting him?"

"No, but I didn't see her this time."

"How was he?"

Bay's voice cracked. "He hasn't gotten any better. He still has a feeding tube and has lost so much weight, he doesn't even look like himself. Of course, the nurses can't tell me anything since Laura's the guardian."

"Wow. That's not much of a way to live."

"No," Bay agreed. "He still can't communicate, and I don't think he recognized me."

"I'm sorry." Maya searched for more comforting words but couldn't come up with any. Doodle Bug jumped up on the bed and started licking her. Maya laughed. "Sorry, Bay. Doodle Bug says hello."

Bay laughed too. "Give her a hug for me."

"Will do," Maya said, leaning over to deliver the promised squeeze. "How are you feeling about your decision to go back to school?"

Bay was quiet. Maya waited, petting Doodle Bug, who snuggled in beside her on the bed.

"I still feel guilty. Not because I left Holden to do it. I think I've made peace with that and I know he's well cared for. I'm guilty because the best days of my life are still ahead, and the only thing in Holden's future is death. I'll be having a good day and then think of him sitting in the nursing home, unable to eat or communicate."

"But Bay, he's 25 years older than you. Some of this is the natural course of life."

"I know, I know. I can't forget about his life before the stroke and all he achieved and experienced." Bay paused. "Now, I also don't want to forget your wardrobe emergency. What's going on?"

"I have an interview this morning in New Bern and don't know what to wear. It's September and almost fall so don't want to wear summer clothes but it will be 85 today."

"First of all—an interview? That's exciting. Who's it with and how professional do you need to be?"

Maya quickly filled Bay in on the Hungry Mother Creek property, how the Coastal Land Trust had become involved and how she found their job opening. "Based on what I saw when Travis and I were in their offices a few weeks ago, the dress code seemed pretty casual. When they're out in the field it's hiking boots, jeans, and baseball caps."

Bay laughed. "You definitely have the clothes for that part of the job. Hey, how's it going with Travis? Seems like every time we text, he's over at your place," Bay said.

"It's wonderful. Sometimes too good to be true. It's still hard to believe someone like him could love me."

Bay interrupted, "Love. Did you say love? Sounds like it's getting serious."

Maya stood and walked with the phone to the windows overlooking the creek. "It doesn't feel serious because we always have fun when we're together, but you're right. Our relationship is getting stronger." Maya paused. "I'm in love with him," she said aloud for the first time.

"Maya, that's fantastic. I couldn't be happier for you."

Maya looked at her phone. "I don't want to make you late for class."

"Oh, you're right. We better get back to our mission for today, but let's talk this afternoon, after your interview."

"That sounds perfect," Maya said.

"Now, do you have a short-sleeved dress with fall colors?"

Maya looked around. She shoved aside a pair of jeans and then held up a dress. "Yes. It's khaki with a small black stripe."

"Perfect. Now do you have a black lightweight blazer or sweater and black flats?"

"Yes. I have both." Maya laid the outfit on her bed. "How come I couldn't do that? It looks great."

"Good. Look at the neckline of the dress and pick a necklace that will accent it," Bay instructed.

Maya already knew the necklace she wanted to wear. "Got that, too."

"Excellent. Now you've got the look, all you have to do is be yourself. This job sounds like it would be a good fit. Remember what we talked about that day we went for a sunset kayak? And you said what you love?"

"Yeah. Being outside and active."

"Sounds like you'd have that with this job."

"I would, and I'd get to use my organizational and people skills," Maya added, mentally preparing for potential interview questions.

"Good luck. I know you'll be amazing. Call when it's over."

"Will do. Thanks for your help."

"My pleasure."

"I miss you," Maya said.

"I miss you too."

Maya hung up with tears in her eyes. Their relationship had come a long way from the days when Maya tried to avoid Bay. Their differences made their friendship interesting but at the core they were similar. She didn't have time to think about that now, though. She only had 20 minutes to get out the door.

All the way to New Bern, Maya visualized herself being calm, poised, and answering the interview questions coherently. She reminded herself of how she could be an asset to the land trust. Maya parked in front of the modest office in a strip mall and took a few breaths to center herself. She was nervous, but excitement was mixed in. What if she got the job? She'd have a role in preserving irreplaceable coastal land. Wow. That would be a better reason to get out of bed than scheduling appointments and filing insurance claims. Maya slammed the car door and walked toward the office.

CHAPTER 18

Maya woke up five minutes before her alarm went off. Travis was lying on his side and she spooned him from behind. She nuzzled the back of his neck and he reached over to hold her left hand. Maya lay there a minute, enjoying the sensation of their bodies molded together, skin against skin. But it was more than a physical sensation. She was safe, loved, and important to someone. A lump formed in her throat with the realization that this was the first time she'd felt this way.

Travis' breathing was heavy and even. Maya gently released his hand and slid away from him. She hated to leave but wanted to arrive early for the equinox gathering so she could meet Sloan and lead her to the Mother Tree. Doodle Bug lifted her head when Maya stepped over her.

"Morning, girl," she whispered. "Travis will take you out in a little bit." Satisfied, Doodle Bug dropped her head and watched Maya get dressed. Maya walked quietly to the door with her flip-flops in her hand.

"Hey, beautiful. Aren't you going to kiss me goodbye?"

Maya smiled and turned around. "How do you know I'm beautiful? It's still dark."

Travis reached up for her hand. "I remember from last night."

Even though it was only the two of them Maya blushed and then leaned down to kiss him on the cheek. "You still paddling up to Hungry Mother Creek for a breakfast picnic after my circle?"

"Yes. I'm bringing my camping stove so we can have bacon and eggs and coffee. What time will y'all be through?"

"Let's see, sunrise is at around 6:50 and we'll start right after that. Be there around 8:30."

"Will do. Have a good meeting."

Maya grabbed her bag by the back door and headed down to her kayak.

***

Sloan parked off the road in front of the Hungry Mother Creek property. It was still dark. She looked toward the woods and tried to push away the image of the man with the Confederate flag belt buckle. She was meeting the women's circle this morning. She wouldn't be alone.

Sloan slammed the car door and turned on her flashlight. A few days after agreeing to sell to the N.C. Coastal Land Trust, Maya and Lilith came by and invited her to join the circle. She immediately said yes, thinking of her great-grandmother GG, and the chance to experience something that'd been important to her. But now she was nervous about fitting in with the others and saying the right thing.

Dawn was a white thread stitched between the black earth and the blue-black sky. Sloan turned on her flashlight and it eased her discomfort with the dark. She followed the narrow beam for a few minutes until the light in the east intensified into red and orange and her eyes adjusted. She walked slowly, being careful of roots, and watched the forest reveal itself as dawn broke. It reminded her of sitting on her great-grandmother's back steps waiting for breakfast in the summers.

"Sloan?"

Sloan froze and gripped her flashlight tighter and then her frontal cortex kicked in and she remembered Maya was hiking out to lead her back to the circle. "Maya, is that you?" She finished her sentence and Maya walked around the corner, her features in shadow.

"Yes. Glad you made it. It's only a five-minute walk from here."

"Thanks for meeting me. I've only walked this way once so it's nice to have your help."

They walked a few minutes single file until the trail widened. Maya slowed and walked beside Sloan. "Are you nervous?" Maya asked.

"Yes. A little bit. I've never done anything like this before."

"I know. This time last year was my first circle. You don't have to speak today if you don't want to. I didn't think I would my first time, but after listening to the others talk honestly about their lives, I was inspired to at least try."

"Since you and Lilith told me about the ritual, I've been thinking about what I want to say."

Maya stopped. "That's the easy part, isn't it? Thinking about things. I've perfected that. Always thinking. It was hard at first to give voice to my thoughts and feelings, but the circle has given me courage. I bet the same thing will happen to you."

"I hope so," Sloan replied. They walked in silence. Sloan thought about GG's small feet pressing into the same dirt where she now placed hers. She trailed her fingers across the bark of an old loblolly pine, wondering if it had stood here when GG walked to the circle.

"Maya, Sloan," Lilith called from the clearing ahead. "Perfect timing. It's almost sunrise."

Sloan stepped into the clearing and the women gathered around to welcome her.

***

While Ella, Violet, and Lilith greeted Sloan, Maya ran to her kayak to get a bottle of water and a dry bag containing the monogrammed box she'd found under the stairs. When she got back to the clearing, the women were preparing for the circle. Ella unfolded the blanket she'd brought to sit on. She patted the spot beside her, indicating Sloan could sit there, and they leaned their heads together in discussion. Today Ella looked like an REI model wearing khaki shorts and a long-sleeved sky-blue shirt. Her blond hair was threaded through a baseball cap. Sloan's hair was pulled up in a twist and she looked elegant and casual at the same time in jeans and a striped Oxford shirt. Her outfit reminded Maya of Hazel. Lilith put a fat pillar candle in the middle of the circle and then placed 10 votives around it and sat down.

Maya took the spot between Lilith and Sloan. She leaned over to Lilith. "Why are there 10 votives?"

Before Lilith could answer, Violet said, "Are we ready to start?" Lilith smiled at Maya and they turned their attention to Violet.

Maya looked at Sloan, who was rearranging her long legs underneath her. Maya knew she was nervous, but she couldn't tell from looking at her. Sloan was calm and dignified, even regal, Maya thought. She was happy Sloan was here, but her presence as the fifth woman accentuated Hazel's absence. Maya looked at the Mother Tree, the feminine face in the bark and the thick lower branches reaching out protectively on either side of the circle. She took a breath and thought of Hazel's kind eyes, her hugs at all the right times, her courage to speak here in the circle about her shame and regret.

Suddenly a bluebird flew into the circle and landed on the fat candle. It hopped from one side to the other and looked at each woman before flying off into the woods behind the Mother Tree. Maya smiled. Now Hazel was here. She looked over at Lilith, who winked at her.

Maya brought her attention back to Violet, who was telling Sloan the history of the circle, just as Hazel had done on her first visit. Violet continued, "And today we'll perform our traditional fall equinox ritual. Beginning on Monday, the official equinox, until the solstice in December, the nights will lengthen and there'll be more darkness than light. This gives us time to slow down, quiet our thoughts and turn inward. Today, when it's our turn with the talking stick, we'll share what issue we want to take into the dark. What is it we need to wrestle with and better understand so we continue to grow spiritually and emotionally come spring."

Maya picked up an acorn lying beside her foot and rolled it in her hand. She knew what she wanted to share but still felt resistance at speaking honestly about her life. This was her fourth circle and it still wasn't easy for her.

Violet laid the talking stick near the candles and looked toward Lilith. Lilith picked up a lighter she had beside her and scooted to the candles on her knees. She lit the fat candle. "This represents our circle as a whole." She began lighting the votives around it. "Five of the votives are for us and we'll each blow one out after our turn with the talking sick. The other five are for women of our circle who are no longer with us. At our last circle, I set the goal of researching and recording the life stories of past members. With help from Violet and Maya, I've gathered histories of four women. Abagail, who was in the circle with Hazel's mother and whose daughter gave us a picture of the circle from the 1940s; Florence, who Violet remembers and whose daughter, Jana, led us to Sadie, Sloan's great-grandmother, and then Edith, Travis' grandmother." As Lilith said each woman's name, she lit a votive.

Lilith paused with the flame hovering over the last votive. "And this one's for Hazel. I know we're all familiar with her story, but I couldn't leave her out." The wick ignited and Lilith slid back to her spot beside

Maya.

Maya reached over and squeezed Lilith's hand. She watched Hazel's votive bow and bend with the wind. The story of how Hazel and her family's money saved the Mother Tree and the circle's legacy lay in her throat. If someone had slapped her on the back in that moment she would have spewed it out. Part of her wanted it to come out so the generosity and financial savvy of Hazel, her mother, and her grandmother would be documented in the circle's history. Maya swallowed. In this instance, the most honest thing to do was stay silent.

Violet closed her eyes and the others followed suit. Maya focused on her breath, filling her lungs with the morning and then adding herself back to it as she exhaled. She massaged the acorn between her thumb and first finger to center herself. She was aware of the women in the circle, the warm sun on the left side of her face, two sparrows conversing. And then only her breath and a sense of emptiness and fullness at the same time. Maya settled here until the chime of Violet's small bell brought her back to the circle.

Maya opened her eyes and saw Violet place the talking stick near the circle of candles. Sloan shifted again, and Ella scooted over to give her more room on the blanket. Lilith watched the candle flames at the center of the circle and never moved.

Maya wanted to be the first one to go today. She caught Sloan's gaze and smiled and then reached in for the talking stick. She laid the stick in her lap and picked up the box beside her. She ran her fingers over the gold monogram and then flipped the gold clasp. She lifted the lid and the hinges creaked. The interior was lined in cloth and contained a satin drawstring bag. She removed a necklace from the bag. It was a silver chain that attached on either side of a silver circle about three inches in diameter. She fingered the necklace and got goosebumps imagining the last time it had been here. Maya felt four pairs of eyes on her and realized she'd better speak because all the women were looking at her with question marks on their faces, especially Lilith.

"I guess you're wondering why I brought this box to the circle today," Maya said. "If it's OK, I'd like to tell you about it before I share what I'm taking into the dark." Violet nodded.

"I found this in a closet hidden under Hazel's staircase a few months ago." Maya still thought of the house as Hazel's even though she'd lived there for six months. "There were tools, household items, and children's toys that looked to be from the early-to-mid 1900s. This box was under a doll's bed and the shiny clasp caught my attention. I thought I found a family heirloom because Hazel's mother's initials were monogramed on the top, and there was a satin bag inside. Instead, I found five tangled necklaces, all with the same silver circle."

Maya held up the necklace she'd taken from the satin bag. "I thought it was strange to have five of the same necklace. I searched the lining of the box, but the only clue I found was a 1943 newspaper clipping from the New Bern paper. The article was nothing special, just a report of a new department store opening up downtown. I cleaned the necklaces and every now and then would take the box out and look at them, wanting them to share their story." Maya paused. "And then the answer presented itself to me."

She held up one of the pictures of the women's circle from the 1940s that Abagail's daughter had given them. "If you look closely, the women in this photo are all wearing this circle necklace." Maya gave the picture to Sloan to pass around. "So that answered the question of why there were five of them and what they were used for, but I still didn't know why the circle stopped wearing them and had them hidden under the stairs in Hazel's house. The best I could piece together from the histories Lilith has gathered and the newspaper clipping from 1943 is that the women stopped meeting for a few years during World War II."

Lilith nodded her head in agreement, as Abagail's daughter had told her this.

"They must have given the necklaces to Hazel's mother, Goldie, at the last meeting and then for some reason they never wore them again. The only thing I can think of is that Goldie forgot where she put them. But, I found them and since we have five members again, I think it's meant for us to wear them."

Maya stood with the box. The energy from Lilith, Violet, Ella, and Sloan was palpable and they all leaned in toward the center of the circle in anticipation. Even the Mother Tree seemed to bow closer. Maya walked to Violet, knowing all the women who'd owned the necklaces before accompanied her. She set the box down and took one out. Violet looked up at Maya with tears in her eyes and bowed her head slightly so Maya could clasp it around her neck. Violet smiled and fingered the silver circle like she'd won an Olympic medal. Maya repeated this with Lilith, Ella, and then Sloan. When she got back to her spot, she put the last necklace around her neck and sat down.

Maya still had the talking stick but remained silent to honor the moment. Lilith reached over and squeezed her knee and Maya knew she'd have a thousand questions about this later. After a couple of minutes, Maya picked the talking stick back up.

"And now back to regular scheduled programming." The women laughed quietly. Maya rubbed the talking stick. The necklaces had thrown her off and she'd forgotten her rehearsed speech. She blurted out instead, "I don't think I know how to be happy." Her neck and cheeks blushed under her tan. "Well, that didn't come out right. What I meant to say is, I realize that it's hard for me to accept the good things in my life. I have a beautiful place to live, the chance at a new job at the land trust," Maya paused, "the love of an amazing man." Maya looked at the Mother Tree and the flickering candles in the middle of the circle before continuing. "It's hard for me to relax and fully absorb the good because I don't expect it to last. I'm waiting for something to go wrong." Her eyes filled with tears. "What I need to take into the dark is my belief that I'm not worthy of a good life. I need to release this and accept that I deserve happiness, deserve to be loved." Maya thought about the blond woman with Travis last week and her jealousy. "If I don't, I could lose everything."

Maya put the talking stick back and leaned forward on her knees to blow out one of the votives. Everyone remained still and silent to honor her words. Maya picked the acorn up again. She had no idea how she would make herself feel worthy, but past experience gave her the faith it would happen. Speaking her intention into the circle and having it witnessed by the other women would lay down a path for her to follow.

In a few minutes, Lilith reached for the talking stick and the attention shifted to her. Violet followed next and then Ella. Ella put the talking stick back and they sat in silence. Everyone focused on the flames of the remaining candles. Maya unfolded her legs and curled them under her. She looked at Sloan out of the corner of her eye. Would she take the stick or pass? A few sympathetic butterflies fluttered in Maya's stomach. How long would Violet wait before ending the ritual? Her question was answered when Sloan leaned forward to retrieve the talking stick. Maya wondered how she felt. She looked calm and serene, like she'd done this many times before.

***

Sloan kept her face expressionless but her hands were sweating. She wiped one and then the other on her jeans and then held the talking stick lightly. She stared at the stick, imagining GG's hands around it. From the moment Lilith and Maya told her about the ritual, she knew she'd speak. She'd even talked with Peter about what she would say.

Now she wasn't sure. She'd thought today would feel like the times with GG under the magnolia tree, but right now it didn't. She'd been naive to think it would. Sitting in the back yard with GG, who'd known her all her life, was nothing like sitting here with four white women she barely knew. Until a few weeks ago, she was their adversary. Would it be safe to share what she'd planned?

Sloan lifted her head. Violet, Ella, Lilith, and Maya were looking at her. She took in each face. Experience had made her adept at discerning a superficial smile that hid judgment or broken eye contact that concealed bias. Sloan saw none of that here. She thought of how they'd been vulnerable sharing their weaknesses and fears. The women must trust her. But could she trust them? What if they told someone what she said? What if word got around and people didn't come to her retreat center?

Sloan's 11-year-old self almost put the talking stick back in the middle of the circle. Her adult self knew that being distrustful and avoiding the truth had limited her ability to connect to others and to experience joy. She had to make a different choice. Sloan took a deep breath to untie the knot in her throat.

"Thank you for asking me to be a part of your circle. We didn't get off to a good start at our first meeting and I'm grateful you gave me a second chance." Everyone smiled at her.

"I'm relieved how everything has worked out. After learning about the Mother Tree, your circle, and my great-grandmother's involvement, I didn't want to log this land but was backed into a corner financially. I needed money to renovate Magnolia Bend," she paused, "and to pay for my daughter's inpatient rehab and had no other options." Sloan swallowed. The knot was gone.

She continued, "Things turned out even better than I expected. I have more money than I'd planned on, this land will always be protected, and you've invited me to be a part of the circle. It's especially meaningful since my great-grandmother was also a part of it. She never spoke to me directly about the circle but we used to talk under a magnolia tree in her backyard. Those conversations transcended the banter that was the norm in our house. It was with her, under that tree, where I could be completely truthful." Tears welled in the corners of Sloan's eyes as she remembered GG and in anticipation of what she was about to share. She held the talking stick tighter and looked at the trunk of the Mother Tree for reassurance.

"The summer I was 18, I told GG something I'd never told anyone and then swore her to secrecy. I hoped that by speaking of this once and then locking it down in the back of my mind that I would be OK. For years, I tricked myself into believing this worked. But it didn't."

Sloan took a tissue from her pocket and wiped her eyes. She felt compassion radiating from the other women. "And that is what I need to share today."

Sloan took a breath and imagined GG as the sixth woman in the circle to give her courage. "When I was 10, my uncle would come into my room at night and lock the door." Sloan braced for their reaction but didn't see any. The circle continued to hold her in their attention.

Sloan shared enough so they could understand her abuse. "During that time and especially during my teenage years, I felt alone and ashamed. I wondered if I'd done something to deserve this. Was I inherently bad? I desperately wanted my mother to find out and protect me, but she never did, and I never had the courage to tell her. I still haven't. We've never been close, and I think it's because I was angry at her for not knowing what was happening to me."

Sloan wished she'd brought some water because her mouth was dry. Maya read her mind and handed over her bottle. Sloan took a sip.

"To survive, I stayed busy and tried to be the perfect daughter, perfect student, perfect ballerina," she continued. "I kept doing this as an adult. I thought if I was successful enough or rich enough, the past would be erased. Now that I'm in Oriental, life has slowed down and it's clear how much my childhood still impacts me, and I want that to change."

Sunlight squeezed through the leaves and fell like glitter into the middle of the circle. Sloan stared at the sparkles of light while searching for the right words to finish. "What I'm going to focus on this fall," she couldn't bring herself to say 'take into the dark' because of what had happened there, "is the intention to heal from my abuse. I'm not sure what that entails," Sloan touched the silver circle around her neck, "but I think my time here in the circle will play an important role in that."

She exhaled, placed the talking stick in the middle of the circle and blew out one of the votives. She closed her eyes in the silence that followed and tears streamed down her face and cheeks. She let them fall to the ground. She was not alone. She was not judged. She was safe.

***

Sloan headed down the trail, back to her car, and Lilith, Ella, and Violet walked to the beach. Maya took a minute to stand by the Mother Tree. She leaned over one of its huge limbs that swept the ground. Between missing Hazel, giving out the necklaces, sharing her goal, and listening to Sloan's story, she was emotionally drained. At least the circle ended on a lighter note when Lilith presented what she'd learned about Abagail, Florence, and Edith. Then Sloan talked about her great-grandmother, Sadie, and the life lessons she'd taught Sloan.

Maya touched the circle around her neck. It was helpful to hear about the past members' struggles and how they survived, even flourished, despite them. Their stores were not that different from what everyone had shared today. Until she joined the circle, Maya'd always felt alone, like the only one with an alcoholic father and abusive husband. Intellectually, she knew this hadn't been true, but when she looked at her classmates when she was younger, and then her co-workers and running friends, she imagined the perfect lives they must have led.

Maya rested her chin on the limb and looked at the outline of the face in the trunk of the Mother Tree. Now she knew different. With varying degrees and circumstances, everyone faced challenges in life. Maybe this knowledge would help her be more compassionate to others, especially the patients in Dr. Allan's office. Maya's heart lifted. But hopefully she wouldn't be there much longer. She had a second interview with the land trust on Wednesday.

"Hopefully I'll get to save more Mother Trees like you," she said aloud and then looked around to be sure no one heard her talking to a tree. Lilith's probably done it a thousand times, she thought to herself. Maya smiled and walked down to the beach. There Lilith was getting into her kayak and Ella was helping Violet with her anchor.

"Maya, looks like you must have a date lined up for this morning," Lilith said and pointed toward the mouth of the creek.

Travis was floating about 50 yards away. Maya looked his way and it felt like a huge sunflower bloomed in her chest. "We're having a picnic breakfast," she said. "The circle went longer then I thought, so I guess he's waiting until I give him the all clear." Maya waved to Travis and he paddled toward her.

Lilith pushed her kayak off the sand, never taking her eyes off Maya. "You two have been spending a lot of time together. I take it things are going well."

Maya blushed. "Yes. Sometimes I have to pinch myself to believe it's really happening."

Lilith back paddled a few strokes to deeper water. "Well, I'm happy for you. You deserve it." She held Maya's gaze and then paddled toward Travis. "Have a good breakfast, you two."

Violet started her motor and Ella hopped off her boat and waded through the water to her kayak.

"Bye, ladies. Have a great day," Violet said. She drove slowly so her wake wouldn't bother Travis and Lilith in their kayaks.

Ella pulled her kayak off the sand into ankle-deep water and got in. "Have a good breakfast, Maya. Call me Wednesday after your interview."

"Will do."

Travis was almost to the beach and he waved at Ella as she paddled by him.

***

Sloan stepped out of the woods, and when she got to her car, threw her muddy sneakers in the back seat. She exchanged them for the Olakai flip-flops she'd purchased last month. She was beginning to enjoy the Oriental dress code. She leaned against the car, her face toward the sun. Even though the air temperature was pleasant, the low humidity and slight southwest breeze made her appreciate the warmth of the sun. A couple cars passed driving into town, maybe to The Bean or the farmers market since it was Saturday.

Sloan took a minute to check in with herself. She'd shared the most shameful and secret part of her life with four women she barely knew. They hadn't caught their breath in horror or looked at her with judgment and she'd felt their support and compassion. Even though it was just her first circle, she already felt a connection to these women forged by the truth they'd all spoken this morning.

Another car passed, and Sloan looked at her watch. She was meeting

Peter for breakfast at Brantley's but he'd have to wait. She had a stop to make on the way. Sloan pulled away from what would soon be the Hungry Mother Creek Preserve and steered toward town. She veered right onto Silverbrook Road and followed the handwritten directions the docent at the Oriental History Museum had given her.

Sloan rounded a corner and then slowed when she saw graves on both sides of the road. The print out from Find a Grave said the older graves were on the left side so she would start there. Sloan weaved between the headstones, trying her best not to walk across a grave. A live oak stood sentry in the middle of the cemetery. Its outstretched limbs covered at least a third of the space and pebbled the ground with acorns. Sloan stepped carefully.

The headstones had definitely been here a while. Weather and time had eroded them and erased some letters and numbers. When she reached the second-to-last row, near the east corner of the cemetery, she saw it: Nellie H. Allegany. Born September 22, 1891; Died February 16, 1924.

Sloan's eyes clouded with tears. She'd tried to prove this wrong to appease her rational mind and keep her friend. She'd searched tax records and deeds, and talked with her neighbors on Magnolia Bend Road, but there was no sign of Nellie except for the one in front of her. The Nellie Allegany on the deed of purchase from 1912 was the Nellie she'd befriended on the pier.

A search through the microfiche files of the Bayboro Sentinel had located an article about Nellie and Issac's deaths. The newspaper reported the same story Nellie had shared about the woman and son who'd died at Magnolia Bend. Sloan wondered if that story was true or if Nellie's husband was the cause of their deaths. She imagined Nellie and her son locked in her bedroom, her husband beating on the door to get to them. Sloan shuddered. Now she understood how a locked door could mean safety, instead of vulnerability.

She blinked to clear her vision and saw a smaller stone beside Nellie's. The letters I and A were all that were on it. Issac. Sloan sat down at the foot of Nellie's grave and studied the headstone again. Her name, and the dates of her birth and death were the only things on it. There were no descriptors, like beloved mother and wife, and no Bible verses to send her off. Just her name and the dates she was here on Earth. Dead at 32. Nellie never had the chance to live without abuse or see her son grow up.

But Sloan had been given that chance.

She'd never thought of her life from this perspective. Her compulsion to stay busy and not think about what happened in her locked bedroom didn't give her brain the space and time it needed to realize she was safe now. By not dealing with her abuse, she'd let it shape her life long after it had ceased. Sloan pulled her knees into her chest and wrapped her arms around them. Things were changing, though. Nellie, and now the women's circle, were helping her heal by listening to her story and not judging her.

Sloan crawled over to Nellie's headstone and pulled the weeds and tall grass that were growing around it and then did the same for Issac's small stone. She stood, clasping the weeds and grass in her right hand. The southwest wind picked up, jostling the limbs of the live oak and layering the cemetery with the sulfuric smell of pluff mud. Sloan sent a silent thank you out to Nellie. She thought of Nellie's unwavering support for the retreat center and pledged to do her best to make it a success, filling Magnolia Bend with positive energy.

Sloan walked toward her car and paused under the large oak. She looked back to Nellie's grave and sighed, still unsettled about their relationship. Did it really happen? Had she imagined the whole thing? Sloan's arms prickled with goosebumps. Someone was watching her.

She looked around the graveyard, and turned to where her car was parked, but didn't see anyone. Then she looked up. There was an owl, an eastern screech owl like she'd seen on her property, sitting on a thick branch about 5 feet above her. The owl held Sloan in her intense gaze and then spread her wings and flew silently over Sloan's head.

Sloan shivered and watched the owl until she disappeared into a grove of nearby trees. She'd never seen an owl this close. Did it mean something? Sloan shook her head. She'd drive herself crazy thinking like this. She would never rationally understand what had happened with Nellie, but her heart did and that was all that mattered.

A trio of motorcycles rumbled past, bringing Sloan out of her reverie. She walked back to her car and dropped the weeds and grass into the ditch beside it. Before getting in, Sloan promised to return with flowers to plant around Nellie's grave, but now she needed to meet Peter for breakfast. Sloan drove away from the cemetery, leaving the past in its rightful place.

***

Travis' kayak slid on the sand and Maya walked over to pull it further onto the beach. "Did you go fishing?" she asked, pointing to the two fishing rods in their holders at the back of his kayak.

"Of course. Sunrise is the best time. I started where Beard's Creek meets up with the Neuse and then paddled back here and fished at the mouth of Hungry Mother Creek waiting for you to finish."

"You catch anything?"

Travis was out of his kayak now. He walked over to her in two long strides and half hugged, half tackled her, causing them to fall onto the sand. "Not until now," he said.

Travis' warm lips countered the cool dampness of the sand under her. Maya parted her lips and returned his kiss. She ran her fingers up the back of his neck and laced them through his hair to pull him closer. The cool creek water lapped at her toes and a kingfisher protested in the distance.

When their kiss ended, Travis propped up on one elbow and looked at her. "Well that was way better than catching a cold, slimy fish," he said. They laughed and Maya pushed him playfully.

"You sure are in a good mood today," Maya said.

"And why wouldn't I be? A beautiful day by the water with you." Travis kissed her cheek and then hopped up. "I'm starved. Let's get breakfast started."

Maya sat on the blanket Travis had brought while he set up the stove. "What can I do to help?" she asked.

"Have you ever used a propane stove?"

"No."

"Then nothing here, but you can get the plates and forks out of my bag. I put some of the banana bread you made in there, too. The water for the coffee will be ready in a couple minutes."

Maya set two places on the blanket with a napkin and fork and put a slice of banana bread on each plate. Travis handed her a mug of coffee and a few seconds later came the sizzle of bacon.

After they finished eating, Maya and Travis cleaned everything up and loaded it back in his kayak. Now they sat, leaning against one another on the blanket, each with a mug of coffee.

"Thanks, Travis. That was amazing. Food always tastes better when you're outside."

"I know." Travis held his mug and stared at the water.

Travis had grown quieter since they finished eating. She didn't mind the silence. It was comfortable with him. The wind picked up, sending ripples across the water. The sunlight broke apart like someone was holding a sparkler under the water. Maya sighed.

"What's that for?" Travis asked.

"I'm happy. Sitting by the water with you, a full belly and a good cup of coffee. Life doesn't get much better than this."

Travis shifted, creating enough distance between them that he could look her in the eye. "But what if it could?"

"Could what?"

"Could get better than this?"

"Well I don't know how it . . ." Maya stopped. Travis dug his right hand into the pocket of his jeans. She couldn't speak and watched him pull out a small square of tissue paper. Travis' hands were shaking and immediately Maya's heartrate doubled. He unfolded the tissue and stuffed it in his pocket. He held a ring in his right hand. It had a round diamond, held in place by four square prongs, and two smaller round diamonds on each side. The band was white gold.

"Maya," he paused. He swallowed hard and his Adam's apple bobbed. There were tears in his eyes. "The only way today could be better is if you agreed to marry me."

Tears streamed down Maya's cheeks and she felt short of breath but never stopped looking into Travis' eyes.

"Maya, will you marry me?" he asked.

In the instant before she answered, their future flashed through her mind: waking up with him every day, their little girl playing with Doodle Bug and Elvis in the backyard, sitting here reminiscing in 40 years with gray hair and wrinkles.

"Yes," Maya whispered.

Travis slid the ring on her fourth finger and it fit perfectly. "This was my grandmother's engagement ring. My mother's had it since Gram died. I asked if I could give it to you and Mom immediately agreed when I told her about the connection you and Gram have with the women's circle."

She lifted her hand and the sun sparkled off the diamonds. "It's beautiful."

Travis stood, and in one motion pulled her to her feet and into his arms. He pushed her hair back from her face and kissed her firmly on the lips. "Now didn't the day get better than it was?"

"Yes." She promptly burst into laughter, needing another outlet for her emotions. Travis put an arm around her waist and waltzed with her by the water's edge.

They stayed on the beach for an hour more, kissing, laughing and making plans. Maya needed time for it to sink in. She was afraid she'd kayak home and it would all be a dream. She held her left hand up and admired the heirloom ring. She turned it around her finger. This was definitely real.

"Are you ready to go?" she asked Travis. Maya was ready now to share her news and couldn't wait to hug Doodle Bug and then call her sister, Bay, and of course her women's circle.

"Yes, ma'am." Travis folded the blanket and Maya walked to her kayak. She paused and watched the water for a few seconds.

"Travis, don't leave yet. I'll be right back."

She didn't wait for him to answer and jogged to the woods. She threaded herself through the saw palmettos and into the clearing. Maya stopped directly in front of the Mother Tree, now fully bathed in sunlight.

Her first time here she was having flashbacks from Hurricane Katrina and was full of conflicting feelings about Steven and her marriage. And today, standing in this same spot, she was at peace with the past and creating a meaningful life for herself. She rubbed the band of the ring with her thumb. How had this happened? She thought of her time in the circle, her relationships with Hazel, Buster, Bay, and of course Travis. She thought of how time alone on the river, and in the woodlands surrounding it, quieted her mind so she could hear her thoughts.

Maya sat down in the sandy soil in front of the Mother Tree, trying to make sense of it. What was the connection between these things and her ability to heal? Connection. Maybe that was it. Since moving to Oriental she'd created connections to other people, herself, and nature, especially this sacred spot on Hungry Mother Creek. But how did that help?

A dragonfly landed in the sand beside Maya. She studied its iridescent wings—aqua then purple—and thought about her conversations with Travis. Could the serenity and acceptance she felt here, the wisdom from her circle and friends, and listening to her own voice all be ways to connect to the God he speaks of? She looked at the face in the trunk of the Mother Tree and wiped a tear that slid down her cheek.

"Maya. Are you all right?" Travis called from the beach.

"Yes. Coming."

Maya stood up. She placed her hands in prayer position in front of her chest and took several deep breaths. The warm sand covered her toes and felt like summer but the breeze that caressed her face held the crispness of fall. The seasons were changing, here by the water, and in her own life. Maya leaned forward in a bow of gratitude to the Mother Tree. A red-winged blackbird called from the river grass. She turned and ran back to the water where Travis was waiting.

QUESTIONS FOR DISCUSSION

1. Maya and Sloan both use mindfulness to manage flashbacks, Maya to her marriage, and Sloan to her childhood abuse. How does being in the present moment help them? Are there times when they are less successful at this and the past interferes with their present? Do you use mindfulness to manage your stress and anxiety? What specific techniques help you stay present in the moment?

2. Maya creates reasons that Travis wouldn't want to be with her and downplays his actual words and actions. When Maya laments she isn't spiritual enough to be with Travis, Bay asks her, "Shouldn't you let Travis be part of that decision, Maya? If he doesn't think you're right for him, why is he taking you out to dinner and putting in all those hours to help you with the Mother Tree?" Why do you think Maya doubts Travis' feelings for her? Have you ever assumed someone thought less of you even without evidence proving this true? Why do you think you felt this way?

3. Sloan tells Peter, ". . . I've had a successful career and raised my children mostly alone. I wouldn't have been able to do all that if I hadn't dealt with it (childhood abuse). I just need to stop thinking about it and I'll be fine." Is Sloan correct, or can you be outwardly successful while still struggling internally? What evidence supports Peter's claim that she has not dealt with her sexual abuse?

4. Two of the fundamental roles of a mother are to provide love and safety to her children. Neither Maya nor Sloan received all they needed from their mothers. Maya's mother was emotionally unavailable due to her depression, and Sloan's mother was unable to protect her from her uncle. How did the relationship with their mothers influence Maya and Sloan? How did they ultimately get their needs for love (Maya) and safety (Sloan) met? Have people supported your growth by providing things your mother could not? Who were they? What did they provide for you?

5. When Maya had drama in her life, dealing with an unhealthy marriage and the recovery from Hurricane Katrina, she was satisfied with her work life. When her life becomes more stable she questions the career choices she's made and says, "I've always taken the path of least resistance." Why do you think Maya stayed in her career in medical records? Why didn't she realize sooner she was unfulfilled in her work? Can you relate to Maya's choices? How did you end up in your vocation?

6. Growing up with a white father and black mother, Sloan didn't feel as if she belonged, even in her own family where they had three different skin colors. She felt the greatest sense of acceptance when she was with her African-American grandparents and great-grandmother in Oriental. In what ways do you think the experience of not belonging shaped Sloan's personality? Do you think Sloan felt a greater sense of belonging after her move to Oriental? Why or why not? When have you felt like you didn't fit it? How did you react?

7. Compare and contrast Sloan's meeting with the women's circle at

her home (Chapter 6) and around the Mother Tree (Chapter 18). What factors contributed to the change in Sloan and the women in the circle? Have you ever changed your first impression of someone after knowing more about their story? Describe that situation.

8. At the first women's circle in *The Mother Tree*, Maya says, "The intention I planted this spring was to get back in touch with who I am and what my dreams are. I think I've lost that over the past few years. ... I spent much of my marriage adjusting who I was to try and keep Steven happy." Do you think Maya is on the path of achieving this by the end of the book? Why or why not? Have you ever lost sight of your dreams trying to keep someone else happy? How did you correct this?

9. Do you think Sloan made the right decision by not telling her mother about her uncle's abuse? Why or why not?

10. Maya and the women's circle view the Mother Tree and land around it as sacred. Lilith says, "The sweat, tears and breath (of women past and present) have infused the Mother Tree and ground beneath her with the wisdom and love shared there for over 100 years. We cannot replace that." Sloan has a different view of the land: "(I) have cut down hundreds of trees to make space for a building that will serve more people than the trees did. I see this in the same light. ... Ultimately logging that land will help me create a retreat center that will serve hundreds every year." Why do Sloan and the women's circle have different views about the same piece of land? Can you understand both perspectives? Why? What factors change Sloan's view about the Mother Tree and surrounding land? Do you think land can be sacred? Why or why not? Is there a piece of land

or water that feels sacred to you? Where is it?

11. Maya feels a sense of peace when sitting by the Mother Tree but is uncomfortable with the church setting. She initially looks at her experiences in her circle and Travis' experiences with traditional religion as incongruent, and a reason that their relationship won't work. How do Maya's beliefs evolve as *The Mother Tree* progresses? How and where do you experience a connection to something greater than yourself?

12. What storyline or theme from *The Mother Tree* resonated most with you? Why?

ABOUT THE AUTHOR

Heather Cobham grew up in North Carolina and now lives with her husband in Oriental, the sailing capital of North Carolina. The Mother Tree is the sequel to her debut novel Hungry Mother Creek. In addition to being a writer, Heather is also a licensed clinical social worker and works as a counselor. She fights writer's block and manages her own stress by running, paddle boarding and reading. Visit her at www. heathercobham.com.